Recklessly His

A Bad Boy Mafia Romance

Nicole Snow

Description

LOVE RECKLESSLY. WITHOUT MERCY, WITHOUT SENSE, BUT NEVER WITHOUT HEART…

SABRINA

He was supposed to be my big break – not my total breakdown. Interviewing Anton Ivankov, the infamous kingpin, was my chance to outrun my broken past. I came ready, determined, but nothing truly could've prepared me for him.

Anton wasn't supposed to be so damned handsome. He wasn't supposed to have a heart. And he definitely wasn't supposed to make me a pawn in his prison break.

Now, he's making me question everything I've ever known, replacing common sense with raw desire. Can I escape before he's done playing wrecking ball – or will this mad need to leap into his bed ruin me forever?

ANTON

I never knew looks could blindside a man until I saw her. Sabrina was destined to be my ticket outta this hellhole and a secret weapon in our street war.

Except I'm not working for family fortune anymore. Every time we touch, it's lightning, dangerous and divine.

Hurricane Sabrina's blinding me to the mission. Her twisted uncle needs to pay big time, but she's got me so distracted I can barely think. I'll kill for this girl, anything to hear her beg for one dirty, reckless, unforgettable night.

Good thing I never fail. I'll do whatever it takes to finish this war and end this Romeo and Juliet crap for good. The only happy ending here is making sure her panties, her heart, her everything are mine, and I'm gonna have it all. I always do.

I: Interview to Die For (Sabrina)

The interview was totally crazy. Nothing less than straight-jacketed insanity.

I knew it, and I did it anyway, venturing to the huge prison about an hour north from Chicago.

I told myself I was ready to do wild things to jump start my career. A girl with an eye for journalism had to do the exceptional to get her name out there. And nothing was crazier than interviewing Anton Ivankov, the infamous Chicago bomber – especially when blood made us natural enemies.

I'd never met the man in my life, of course. But that didn't change anything.

We Ligiottis were born into rivalry and danger, the price of enjoying all the wonderful things the underworld has to offer. For us, nobody was bigger and badder than the Ivankovs, latecomers to the Chicago crime scene, vicious Russian bastards who made everything my family did for cash look like a gentle Florentine opera.

So I'd been told, anyway. I wasn't *really* privy to what went on behind closed doors and inside dark alleys to make us rich. Uncle Gioulio saved me from getting too close to the family business, a promise he'd sworn to my late parents.

Honestly, I didn't mind being sheltered. Partaking in the madness, the fear, and the murder didn't appeal to me. Raw, personal history did, and nothing was a bigger coup for me than when the letter showed up last week from Anton Ivankov. It was just a date and a time. Today's, five minutes to three o'clock sharp, plus two crabbed sentences.

ONE HOUR. NO RECORDERS.

By some insane miracle, he wanted to talk after more than a year in the slammer. Hell, he wanted to talk to *me*. I couldn't stop wondering how I'd gotten so lucky. I'd omitted my last name in my request, and he'd taken the bait.

All he needed to know about me was that I was just another young, hungry girl looking for a story. I wasn't about to fuck it up by spilling the beans about our families being mortal enemies.

Right place. Right time. Right luck? Well, it was time to find out.

A warden named Charlie walked me down a narrow row of lean, brutal men in their cages. Their rough eyes leered at me from the shadows. I suppressed a shudder, tried to tell myself it was about what I'd expected. It wasn't unusual for men who'd been locked up for a few months to eye any woman the same way a starving man gazes at a piece of prime rib, right?

Damn, if only there was an easier route to the visiting room. But it was an old prison, as Charlie explained, and there was no choice but to lead me through the small section where they kept their overflow creeps, felons, and killers.

"Right here, Miss Ligiotti," he said, pulling open a heavy steel door. "You've got an hour. Mind if I ask whose balls you busted to make him talk to you?"

I smiled and shook my head. "Call me Sabrina. No balls were harmed making this happen, I can assure you. I just got lucky."

"I'll say! All right, I'll let the chef keep her recipe a secret." Charlie's wrinkles doubled as he beamed me a smile and a wink. "Good luck. Try not to rile him up too much – don't want to ship his ass back to solitary. He's only been out a week."

Charlie closed the door behind me, and I was alone, taking the middle cubicle with the low, worn wood beneath the glass. Perfect spot for my notepad and the crappy marker clenched in my hands, the only things I'd been allowed to bring inside.

I'd read up on prison regulations before the interview, but I still didn't get it. The cameras were on us the entire time, so I couldn't smuggle anything in even if I wanted to. Besides, this glass between us looked thick, like something you'd see holding a gorilla at a zoo.

Bulletproof. It had to be. And if it could stop gunshots, then surely it could absorb the blows from a man's fists?

The door behind the glass squeaked open on the opposite side. When I saw Anton for the first time, I wasn't so sure about the barrier between us anymore.

I wasn't sure about anything.

Imagine a tiger walking on two legs, suppressing its instinct to rip apart the first tender flesh it finds, if only for a moment. That was him. He moved like he owned the place, instead of being its captive.

I doubted the neon orange jumpsuit he wore even came in a bigger size. And there was a lot stuffed into it – so damned much.

The fabric over his torso stretched like it was about to bust at the seams each time he stepped towards me, the tree trunks he had for arms clasped in front of him, held together by flimsy looking chains. It was the only skin he had exposed besides his face. I couldn't begin to make out the jungle of dark, evil looking ink plastered on those granite muscles.

It rolled up into his sleeves in hypnotic waves, serpents forever bound to his skin. His shoulders were broad, making him a man sized battering ram. Damn if I didn't slide my hand forward and press against the glass, checking to make sure it didn't budge.

Nothing. If this mountain of a man went manic, maybe I'd be safe.

Maybe.

Then there was his face. Short brown hair topped a powerful, angular jaw, a face made for taking a big bite out of the world and spitting it out however he wanted. He'd done that with human lives, I reminded myself, the whole reason he was here.

He didn't have the eyes of a killer. The gems in his head were the clearest baby blue eyes I'd ever seen. For a man who'd rigged up explosives that killed twenty people, I'd expected them to be glazed with death, glassy and mad.

The burning blue fire around his pupils surprised me, melted me in my seat. It flickered with a conscious, eager energy that was almost as scary as the intensity rippling through the rest of his face. The fire held me, forced me to recognize its strange beauty, calling me to look and marvel. I barely caught a glimpse of the faded scar going up his right cheek that completed the ensemble before I forced myself to look down.

Gazing at him too long was like staring into the sun.

Jesus. What happened? Was I seriously getting hot and bothered by this sick demon who'd rip me limb from limb if he knew who I was?

I didn't understand the illusion in my brain, and it scared me. When I looked up, he was close, and I forced myself to see him for what he was: a giant, a killer, more dangerous than a tiger – now separated by only inches of glass.

The identical chair on his side was small for me, but it looked like a child's seat when he plopped down in it. I swore I heard the legs groaning, ready to bust apart under the heavy, livid muscle piled on it.

That shudder I'd suppressed earlier was back. I barely caught myself before I started shaking in front of him, gripping the little notepad until my knuckles were white. He turned his head slowly, a sly smile pulling at his lips, motioning for the phone next to him.

Of course. There was an identical one on my side.

I ripped the old phone off its receiver and pressed it to my ear, watching as he did the same, slower and more fluidly than me. When Anton's face was level with mine again, that smile was bigger, but it revealed nothing.

I held my breath, waiting for his first word.

"You're Sabrina?" He asked, so much like a king talking down to his subject.

The whole world ended in the thud of my heart. I took a long, jagged, ice cold breath. Hearing my name on his lips brought a sick pleasure humming to my skull, like he'd just whispered some dirty, private secret in rich, smoky baritone.

Jesus, girl. You're losing your shit. Screw your head on and remember why you're here.

Don't blow this. It's your lucky day.

It was hard to obey the voice in my head. But I met his eyes and forced my lips to work.

"Yes. Thank you, sir. Thanks for agreeing to talk to me today."

"Sir? Nobody's called me that since I was a kid, playing assistant manager at my father's club." He smiled, this time wider, baring several square white teeth. "You've gotta be fucking with me. Come on. Get on my level. You wanna interview me, or sit there worshiping my dick all day?"

If I'd been drinking something, I would've spat it out. Bastard. He had my attention.

I stood a little taller, hid the red blood raging to my cheeks, and nodded.

"Then cut the shit, Sabrina. Call me Anton and let's get this fucking show on the road. You're here to find out why I blew Club Duce to kingdom come, right?"

"Only if you're ready to tell me," I said, trying to keep the calmest voice I could.

Good luck. The last couple words ended in a tremor. It didn't help that his eyes stayed on me every damned second, heating my skin like he had x-ray vision, a super villain power to match his evilly long gaze. His eyes started where my middle met the little table and went up, stopping at my face.

He was inspecting me – every inch of me – right through my clothes. Fuck.

Yep. My skin was on fire, roasting in his baby blue beams.

"All right. I'll talk. Let's make this quick, clean, and easy."

Shit. If I thought I was going to keep my breathing steady, I'd just lost my last chance. I held my breath, reached for my marker, and pressed it to the paper, waiting.

"It was a simple job. We were gonna decapitate the Ligiottis in one strike, finish this little war going on between their fucked up family and mine. Gioulio and his boys were gonna be there. Our intel was always good, never failed us before – until that night. The old bastard decided to host a big dinner party for his biggest, best clients. We ended up with a buncha dead businessmen, a couple fucks on the city council and the school board, some Naperville high rollers. No Italians, though – unless you count the bartender, who was supposedly a distant cousin or something."

Distant was right. I heard about Raphael getting killed in the attack, but Uncle Gioulio wouldn't let me attend his funeral. Too dangerous, he said, and why did I want to waste my day on a second cousin I'd only met three times at reunions anyway?

That was before Anton was singled out on the security footage, backing the explosive into the club's loading dock. The danger faded everyday after he was arrested, and soon my Uncle wasn't handing out constant warnings. If only he knew I'd gone right into the tiger's den.

"So, you slipped up?" I asked, tapping the marker on my notepad. Wasn't much good for writing anyway, and I was too glued to his rough face to remember to move it.

"Yep. Me and my brothers fucked up bad. Worst mistake we ever made, short of giving the go ahead plastered after our last bash. We were drunk and naked. Took turns on every one of those bitches just flown in from Europe. I fucked them *deep,* Sabrina. Took my time railing 'em, feeling my balls bouncing on their asses, gave 'em a hello and welcome to America they'll never forget. Damned good thing too, considering where I'm at now. Last hot piece of pussy I might ever have."

I blinked. The fire his eyes kindled on my skin became an inferno. I shook my head, wondering what the hell just happened.

He's talking about sex. Fucking. Trying to throw you off.

"Um, you want to say that again?"

Anton threw his big head back and laughed, fixing his gemstone eyes on me when he came back down. "What? You think all this fucking and killing makes me a bad man, don't you? I'm waiting. You gonna call me on my shit, or just lay down and take it like those Latvian whores?"

Bastard! He was testing me after all, making me sort the truth from fiction. And, so far, I'd been too frozen in his bad boy good looks to be anything more than a toy.

I bit my tongue, pumped my hips to get myself an inch closer to the glass. "Tell me about your regrets, Anton. You killed twenty people, many of them highly respected in their community…"

"Regrets are for civvy fucks, Sabrina. Not outlaws. When Ivankovs go to war, they don't regret shit. You think my grandpa regretted cutting German throats out at Stalingrad? He personally killed a hundred men defending his country, his family. You can check the records if you think I'm bullshitting, though record keeping in the motherland has always been shit, and I never learned the language."

I didn't answer. The smile was gone, and now he looked truly serious. His fists hit the table on his side, rocking the wood between us, deafeningly loud with the steel chain slapping wood.

I jumped. I gasped. The second I caught myself, I wanted to hate him for making me crack, but I was too busy fighting the dizzy tingle pure adrenaline pumped into my blood.

He was too good at this. The very second I'd tried to take back a little control, he'd ripped it away from me, and now the ball was in his court again.

"You're a shit interviewer, Sabrina. Look at you," he said quietly, almost a whisper, voice filled with disgust. "I've got this whole fucking thing by the balls. I'm asking the questions. I'm steering you like a bitch on a leash. When I got your note asking for this shit, I thought I'd get a young, plucky, hot little thing who's hungry for my story. I was ready. Instead, I've got some chick who can barely talk because she's too fucking busy trying to put out the fire in her pussy."

Asshole! It was my turn to curl fists.

Criminal or not, Ivankov or not, nobody talked to me that way. There was more truth in his words than I wanted to acknowledge, sure – plenty to leave me ashamed for the next ten years – but there was no way I was walking out of here after letting him walk all over me.

"You're an animal, Anton. That's why you're in this cage. I'm a professional. I'm a free woman. I don't think you're ready to tell me any story at all today. This is all just a big joke to you. Guess I can't blame you – prison gets boring, right?" I slapped my notepad shut and stood, pushing in the chair.

His eyes widened. He looked...surprised, as if he couldn't believe I was the one ending this crap instead of letting him screw with me a second longer.

"You gotta be shitting me, babe. You're giving up now? Just when I was ready to get to the good stuff?"

"Start talking," I hissed into the phone.

The metal felt like it was scalding hot against my ear. But it was just my own blood, heated to boiling point, all the fear and nasty heat he sparked beneath my skin.

"Okay. I'm not as hard as my gramps. I'll tell you that much. Prison's rough. You're right – it's boring as all fuck. My old man brought us over here when we were just kids. Guess me and my brothers have been in the US of A too long to be as cold as our Siberian forefathers. You wanna hear about my regrets? Just one." He held up a pointer finger.

I waited. Fighting off another round of shaking knees, I slid back into my seat, pressing the phone so tight to my ear I thought I'd leave a permanent imprint there.

"I'm listening. What is it?"

"I regret ever responding to that fucking note in the pretty pink envelope. You're young and beautiful, Sabrina. You ought to be writing about fashion and eccentric artists. Shit, maybe slipping on some pretty lingerie and posing for the magazines for some side cash. Not spending a bright autumn day chasing down monsters in this fucking place. Go home."

I stopped, stared, and felt my nostrils flare. Before I could say anything, he slammed his phone into the wall and shuffled up. He never looked back once as he walked to the door, slow and steady, moving like a stuffed orange tiger who'd just had a good meal.

You can guess who. Ugh.

He never looked back, not even when I smashed my phone down and ran a trembling hand across my face. I had to fight every urge to pick the phone up and begin smashing it to bits against the wall.

This asshole frustrated me in all the wrong ways – mentally, physically, sexually. Admitting that last one made me want to try to break through that glass slab myself so I could follow and strangle him.

No, no, no, this couldn't be happening. God damn.

I'd lost my story and my pride in one blow. I certainly wasn't going to write about how I'd just gotten completely owned by the twisted asshole who'd demolished my Uncle's best bar and lounge to become the biggest terrorist in Chicago's recent history.

I spun, flustered, fighting down the lump in my throat. Charlie the Warden was already standing there with the door open, an apologetic look on his face. I didn't care about making a scene. I hurled the unused notepad into the little waste bin on my way out, stomping past him so quickly I didn't care about the dark, cruel eyes in the dingy cells ogling me as I marched to the exit.

I sat in the Silver Pear downtown, enjoying my second martini on the house. Free drinks at the family's bars were the only perks I allowed myself for being a Ligiotti girl — not counting the fat trust fund dear old dad left me before he ODed one cold winter night half a decade ago.

I was his legacy. I wanted to make him proud, and Uncle Gioulio too. The interview was supposed to do that, and I'd fucking blown it.

The glory would have to wait while I licked my wounds and regrouped. Right now, all I was concerned about was dousing my belly in as much alcohol as I could get without falling off my chair.

My heels rubbed together, close to starting a fire beneath the leather booth, but it wasn't half as hot as the ridiculous furnace beating in my belly. I dreaded the call from Richard the blogger. Just dreaded it.

Not only would I have to tactfully admit I'd bombed the one story good enough to get me an in with his wildly popular blog, but I knew I'd feel the failure all over again. I couldn't just swallow the humiliation and move on.

Nobody treated me like Anton did — nobody! Sure, growing up a second generation crime princess made me as entitled as they come. But Anton Ivankov had knocked me to the floor as a *journalist* and wiped his feet on me.

Shallow, angry sips slid down my throat. I wished I'd ordered something stronger. If I wanted to be brutally honest — and I did — the bastard stirred up more than humiliation.

The coarse, filthy way he'd talked was burned into my head, like he'd pulsed those words against my skin with his rough lips. He was masculine power personified, stuffed into a bright orange jumpsuit. I couldn't remember the last man who'd really made me ache, pulsed a sultry tension through my core, folding everything inward.

Probably because there wasn't one. Anton had done the unthinkable, and it was just my luck that he was the one man on planet earth who was totally off limits.

Maybe being twenty-two and a virgin does crazy things to the mind.

No boys had the balls to ask me out in school. Word travels fast when you're a dead mobster's daughter, a living crime lord's niece, and you get chauffeured to prep school everyday by two big Roman bulldogs who'd knock some gangly kid's teeth out if he even looked at me the wrong way.

Well, fuck them. I didn't want a coward. And screw the goofy frat boys I'd been tempted to have a quick, drunken tryst with in college. They obviously hadn't tempted me enough.

I was holding out for a *man*. One who could pull my hair, drag me up to his level, and fuck me into the mattress until I couldn't remember my own name. Anton offered it all, if only he wasn't behind bars.

Unfortunately, it seemed like all the real men lived in the blackest corners of the underworld. Darker than anything I'd experienced. And that made me sad because it called me to tip-toe into them, go to all the places my father never wanted me to visit, into the shadows I'd determined to avoid.

My head was spinning. I was still hot, crazed, and slightly wet, no matter how much I drank.

Bastard! He'd gotten underneath my skin, into my blood, crawled up inside me when I wasn't looking.

That call with Richard didn't seem apocalyptic anymore. No, what really worried me was a freak possibility of a second interview with Anton.

If he could leave these kinda scorch marks on me in a taunting half hour session, what would he do next?

Nightfall.

I took the call from Richard and talked it up like a triumph. It wasn't just saving face – it was keeping my face from getting peeled off in the cutthroat world of weekly features and ad-driven exclusives.

He only sounded half-convinced. Too bad. I'd find some way to *make* this thing a win. I had to.

First, though, I had a two block walk home to my little condo, and then a few more shots of whiskey before I passed out early.

Anton came to me in the sleek, cozy darkness when I laid down. My brain wouldn't let go of his feral energy. He leaped into my bed, pushed between my legs. I reached down to bat his hands away, but he just jerked them up above my head in his huge fists, growling as he smashed them into the pillow.

"Stop fucking fighting me, babe. This is what you want. Your pretty mouth can tell all the lies it wants, but your pussy's all truth. Shit, I've always wondered what an Italian girl feels like." He hovered over my lips, breathing hot breath, one bite away from getting his teeth on my tender flesh. "Do you fuck like your family does business? Sneaky? Sloppy? Merciless? Or are you gonna drain my balls like an Ivankov's girl, fuck me like it's the only time you're ever gonna have a dick this good in you?"

I tried to let out a scream, but he smashed his lips to mine. A bomb went off in my belly. Before I knew what was happening, my legs trembled. I couldn't feel anything except the fire between them, a rising fire he controlled.

"What's the matter? Haven't you ever been fucked before?" Rearing up, Anton's dark eyes flashed. He rocked his hips against me knowingly, raking my throat with his stubble.

To my horror, my hips rose to meet his. I grunted, throwing my weight into it, grinding my sopping wet panties on his cock.

It was all he needed. With another growl, he reached down, ripped them down to my knees, and shifted his weight until he was totally on top of me. His icy eyes glowed with the same playful fire during the interview, and then he tugged on a zipper, shoving down his pants.

His cock pressed against my folds. So damned big, harder and hotter than anything I imagined.

No! It's going to hurt me. It's going to rip me apart.

No time to dwell on those thoughts. He covered my mouth, giving me a wink like he knew how to read my mind. Guess he did since he was a figment of my own lust.

"No!" I screamed it through his fingers, and it came out like a feeble whisper.

"Yes, yes, yes," he said, rubbing his length against my clit, harder with every word. "You fucking asked for this, babe. Now I'm gonna deliver exactly what you're hankering for. You want it hard and rough. And if you don't, you sure as fuck will after this."

His cruel blue eyes froze me with fire as he pulled back. Then his hips slammed down, throttled against me, tearing me open for him. I arched my back and –

"Fuck!" I bolted up, hurling the heavy blanket off me.

Crazy, crazy dream. It was like he was really there, truer than any nightmare. I was burning up a second ago, but now I was freezing cold. Folding my arms, I felt the clammy heat on my skin, wondering why I was so damned cold.

I wondered, but I already knew. Anton Ivankov had officially gotten into my head like a parasite, an evil, sexy intruder I was sick and insane to want.

My body jerked again when the phone rang on my nightstand. I picked it up, grinding my teeth, reminding myself to pick a different ring-tone later on. Hearing the *boom-boom-boom* of some stupid pop song screaming at me this early was officially too much.

"Hello?"

"Brina, it's Richard. Listen, I wanted to apologize for being such a dismissive asshole yesterday. I'm sorry I ever doubted you." He sounded excited.

I frowned. "What? What are you talking about?"

"We just got a lovely thank you here at the office from Lake Federal Correctional. Dunno what the hell you said, but it must've left a mark on Mister Ivankov. He thanked you, thanked the blog, and he says he'd like to do a followup soon! Can you get your draft over to me today? Can't wait to see what the hell you've got."

"Sure."

"Fantastic!" The word burst out of his mouth so loud I had to hold the phone away. "This is fucking gold, Brina. Keep it up and you're gonna be getting exclusives with way more than the Chicago bomber."

The call went dead. I flung the phone down on my mattress and collapsed headfirst. All the blood seething through my loins was racing up my spine now, pooling in my head, trying to cool the evil burn building in my brain.

I had to see him again. There was no going back. And – worse than anything – he wanted to see *me*.

Why, why, why ran through my head, touching all the horrible possibilities. I shook my head, trying to understand, and failing.

I thought I was going for a real hard hitting exclusive with a hardened criminal. Instead, I was becoming a prisoner myself with a bigger, fancier cell, a whole universe compared to his tiny six by eight world.

Unlike him, though, I had a way out when all this was over.

I had strong family ties and a clean record on my side. If I mined him for gold, I could do anything I wanted.

"You can do this," I whispered, clenching my fists as hard as I could.

Yeah, I could, and I had to. If I could get it over soon, then I'd come out of it with a story as awesome as Richard imagined, or fall right on my face. Whatever way it went, it would end there, wouldn't it?

Anton had gotten his hooks in me for sure. But I was determined to dig them out, throw them away, and never, ever fret over the big handsome bastard in the orange jumpsuit again.

II: Strings (Anton)

I lay in my cell, wondering who the fuck I'd pleased up in heaven to drop this miracle in my lap. The Ligiotti girl was beautiful, hungry for my every word, and also dumb as a stump.

Well, at least as far as what came next was concerned.

Blowing up those twisted fucks at Club Duce must've scored me some points with the angels of justice and death. Yeah, the media loved to beat their chests about the twenty upstanding citizens I'd slaughtered. Nobody except my two brothers and I knew upstanding citizens don't visit a place like that after hours, owned by an Italian mob boss with a love for making easy money off slave pussy.

No point in talking about that. It wouldn't buy me parole. It sure as shit wouldn't win me any points with the sassy little beauty queen I'd just invited back for a followup.

I had to make shit happen myself if I ever wanted to see the light of day again. My brothers were on the outside waiting, scheming, looking for a sign. I took the fall for

Lev and Daniel like a good elder brother should, and there was no fucking way they'd leave me high and dry.

We had a plan for these situations. You do a lot of goddamned planning when making good money puts your ass on the line in all the worst ways.

Escape was barely harder than whispering it. They were just waiting for me to give the word, the signal. And I couldn't wait to see the crazy ass look on their faces when I busted out and dumped a Ligiotti girl right in their laps.

Vengeance wasn't supposed to be this easy. Neither was a second crack at fuckface Gioulio.

I grinned, slapping my stress ball from one hand to the next. It was my fifth ball in the last six months I'd gotten trading petty shit with different fractions, something to keep the bones in my hands strong and my mind happy. Came in handy when the urge to grab some fuck by the throat and squeeze him 'til his head popped off got too strong.

And when I wanted to fuck? It was a godsend. Tonight, the little ball was my faceless angel, crushed in one hand and then the next, back and forth, long after my knuckles went numb.

Sabrina looked far hotter than the daughter of my sworn enemy had any business being. Or maybe my brain automatically saw a perfect ten *because* she was a Ligiotti. The hourglass hips, big ripe tits, and hazel eyes beneath her raven hair just completed the ensemble.

Perfect ten. Perfect tease. Perfect for me to fuck one day when I got outta here.

Christ, it was gonna be a fuck to remember too. I'd start an earthquake right in the middle of goddamned Midwest when my hips went to work on her. I hoped to hell she'd cling onto me and take it like a slut, ride the seething volcano of testosterone pent up for way too fucking long.

If she didn't? Tough. Shit.

Nothing was gonna stop these fists from hammering their way outta this hellhole. And a few smooth caresses sure as hell wasn't stopping my dick the instant it was pressed up against soft, wet female flesh.

I almost popped the stress ball like a fat water balloon, thinking of all the ways I'd dig my fingers into her ass while I slammed into her cunt, showing her Ivankov's fuck hard, long, and honest.

"Hey!" A fist pounded on the bunk above me. "You still down there jacking off to that reporter girl?"

I grinned in the darkness, throwing the ball to my opposite hand, hard enough to make a resounding *slap*. "Go back to sleep, old man. You know I don't spend precious energy jerking off. Don't need to waste my jizz in my own fucking fist. Pussy's on the menu for me soon."

Dino snorted. "You planning something, Russki?"

"Nothing you need to know about," I growled, pinching the ball in one fist. "I'll send a Christmas card to your crew if it all works out."

The old biker chuckled. "Don't think the Devils up in Des Moines want much to do with you Russian bastards in Chicagoland. But yeah, give 'em my regards."

I grunted, wondering if I'd look half as good as the leathery fuck above by the time I pushed sixty. Whatever. I had about thirty years to find out, and I sure as shit wasn't spending them behind bars.

Old Dino had a whole crew waiting on the outside, tons of biker buddies in the notorious Prairie Devils MC, who ruled the plains out state. Here, it was just me and my brothers, and we owned a piece of Chicago.

If everything went as planned, we were gonna own a whole lot more soon, carving out prime cuts from the late Ligiotti empire.

Shit, maybe I'd really make off with Sabrina in the process. I deserved a pretty trophy after a year rotting in courtrooms and cramped cells. There was so much left to experience on the outside, starting with whether or not a dark Italian princess could keep up with my Slavic need to fuck around the clock.

A couple days later, I saw Charlie walking up to my cell. We'd just gotten through our time in the prison yard. Maybe the extra sheen of sweat from all that iron I'd pumped would turn Sabrina's head harder. Good looks have always served me well, clouding up the minds of opponents and prey, if they're female.

I worked hard on being ripped, and I wielded it like a weapon. Real strength comes when you can stand up and watch a lesser man cower. I wasn't interested in flexing guns for girls, but making them as hard as I fucking could to beat any bastard who crossed me into the floor.

Of course, having a killer bod to match the bloodlust in my veins drenched every panty I ever came across without lifting a finger.

Sabrina's were gonna be the latest on my list. Playing with her last time, watching her get flustered, hit the fucking spot. I knew there was more to the girl's blush than raw anger when I saw it. She would've jumped my bones and started grinding on me if it wasn't for that fucking glass.

Today, it was time to shift into a different gear, give her a better chance to lead the questions. That damned interview had to get published, after all, if I was gonna swing the trap.

"Come on. She's waiting for you," Charlie said, giving me a suspicious look.

I felt the hair prickling on that bastard's neck every time he walked me down to the visiting room with his underling guard. They had me in the middle, standard procedure, good distance between us, but I knew that fuck always wondered if I'd lunge, grab him by the throat, and slam his face into the ground. He'd be dead before anybody could get off a shot.

Killing his ass wasn't on my schedule today. I didn't have it in for these fucks, even though drawing their blood sounded good after a year of them herding me like a goddamned sheep.

He held the door open and I walked in, then slammed it tight behind me. It took my eyes a couple seconds to adjust to the bright white fluorescent light. Then I saw her behind the glass, and cracked a smile as I approached.

Fuck, she was young. I had to check to make sure she was really outta college, and not just a freshman straight outta daddy's penthouse. Though her old man was long gone, so it would've been her uncle instead.

Gioulio Ligiotti. Latest lord of the city's leading Italian crime family. Also the fuck my brothers and I were gonna kill, one way or another – but that was getting ahead of myself.

I plopped down in front of her, resting my chains on the small wooden desk, reaching for the phone. The girl already had hers up against her ear, patiently waiting for me.

"Didn't expect you'd come back so easy after last time," I said.

"You wanted me to. I think you're sorry for what happened." Surprising confidence rang in her voice.

Surprising, because it was fake as shit. She thought she could grab me by the balls and give them a good twist by looking me in my blue eyes, pretending to be stronger. I had to play along, even though I would've liked nothing better than to pop outta my chair and slam both fists on the glass. It was tempting to remind her who was in control here.

Would she topple over, giving me a perfect view of those sweet tits beneath her sweater? Or would she high tail it to the door, shaking that fine ass, leaving me to grip the ever living shit outta my stress ball?

Later, I promised myself. *Keep your cool and maybe you'll find out. Maybe you'll get to do things to little Miss Ligiotti that'll make your brothers cry with jealousy.*

"Sorry? Whatever. I agree it's good to start over," I said coldly, flashing her a thin smile. "I'm ready to be a good boy this afternoon. Are you ready to listen?"

She nodded, a fresh new notepad in her hands. "Let's take a different approach. I know, we've already figured out you don't do remorse, regret. So, do you actually feel proud of the things you've done? The bombing?"

Good question. I leaned in, tightening my fists, pausing just long enough to see the nervous uncertainty light up her eyes.

"I'm proud of serving my family. My people. This fucked up world doesn't have many places for men anymore. I can't run off to the battlefields like gramps did for the motherland. I'm American through and through. Haven't been to Moscow since I was a baby. Still, the values are the same, especially here in the land of opportunity. Best thing I can do is make my family proud, doing what we do best."

"Yeah?" Her eyebrows lifted. "And what's that?"

"Making bank. Spilling blood, sweat, and tears, getting our piece away from the rest of the mad dogs chomping at the bit in this town. You ever heard of the Red Eagle?"

She shook her head.

"It was a little vodka bar my Uncle Volodya started right off Fulton, back in the late nineties, about the time I figured out I could do a whole lot more with a woman besides stare at her pretty dress."

I dropped my eyes, a blatant attempt to catch some tits hidden behind that fabric. It was too high to see any skin, but fuck if it wasn't tight enough to see her curves, make out the plush outline of those tits my hands burned to ravage.

Shit. It was way too early in the interview to let my dick get this hard, snapping at my orange pants, too stupid to know throwing her to the wall and fucking her wasn't an option right now. Not just yet.

Good thing reporter girl was just as flustered. Her cheeks got a little brighter, and she lost my gaze, darting to her notepad and then back up, trying to clear the steam throttling her brain – or maybe oiling up her pussy.

"Uncle Volodya tried to go legit. He was a good guy. Funny, generous, dedicated to his work. He got rave reviews and tons of tourists. He was making money hand over fist, and for awhile my old man was looking at getting into the biz himself. Then one day a pack of Yakuza put three neat holes in his chest and popped about as many heads as they blew vodka bottles. You wanna talk about massacring innocents? This family lived it. We let our guard down. After Uncle Volodya, we learned there was no going back."

I paused. She scribbled furiously – probably trying to keep her pure eyes off me. I sure as shit didn't keep mine off her. No, it was the perfect opportunity to watch her tits bobbing underneath that shirt, watch her plucking at her glossy bottom lip with those little teeth.

I'd suck that sweet flap between my lips ten times harder. Fuck, I'd bite it, sink my teeth in, taste her and memorize it before we fucked ourselves crazy.

"Tell me about your brothers. Family's obviously important to you." She looked up, tucking a loose strand of that silky black hair over her ear.

"Lev and Daniel are my blood. They've got my back and they always will. I watched them come up behind me as a kid. They cried just as hard as I did when our parents died. They celebrated like fucking maniacs right along with me every time we won something new for the family. They're my brothers, in blood and spirit. The shit we've done...it brings you close, Sabrina. Closer than anybody living a nice, quiet life on the outside will ever understand."

There was that nervous flash again in her hazel eyes. I smiled. She didn't know that I knew exactly who her family was. Just like she didn't realize I was staring at my ticket to a family reunion really soon.

"I want you to give me a moment," she said, twirling the marker against her lips thoughtfully. "Sometime when you knew this was the life for you, and there was no turning back. Was there one?"

I nodded. She did a damned good job of changing the subject, deflecting the shit I said about criminal lives. This little reporter knew a helluva lot more about it than anybody else who'd be sitting in that chair for a sensationalized bullshit rag.

"3:30 PM. A cold Wednesday, about four years ago. That was the day I held my old man as he coughed up blood and shuddered one last time, on his way to meet the reaper. It was a hit and run. They did it quick while he was walking on a busy street, slammed him to the wall and sliced his throat with a piano wire. Sloppy as shit. He played dead. Took him about a half hour to bleed out and go cold. Long enough for me to come running when I got his garbled call. Not long enough for the medics to do shit. It feels like it was yesterday, and it's still gonna feel that way next week too."

Sabrina stiffened. She sat straight up, a dark sympathy swirling in her eyes. Good thing they were so bright just then, because with her sitting up like that, my eyes wanted to fall instantly to her tits. My hands hurt, begging to flatten themselves against the glass, wishing to high hell they could find their way through and squeeze her nips.

"And how did that make you feel?"

Fuck, was this chick even wearing a bra? I looked down, giving her my best sad puppy dog face, hoping it wasn't too fucking unbelievable. No, she had a bra after all, but it didn't do anything to hide her curves and edges. Thorns scraped my veins, a horny numbness, aching to get outta this cage, lay her down, and fuck the living shit outta her.

Patience, you bastard, I thought. *Finish this shit right, and you might get your chance in another week.*

"Alone," I said. "Like I'd been thrown in solitary, except nobody was ever coming back. I was the only one of my three brothers who got to say goodbye to papa. I gave myself a day to be quiet and sad at his funeral, and then…"

When I wouldn't finish it, burying my face in one hand, she tapped the glass gently. I threw my hand down, making her think I'd swept a fake tear from one cheek.

"Then what, Anton?"

"I swore I'd storm heaven and hell paying back every last fucker who did this to him, to our family. Before papa bit it, I thought I might try to do some shit like Uncle Volodya, without letting my guard down. Maybe I'd learn to set guns or run a chop shop for motorcycles, something with a connection to the hard world I'd grown up in, without having to do outlaw shit into my thirties. That all went out the window the day my old man died. His death left us to head the Chicago clan. Ivankovs have a way of burying their own dreams for family blood. For honor. For all the shit that matters."

She nodded, scribbling a few more notes. Had to look away when her tits pressed together, bobbing again, hypnotizing me to do something stupid that would blow this whole fucking thing.

When she met my stare again, her eyes were darker, reluctant, like they were holding something in. "You look like you know a thing or two about loss," I said.

Sabrina shrugged. Smart girl. She wasn't throwing me a bone and turning over any control to me – not after she thought I was giving her everything.

"What? I thought you were gonna ask me all the hard stuff," I said. "Looks like you're trying to protect my feelings. Don't bother, babe. I don't fucking have any."

Liar. I had feelings for this chick, all right, but right now they were all concentrated in the red hot lava throbbing in my dick.

She bit her lip, and then pushed her chair in, closing the last tiny distance between her and the glass. "How does it feel knowing everything you wanted to accomplish is in your brothers' hands now? You're serving a life sentence, Anton. The bombing was too infamous. If there's ever any parole opportunities, you'll be an old man."

Fuck. I'd underestimated her. She really knew how to sling arrows at a man's heart, and not all of them hit with a heart shaped kiss from cupid.

"How the hell do you think it feels?" I growled, letting more anger than I intended slip out. "I...you know what? Fuck this!"

Time to run with that anger. I jerked up, watching as she threw herself back fearfully, and then jumped when my chains slapped the glass. One day soon I'd break that shit and waltz outta here. Just not today.

"Question time's over! You got what you wanted. Get the fuck outta here!" I kept my angry eyes blazing on her as she stood and gathered her things.

I heard the door behind me burst open. Charlie and some other guys were coming in to get me the hell away from traumatizing the poor girl.

"Come on, big guy. Visiting hours are over when you start acting like an ape," the old warden said.

I turned, beaming death rays at him out of my hateful eyes. I started to walk before any of those fucks could lay a hand on me. Shit, I'd gone way past pretending here – my veins throbbed with a bloodlust I hadn't felt since knocking out the shithead's teeth who'd landed me in solitary.

He had it coming when he thought he could have a piece of me in the shower with his crew. Bastard became my relief valve for a whole lotta pent up rage when I broke his jaw, ramming my fucking head against it while I let his guys hold me down. They got a few bruises of their own before the guards broke up the brawl, and I walked away with my virgin asshole intact.

"This isn't over! You come back next week, Sabrina!" I roared, turning back to her before I was through the door. "Wednesday afternoon. I'll give you the rest. Everything you ever wanted and a lot fucking more."

She looked shaken up through the glass, but not so fucked she'd avoid me. I hid a smile from Charlie and his boys on the way to my cell.

It would be at least another week before I got to grab her soft dark hair and pull it while I fucked her, but I already had her tangled around my fingers. She was in my fucking trap, and now all I had to do was swing the gate.

Dino was snoring that night before I started on the stress ball.

I'd lied through my fucking teeth, and the Ligiotti bitch ate it up. If she didn't come back next Wednesday for the finale, I'd find her later and spank that nice, full ass when I found a different escape line. And if she did, I'd have my cock so far down her throat in another week that I might forget what solitary felt like.

The plan was perfect. Daniel would figure it out when he saw the shit on the blog. He'd always been the real brains behind our operation.

My Uncle Volodya never owned a vodka bar called the Red Eagle. That was a code to my brothers, and they'd see it as soon as this part of the story went live.

Everything else I'd told her was true – or true enough. Gioulio and his bastards probably kept her shielded from the nitty-gritty details about the war between our families. Didn't think she knew it was his men who'd sliced papa's throat and left him to bleed out in my arms in a cold Chicago alley.

It took four years after he was buried to blow that fucked up club sky high. I'd paid for my act of terror, and I was serving my time accordingly, but fuck if my work was done. Not while Gioulio was breathing.

He was number one on my hit list. Lev and Daniel couldn't do him without me. And Little Miss Blogger was gonna be the pretty key up my sleeve for getting at him –

right after I fingered, twisted, and bent her all around my dick.

One last humiliation for the Italians who'd fucked us and spilled our blood. My stone cold heart said I should have my fun, use her, and then kill her to finish off their Chicago bloodline forever.

But I didn't like the way she looked when I hopped up and pounded on the glass. It wasn't just the cruel lust in my veins knotting my brain. Something about seeing this devotchka scared caused an ounce of guilt to curdle my savage blood.

Just an ounce, and nothing more.

I wasn't slowing down. One more week, and I was busting outta here. I'd be reunited with my brothers and my quest for vengeance, right after I reunited my starving cock with some tight wet pussy.

I squeezed too hard. The ball popped in my fist, exploding grainy stuffing all over my chest. Fuck.

Another one ruined.

Dino coughed above me, woken by the sound. He rolled in his sleep and flopped over before he began snoring again. Soon, it was all quiet in the prison, nothing but his steady growl to keep me company.

The countdown started in my chest. Seconds slipped past with every rampant heartbeat. I couldn't wait to find out how fucking good she felt against my skin, and I wanted it as bad as breathing the fresh air outside without my ink covered up in eye-bleeding orange.

III: Buckle Under (Sabrina)

It was a long drive home. I got inside my condo, threw my stuff down, and set myself to work transcribing the interview from my recorder. I'd kept in my pocket, concealing it from him, deliberately using the one thing he'd forbidden.

It was the only way I was going to remember every shocking detail just perfect. The notepad was worse than useless – nothing on the paper except nervous squiggles – all I could do to keep myself fearless and focused.

It worked, right up until the end. Then he threw his tantrum and made me question whether or not the thick glass would hold if he really went berserk. He only slapped it once, but the boom was like the end of the world.

I walked out of there as he yelled after me, shaken like an animal who'd just escaped over a busy road. I barely had time to catch my breath and stop before Charlie came in to escort me out.

I worked on the transcription without thinking. Hearing his rough, smooth voice again on the speaker made it even harder. But I sat down and did it, promising myself a nice, tall drink after I was done.

I knew I'd need several to fall asleep tonight, as soon as the draft was off to Richard's inbox. I'd have to get totally plastered to avoid the dreams like the first time I'd interviewed him, especially with his voice here in my own home.

He dominated the silence. I'd never met a man whose presence twisted the atmosphere into submission with just the sound of his voice or a single glance at his massive body.

But that superpower was Anton Ivankov's specialty. And he'd rooted himself deep in my life like a supervillian.

My fingers whirled across the keyboard, digesting the interview, re-living every word. God, he'd acted so different this time, and I still sounded weak on tape. I'd bristled when he suggested I knew nothing about the underworld – the only thing I could do. Any other reaction threatened to show him who I really was.

Then there was the way he'd exploded against the glass at the end. How much fiercer would it have been if he'd known I was Giovanni Ligiotti's only daughter? Would I have made it out of there without getting torn to bits in flying glass? Would I have made it home alive?

I wasn't sure. All I knew was I worked without breaks. I only stopped when he pounded the glass at the end, followed by his muffled shout, and then the final minute or two of my own hurried footsteps mixed with heavy breaths.

It was night when I was finally finished. I sent the transcript off to Richard with my commentary and stepped outside. I'd never been so grateful to breathe the cool Chicago air.

I stuffed some easy cash in my purse for tips and cab fare before I was off to the Silver Pear. I'd need them later, when I was so sauced up I could barely stumble out of the elevator at my place.

I'm going to forget Anton Ivankov, I vowed. *No matter how much it makes my liver cry in the process.*

I ordered heavy, strong drinks, one after another. Someone was looking out for me near the end – probably my Uncle's manager, Vitto, who came out and personally thanked me for the family visit.

I wanted to throw my empty shot glass at him.

"Bar's closing early, Miss Ligiotti," he said, offering me a big apologetic smile.

"Sure it is." I turned away with a haughty sniff, leaving the waiter a good tip. It wasn't his fault this asshole was one more extension of my Uncle's eyes and ears, reaching into my life where it didn't belong.

"Wait, wait," Vitto pleaded, running after me when I slid out of the booth and marched toward the lobby. "He's waiting for you, Miss Ligiotti. No need to call a cab."

I stopped in mid-step, turned, and nodded. Shit.

One more pivot and I saw him sitting in the entryway, two stoic faced thugs in leather jackets at his side. I hadn't seen Uncle Gioulio since a cousin's wedding almost four months ago.

He was out of his chair and heading toward me before I took another step. He was a tall, lean, balding man with a scar on his cheek. He always joked it was from a bar brawl in his younger days, but I suspected something worse.

The expensive suit covered up the belly he'd been developing in his fifties nicely. His well polished shoes completed the ensemble, always immaculate.

"Sabrina!" His cold hands folded around me, and I returned the hug, bracing as he kissed both cheeks. "It's been too long, my niece."

"Far too long," I agreed, letting my drunken tongue sound more enthusiastic than I really was.

"Come sit. There's something we need to discuss. You know it's not like me to drop in personally without notice, but tonight, I couldn't resist."

My knees felt like rocks as I followed him to the empty chairs. The whole bar staff cleared out. They knew to keep their distance when the real owner showed up.

I sank down on a bench a few feet across from him, watching as he sat between his men. He fished out a pomegranate and a small silver knife. He took his time, slicing away the top, opening it up, using the blade to help dig out a few seeds, which he popped into his mouth and chewed before he looked at me.

"You're a good girl, Brina. My favorite niece. When will you go off and find a good man to marry? I'm surprised you're still here and not traveling abroad. You ought to be putting your heels far and wide while you're young enough to enjoy it."

I smiled – all I could do to settle the unease in my legs. Damn, maybe I should've skipped the last two drinks after all.

"Can't do that until I've got some stuff published, Uncle Gioulio. I'm –"

He cut me off, holding up a finger, chewing a few more seeds. "You're busy sticking your pretty head in places it doesn't belong."

"You're talking about Anton Ivankov?"

My Uncle bowed up when I said the name. He looked at the bulldog on his right and handed the pomegranate to him, then leaned forward in his seat, folding his hands. The knife rested on the arm rest next to him.

"You know I am. Why didn't you clear this with me first, Brina?"

Because there's no way in hell you'd let me go through with it, I thought.

"He's locked up," I said quietly. "I didn't think you'd have a problem."

Gioulio's face darkened. He shook his head, like I'd just smashed one of the regal portraits of our ancestors at his city estate.

"The problem isn't the Russian behind bars. He's got two brothers walking free. They're all very much alive and active, I'm sorry to say. Tell me, Brina, what do you think would happen if he found out who you are? Hm?"

I swallowed. He had me. Nothing good.

"That's right," my uncle whispered, standing up. "I get it. You're young. Hungry to make a name for yourself. Maybe do something that'll get this family some positive buzz in the press, outside the trendy reviews section, I mean."

Our clubs always got glowing reviews. I wasn't sure if he bribed them, or if the quality was really just better than everybody else's. It almost made up for the odd story that slipped out about our mafia doings.

He crossed the room and kneeled. He grabbed one hand with both of his, held it. I couldn't suppress the shudder. He was so damned cold, his fingers like stubby icicles.

"You got your interview, my niece. Two of them, and that's plenty. No more followup. Visiting him twice was dangerous and stupid," he said coldly, pinching my fingers in his. "This will be a one off, an exclusive, whatever the fuck you call it in your business. And if you ever decide to have talks with an Ivankov associate again, you'll come to me first. I'm not going to treat you like a kid, Brina. You're a mature, beautiful woman now. But I'm *not* going to be the idiot responsible for something bad happening to you while you're young and stupid. I promised Gio I wouldn't let that shit happen, and I'm sticking to it."

I turned my face away. Hearing him talk about my father hit me harder than it should in this state. The alcohol numbed everything else, but not this, apparently.

"Uncle, don't." I extracted my hand from his, warming it in my other palm.

"I won't, Brina. I don't need to. I know you understand, don't you?"

It took me a good ten seconds to meet his eyes. Finally, I nodded.

The glacial frown on his face thawed, and broke into a smile. His small, too perfect white teeth glistened in the dim light.

"*Magnifico!* There's my good girl." He reached around me, pulled me out of my seat, and held me tight. "Stay away from the Silver Pear for awhile. Don't let an Ivankov poison your good mind, Brina. Drink some water. Get some sleep. I'll have Silvano take you home. He's waiting for you outside."

His grip was cold, but it was reassuring after the day I'd had. What could I say?

I wasn't making promises I had no intention of keeping. I hated being looked after like a kid, but I couldn't deny his intentions were good. Uncle Gioulio was more experienced, a man who'd spent his whole life precariously perched between two worlds, criminal and civil.

"Thanks, Uncle." I gave him one more squeeze and then headed out to the sleek black sedan with the chauffeur out front.

When I looked through the Silver Pear's glass just before the car pulled away, he was still standing there, thumbing his knife's handle. The big flat blade tapped on his thigh the same way an angry cat thumps its tail.

I took my vitamin and guzzled several big glasses of water before I collapsed in a long, dreamless sleep. Richard's call woke me the next day way too early.

The hangover almost killed me when I sat up, but I managed to reach the phone. "Hello?"

"Brina, baby, this is fucking gold! And it's going live today."

Mission accomplished. So then, why did that make me feel so nauseous?

"I'm glad you like it. He said something about a followup on my way out, right after the part where he scared the hell out of me."

Richard laughed. Easy for him to chuckle when I'd done the hard part, feeding content to his fifty million daily viewers while he hadn't done an interview himself in the past decade. And never one with a savage creep like Ivankov.

I shouldn't have said anything about the followup, my last heart pounding moment with Anton. Richard said the dreaded words.

"We'll make this a three parter!"

Fuckity-fuck. That headache rumbling in my head growled louder. "I don't know. Are you sure people really want that much on the Chicago bomber? I didn't know the appetite was so strong."

"What? You kidding?" He sounded like I'd just spoken complete gibberish. "I've been in this business a long time, Brina. If there's one thing I've learned, it's that the people *love* freaks. They want their killers, psychos, and terrorists up close and personal. Candid or off-the-walls crazy, it's all good. It's our job to keep the carnival running as long as possible."

"Okay. One more interview," I snapped. "Next week. Then that's it."

He paused. "Brina, what's going on? You sound stressed."

He didn't know the fucking half of it. Anton was a murdering thug who sent chills up my spine. I could explain that, but I'd never admit to the sharper chills electrifying my bones whenever my brain was free and unchained at night. I wasn't about to tell a top ten roller in the new wave media that my sick brain wouldn't stop having sex dreams about the fearsome Russian killer.

"I'll get through it," I promised, taking a deep, silent breath. "These sit downs with him are very intense."

"Oh, no doubt, girl. And that's why I love 'em. Just keep doing what you're doing. Rest up and be ready for the final act with him next week. I know you won't let me down, Brina. This *is* your big break. And I'd be saying that without a third act to look forward to."

"Thanks, Rich. I needed that."

No answer. I held my phone away and saw it was dead. Great. I angrily slapped the key and headed for the shower.

A nice, hot steamy fog would do a lot to sweat out the fever Anton fed in my skin. Then maybe I'd have the strength to face the next few days sober, right after I called the correctional facility and set up the Wednesday afternoon he'd suggested.

If I wasn't such a scared, high strung virgin, this would've been the perfect time to go out and get laid. In the shower, I couldn't stop craving a man's thick, strong hands roaming my curves, all the dirty yearnings I'd been too scared to face head-on.

Big mistake. Little by little, those imaginary hands became *his*. Anton's fingers pinched my ass until I cried with pleasure, slamming me against his hard, rough body, pressing my face to his hard, unapologetic lips. His tattoos were a hypnotic world on his skin, alive and dangerous as the rest of him. And his cock – when it brushed against my belly, hot and big and brutally hard, I melted.

Fantasy Anton moved like lightning, fisting my hair in one rough pull, holding my face underneath his. "Stop fighting this shit. I know all the nasty things you think about me. I know you pretend to be a good girl, Sabrina, divorced from the shit you were born into. Stop fucking fighting it. Stop fighting me. You're a crime girl, babe, and a starving little slut to boot. You want your goddamned exclusive? Then I'm gonna give it to you hard and deep, just like those Latvian chicks. I'll pry your pretty eyes open, make 'em see everything with one hard fuck."

I screamed when he pushed between my thighs, taking me, driving me insane. It should've hurt, but my clit hummed pleasure, throttling beet red ecstasy to my head.

"No. Yes! I mean *no!*" My fingers were shaking. Wet, clammy, and not just from the water.

The fantasy bad boy was gone.

I jerked in the shower and hit the wall, wrinkling my nose when I pulled my hand out from between my legs, Anton's rough features still burning in my mind.

Jesus.

I had to finish this crap next week and check myself in to see a shrink if the sadistic fantasies didn't stop. I couldn't go on like this. He'd struck nerves I didn't know I had, twisted them in knots.

All these years avoiding the shadows of what my family was and what it did hadn't truly saved me. I was drawn to the darkness like a mirror to my own black soul, and Anton Ivankov promised to reveal everything.

I survived the week. Lots of drinks at home, bad TV, and then some sobering up with good Thai takeout. I got up early Wednesday, ate breakfast at a good greasy spoon place a few blocks down the street, and told myself I'd kick this interview's ass.

I'd kick it so hard Anton would stop invading my dreams. I'd leave my bad boy fantasies to action shows and romance novels, maybe invest in a *really* big dildo until I was ready to hit the dating scene again. I'd heard those vibrating wands could do wicked things.

The prison was strangely quiet when I arrived. The prisoners tucked back in their cell blocks barely raised their eyes as I passed, too wrapped up in something heavy hanging in the atmosphere, like the charge before a storm. Charlie seemed more solemn than usual as he led me into the visiting room. I noticed a small dent in the glass about half a foot above my head.

"Hey, what happened there?" I asked, pointing. "Don't tell me that's from him last time?"

The graying warden smiled and shook his head. "Nah. Don't worry. Another guy named Rasch went ballistic a couple days ago. His brother told him his wife was screwing around on the outside. He snuck in a hammer, started beating on the glass. Bastard took a few swings at my guys' heads before we managed to get it away."

I swallowed hard. "It's still safe? Even with this damage?"

"Safe as can be," Charlie said with a wink. "This glass is designed to hold back a raging bull, Sabrina. Hey, I can post a couple extra guys outside the door if you're worried he's going to try something."

"No. That won't be necessary." I hoped to God it wouldn't.

Charlie shrugged and disappeared, locking the door behind him, standard procedure. One more layer of security I should've felt good about – except if something blew through the glass and the guards couldn't get to me in time, I'd be stranded here with him.

I waited, waited, and then waited some more. What was the holdup?

Footsteps thundered outside the door, and I caught a glimpse of something long and black moving through the hall. My heartbeat spiked. I stood, walked over, and pressed my face to the glass.

The faint buzz I thought was just in my head was actually an alarm blasting in the hallway, muted by the thick door. Orange and black blurs mingled like tornadoes, prisoners grappling with guards in uniforms. Some wore thick armor, the heavy black stuff I'd seen blurring by the first time. Riot gear.

Holy shit. I remembered the way the prisoners looked like they were sitting on a dynamite charge and my blood ran cold.

I was about to freeze up and let panic set in when there was a loud bang behind the glass. The door on the other side opened, and Anton stepped in, a knowing smile on his face. He was still in chains, but his fists were bloodied.

Oh, God. Oh, no. This can't be –

Can't be what? Happening? It sure as hell was.

He'd dropped Charlie's limp frame behind him on the way in. I didn't know if the warden was alive or dead, but his face was really red, like he'd had all the blood shuttled to his head and then abruptly cut off there.

Anton's heavy footsteps were slow at first. He waited until I was fully in his sights before he lunged, slamming more than two hundred pounds of pure muscle against the glass. He went right for the weak spot.

His wrist cuffs smashed the dented glass again and again, a thud like lightning striking a sheet of ice. I stood there watching dumbly, my heart throbbing in my throat. Eight deafening whacks and the entire sheet splintered, caving in the same way as a shattered windshield.

The entire wall separating us came down. He punched out the last few pieces and climbed over the table, slightly clumsy because the chains bound his wrists together.

I fumbled with the tape recorder in my pocket – all I really had to throw at him. It fell, smashed into a couple of pieces on the hard floor. I hit the ground after it, throwing my arm over my head, shaking.

He took a good look and laughed. "I thought I said no fucking tape recorders?"

"Please don't hurt me!"

"Babe, I wouldn't dream of it. But you're gonna help both our asses out right now by climbing over the glass and getting the warden's keys outta his pocket." He waited, tapped his big foot near my face for about five seconds. "I mean *now.* Get the fuck up!"

I didn't comply. I was too numb.

This wasn't happening. But it was, and all the grim denial in the world wouldn't change it.

My worst fears had exploded too abruptly to process. I was really, truly in the middle of a prison break. No, worse. The man who'd stirred *so much* emotional shit in my screwed up brain was asking me to aid and abet his escape.

"Shit. Looks like I'm gonna have to drag you kicking and screaming. Good thing I like it rough."

I looked up just in time for him to stick his bloody fingers in my hair and pull. Hard. I stumbled up on my feet, fighting him, screaming like a lunatic.

Soon as I was standing, he slammed me into the wall. Anton's enormous bulk was so much heavier than anything in my depraved fantasies. I couldn't have escaped it if I tried. He pressed hard, flattening my breasts with his immense chest, somehow forcing my wrists up above my head.

"I told you I don't even wanna think about hurting you, babe. But I'm not promising shit if you don't do what I say. Right fucking now." His breath was hot on my face, his baby blue eyes burning like gas furnaces. "This isn't a goddamned game. I let you lead last time, but I'm the one calling the shots today. I'm in control. Every step you take begins and ends with me telling you where. I fucking own you now, Sabrina. Judge, jury, and executioner of how you're gonna spend your next days on earth. Is that crystal fucking clear?"

He rocked his whole body against mine. A harsh smile pulled at his lips. It must've been hard for him to force it down.

Damn it, the numbness in my nerves tingled sharper with him pressed close like this, sexy and dangerous as hell. My body betrayed me. He must've felt how hard my nipples were beneath the sweater and flimsy bra I'd chosen. All the modest clothing in the world couldn't hide how my flesh and brain and soul were mutinying against me, offering me up to this monster.

He swirled, still holding my wrists in one hand, his chain clacking near my ear. We both turned, and he marched me to the table, flattening me on the big desk previously separated by the busted safety glass.

"Climb the fuck over it, and go see Charlie." Something heavy hit the door next to us, and a man's muffled scream came through the wall. "Hurry the fuck up!"

There was a certain peace in my surrender. My brain found its survival setting through the lust and terror obliterating the last few shreds of resistance and common sense I had left. I carefully climbed over the destroyed break in the rooms, listening as he followed me through the gap, and then walked over to Charlie.

He was warm when I touched him. There was a tiny bit of relief when I felt him breathing. Whoever Anton had beaten to a pulp with his monstrous fists, it wasn't this man. Charlie would live with nothing worse than a cold blow to the head and a few scrapes.

"They're on his belt. All that shit's there, fixed to the same chain."

It all happened like a sickening, fragmented nightmare. My hands moved on auto-pilot, unclasping the guard's keys, finding the one Anton demanded, and unlocking his cuffs when he held them toward me.

Then he pushed me aside and dropped to the guard's limp body. I watched as he started undressing him, wondering what the fuck he was doing. I didn't completely shake off the stupor until Anton stood, and immediately began tearing off his bright orange jumpsuit.

He was naked except for the tight boxers clinging to his strong ass. The ink covered him more fully than anything I'd imagined, lining his entire body, sharp edges and furious phrases written in English, Latin, and what looked like blocky Russian Cyrillic.

He rolled the pants on before he started on Charlie's shirt. He turned, and I caught a flash of a huge predator bird on his chest. Maybe an eagle or a hawk, or else something more mythical. A phoenix wouldn't have been out of place if he actually pulled this off. His blue eyes flashed, and he gave me a grin, casual as if this whole thing were just filming a movie.

"What the fuck's the matter? You look like you've never seen a dude naked before. You always stare at guys who order you around like this, or is it just because I've got the biggest dick you've ever seen?" He reached for his crotch and squeezed.

Gross! Or, rather, it should've been, if only he didn't look like an Adonis who somehow used his sick confidence to look even more handsome. Infuriating was more like it.

I swallowed, fighting the tears. Bastard. How dare he.

How fucking dare he. How *dare* he accuse me of anything, remind me of this grotesque attraction, as if he hadn't already ripped my whole world apart by the throat.

He grunted, trying to do the buttons. The shirt was way too small. To my surprise, he shrugged, leaving it open and tearing the keys out of my limp hands.

"Come on. This shit'll do the job I expect, doesn't have to be perfect. We gotta move fucking fast. You follow me. Stay close. It's your only way outta here in one piece. One wrong move is all it takes to get hurt – and I'm not talking about me laying the pain on. There's a full fucking prison riot going on outside. You step outta line, you'll find out how fast it takes to find some fuck's knife in your leg or an elbow flying for your nose." He reached out, still wearing his trademark smile. "Shadow me, Sabrina, and you'll never have to worry about that pretty face getting broke. I won't let anybody else near it."

He walked behind me, pulling me close, protecting me from all my vulnerable sides. I moved with him dumbly, stopping as he unlocked the door leading into the corridor.

Hell waited for us.

Smoke burned my nostrils as soon as we were out. Half the sparse cells lining the little walkway to the visitors' room were open, empty. We went through another door, and then a split in the hall, leading me towards some place I'd never been in the prison.

The long delayed thoughts I had about escape were shattered the instant something heavy slammed into my side, tearing me from his grasp. It knocked me all the way to the wall.

"Anton!" I screamed his name, landed with an *oomph!* and felt fire racing up my shoulder.

"Stay the fuck off her!" Anton roared, slapping the fat prisoner who'd crashed into me.

I watched him force the round man against the opposite wall head first. There was a sickening crack as his head connected with the brick. He fell on the ground, gurgling, jerking one more time when Anton brought his foot into the man's ribs.

One good stomp was all he needed. He looked down, satisfied, and then he was reaching for me again.

Rough hands tugged around me, tighter than before. "Come on! Keep moving. We're almost there."

He said it with a weird tender quirk in his voice. Like he was guiding along a scared puppy. Fitting, I guess, because I was terrified out of my skin, and just as obedient too.

It wasn't Anton threatening ruin anymore. I did it to myself by being too scared to fall out of line. I followed him without skipping a step, into the cool October air that hit me in the face as we swirled outside.

It was some kind of loading dock. The prison brawl hadn't spilled over out here, and it was eerily quiet except for a loud semi rumbling a few feet away. Anton dragged me towards it, stopping at the closed backside.

He banged on it with his fists. "Open up, you bastards! We're here. Red Eagle. Red fucking Eagle!"

The door swung open. Anton spun me around, swung both hands around my waist, and leaped into the truck backwards. His huge body shielded me from the blow when we landed on hard metal.

A man near the door yanked it shut, and the loud rumble in the empty trailer doubled. I rolled in his arms, realized we were moving. Probably picking up speed pretty fast if the loud squeal of the metal underneath the engine's growl was any indication.

Suddenly, Anton's iron grip broke. He let go, stood, gaining his balance as the truck shook. I watched him walk over to the two big men crouching by the trailer's door. The other two stood, and all three men huddled in a big, manly embrace.

"*Skol'ko let, skol'ko zim!*" One of them said.

"Fuck you, Lev. It's been too many years and too many seasons. I never thought I'd get outta that fucking place." Joy rumbled in Anton's throat as he growled.

Another man lifted his head, and it was almost as big and powerful as Anton's. "Three hundred and ninety days. That's how much time you did in there, you magnificent bastard."

Their faces were similar, minus Anton's scar on the cheek. He laughed, ruffled the man's longer, wavier hair. "Leave it to you to track every fucking second, Daniel. Fucking brainiac. You timed that shit with Rasch perfectly. Can't believe they didn't notice how bad he fucked up the glass with that hammer you smuggled in."

Daniel smiled. "Him and his brother are great actors. Good smugglers too. There'll be something extra in their checks once the cops' heat is off them."

Crap. I realized I was staring at all three Ivankov brothers. If there was anything more imposing than Anton's flaming blue eyes and skull crushing muscles, it was having three sets of them just feet away, three big men who looked like they could bring the entire world down to their knees.

"Lev made me. I think he missed you more than I did," Daniel said with a smile.

The third man stood up out of the huddle, even beefier and slightly shorter than the other two. He was top heavy like a bulldog, slabs of muscle rippling above the waist, unlike Anton's which was oh-so-evenly-distributed. His hair was darker too – short and almost black. He looked at me with the same bright eyes.

"What's the plan for the *devotchka?* She gonna keep her little mouth shut, or will we have to make her?"

Anton gave his brother a shove, rougher than it was playful. "Fuck you, man. We don't need to hash this out in front of her. She helped me outta the slammer. Calmer and more cooperative than I expected."

Ugh. I really had, hadn't I? The realization made me sick. I wondered if I'd be charged with crimes myself for helping him, assuming I ever fled back to the normal world again. I tried to struggle up, but my whole stomach was knotting inside-out. My pathetic contribution to reuniting the Ivankovs joined with the trucks rough motion across what felt like a highway.

"That doesn't sound like you, Anton," Daniel said. All their eyes were on me now, icy and unbearable. "You tie up your loose ends fast. What's going on here? You falling for this Ligiotti bitch or something?"

What? What did he just say?

Time almost stopped, along with my heartbeat. My eyelids fluttered and I watched an evil, knowing grin break out across Anton's face. He sat up from the bench where they'd flopped and stepped forward. I fought to scurry backwards.

My hand slipped, and I crashed down, almost banging my head on the rusty metal floor. It was his cue to flop down on top of me, hold me down, pour his hot breath across my throat.

I really struggled this time. I gave it everything I had, kicking and scratching, trying to bite his shoulder while my screams died against his thick skin through the open shirt.

"Shut the fuck up, babe. Can't have you bruising your sweet face on this shit before we've pumped it for information."

I couldn't breathe. When I stopped thrashing, he finally let my head roll to the side.

"You knew!" I sputtered. "The...the whole fucking time...you knew who I was."

Anton smiled, and his eyes narrowed, a confession in his droopy lids. "Yeah, I did. There was no mistaking a Ligiotti girl. Didn't have any doubt you were the finest piece of Italian mob ass I'd ever seen the second I walked in and saw you behind the glass."

That set me off again. Anton sighed, his heavy chest shifting against me, holding me down. He grabbed my wrists and pinned me. Meanwhile, his wicked brothers laughed. Their harsh chuckles echoed in my ears.

"Let's be honest, your name's the reason you're here. I've turned down dozens of interviews before. Shit, I wouldn't have given you a fucking second of my time if you weren't a Ligiotti princess, Sabrina. I played dumb. You took the bait. I won."

Bastard! I thrashed against him and finally found a soft spot near his exposed shoulder. I bit him as hard as I could. I felt bone between my teeth, and then the iron sting of blood.

Anton grunted, laughed, and pushed himself against me. He shoved his shirt aside, giving me more space to bite him. My jaw went numb and relaxed at the insane reaction.

"Fuck yeah, baby. Suck it all out. I like this shit so rough it leaves permanent marks." When he moved against my thigh, I felt how hard he was.

Jesus. He wasn't just screwing around. He was really getting off on my desperate struggle. Panic came down in an avalanche.

Nothing gets to this bastard, does it? Nothing!

Hot tears burned in my eyes. They spread through them, sizzled, turned my vision blurry. I stopped fighting.

"You done yet, babe?" He waited a few more seconds. "Okay. Good. Just lay back, Sabrina. Fucking relax. You keep doing what I say, and nobody gets hurt. Well, nobody except your asshole uncle."

I shook my head, trying to comprehend how the hell I didn't see this coming. I was too selfish, too drunk, too focused on jump starting my career with that stupid blog. Now I'd screwed over my entire family.

For a second, I wondered if I'd been adopted. No one with Ligiotti blood should've been this stupid, this oblivious. This trusting.

God damn it.

"Shhhh," Anton's coarse stubble scratched my cheek as he leaned to one ear. His voice was so loud with his lips against it, even when he was talking to me like a baby.

"You're gonna be okay. No bullshit. The worst is almost over." Behind him, his brothers snickered again. "Just cooperate. We make a good team. Fuck, babe. You wanna sink those little teeth into me anytime, go ahead. You like the feeling us up close and personal just as much as I do, right?"

He rocked into me, shifting his hips from side to side, forcing my legs apart. I felt something hard and rough raging beneath his pants again. It sparked a savage fire below my waist.

"Yeah, you do," he whispered. "Yeah, you fucking do."

My pussy thrummed and swelled as he rocked, dry humping me between my black slacks and his jeans.

He knew. The bastard *knew* exactly how my body turned against me – and he loved it.

"Yeah, babe. Least your pussy's honest. Those pretty little lips can tell me a lot of lies, but your body doesn't. Shit, I can't wait 'til this ride's over. Can't wait to get you home. Cannot. Fucking. Wait."

I braced for another earsplitting scream, lust and betrayal and terror steaming in my veins. I slapped my fists into his huge arm one time, but it was like pounding a padded wall. My arms went numb, alternating between punching him and the truck's steel floor.

Soon, my energy was all gone. I collapsed.

Everything went dark. My brain shut down.

I had to save my strength. Wait for a moment when I stood a chance against him, when a well timed bite or scratch would do something. Maybe when I could get something in my hands a lot more powerful than unprotected knuckles.

He could take my body the same way he'd busted out of prison. No doubting that. But if I had anything to say about it – any last shred of Ligiotti strength and cunning – I'd never surrender willingly to his ruthless strength.

Bide your time. Wait. Just like he did. Then when he least suspects it, strike out. Hit him until he stops breathing. Bash his brains out until he can't even think about making more of those harsh, filthy threats.

If it wasn't for his masculine taste still tingling on my numb lips, taunting me, I would've smiled.

At some point during the ride, I really blacked out. Maybe I fell asleep or went comatose or something. I didn't understand what was happening to me anymore.

Twenty two years of crime and sin concealed me from the same fate as my forefathers. I never had to face their agonies, their risks, their consequences until today.

I expected to wake up in a dungeon. When I opened my eyes, I was in a room, dim lit with what looked like candlelight. Silky sheets clung to my legs. I felt...cleaner somehow.

Jerking up, I threw the sheets off. I'd been stripped, washed, and thrown into a nightgown. Nothing except the bra and panties I had on were familiar.

It was a huge canopy bed, like something you see in movies depicting Victorian times. I could barely make out anything behind the burgundy curtains, but someone was moving in the silence. I drew up against the headboard, tightening my jaw, pressing my hands together.

Please don't let it be Anton. Please, please, please...

The curtain ripped open below my feet. My prayers fell to pieces. He pushed his way through the gap and grinned, wearing nothing but a set of dark trousers that fit him better than what he'd stolen from the warden.

"I was wondering if you'd wake up tonight." He smirked, looked down, and lifted the glowing tablet in his hand. "Beast of a bomber, huh? A devil in a dingy prison, out of sight, but never out of mind. He's no less sinister today than the night he murdered twenty powerful men in cold blood."

Anton stopped. My head spun. I realized he was quoting my article, and I tried to reach for the iThingie in his hand. He jerked it away from me.

"Did you write that shit, or did your editor?"

I swallowed a thick lump. "He may have embellished. Only a little."

Anton snorted. "Good answer. You keep being a good girl, and maybe you'll get a chance to read this shit sometime yourself. But not today."

He pulled the curtain open at his side and tossed it to the floor, carelessly, as if it was nothing but a cheap magazine. I folded my arms, feeling new adrenaline pulse through my veins. The light did evil things to him, made him look far sexier than he had any business being just then.

He'd taken me, forced me to break the law, pulled me into a world I'd tried so hard to avoid. Damn it! I had a hundred reasons to hate him, but my eyes disagreed with my heart. They only saw a beautiful, damaged, heavily tattooed angel with a scar glowing on his cheek, dark as the ink going up his arms and meeting in the firebird on his chest.

"What the fuck do you want from me?" I wasn't sure why I asked the question.

His hungry eyes already held the answer. They looked me up and down, following my curves, burning my contours into his screwed up brain.

He wanted to fuck me, use me for his pleasure, and then use me again to get at my uncle. I was his secret weapon in a war that started before I was old enough to realize what it was all about.

"Your cooperation," he said. "Same fucking thing I told you I wanted in the truck. Believe it or not, part of me wishes it didn't have to come down like this, Sabrina. I would've fucking loved wining and dining you in another life – one where wasted family blood doesn't make vengeance my only obsession."

His tongue quickly flicked across his lips. Just then, I didn't believe fulfilling an old vendetta was the only fixation on his mind. He stepped closer, putting his knee on the edge of the bed, closing the distance between us.

There was nowhere to run. Nowhere to hide. I didn't give a crap about finding out what was behind the curtain – probably some luxurious room with locks on every door. He'd broken out of prison, for Christ's sake. No way would he screw up something so simple when he had an enemy in his bed – if it was his bed – and his brothers wanted me for more than just satisfying Anton's dick.

My eyes darted to his crotch. There was a noticeable bulge, bigger and meaner than anything I'd seen in my nightmares. Those stupid fantasies felt like they were in another lifetime, now that I had the real thing staring at me in the shadows.

"My beef's with your uncle and his crew, babe. Not with you. You know that, right?" The bed sank beneath his weight, and he crawled towards me, running a confident hand through my hair.

My head snapped away from him. I watched his smug smile melt out of the corner of my eye.

"I don't know *anything* when it comes to you. I don't want to, really, unless it has to do with when you're going to set me free."

I met his blue gaze. His eyes rippled, fiery and intense, longing and frustrated. Two small oceans of contrasts.

"You gotta give this a chance. You work with me, you can have it all. My brothers and I are gonna put your asshole Uncle outta business, whether you sign off on it or not. I'm giving you a chance – one fucking chance – to minimize the damage we've gotta do on the way to the prize. Come the fuck *on,* babe. Work with me."

"I'm not your babe!" I sat up, taking a swat at his huge arm. "You know what? We already know which way this is going to go. You're going to take me, use me, and probably end up killing me when I don't go along with any of it. Fuck it. Here. Let's get it over with."

My last shred of sanity snapped. He couldn't invade me if I gave myself up willingly, taking away his pleasure, his conquest. Anton looked at me like I'd sprouted a second head as I slid my legs off the bed, stood, and stopped.

I fingered the straps to the gown on my shoulders, letting it fall. His blue eyes widened when he saw me almost naked, instantly drawn to my hard nipples beneath the bra.

"Take it. Lay me down and rip me apart. I won't fight it. I'll lay there like a rock. You'll fuck me. I'll hate it. I won't even acknowledge you're in me." I sniffed. "I'll be too busy thinking about how I'm going to get out of this, and let Uncle Gioulio know what you did so he tracks you all down and puts a bullet in every one of you."

Anger rippled through his muscles. For a second, I thought he'd pounced, maybe do something a lot worse than shove his hips between my legs. He got up slowly, rounding the bed, taking patient steps.

When he was only a couple feet away, he laughed. I fumed. Once again, I'd completely misjudged how fucking dark and evil the depths of this man's brain went.

"That's cute, babe. You think you've got a choice. You think you'll be able to keep it together when I'm fucking your goddamned brains out your ears." He paused, shook his head. "You think this is a fucking game, don't you?"

I didn't answer. I was steeling myself for the inevitable, trying not to shake while my heart pumped scalding fire through my veins. We locked eyes, and I tried to tell myself I wasn't afraid, that I was ready to have him pressing me into the bed, fucking me like a depraved animal. I told myself I wouldn't feel anything except hate.

But I knew it was a lie. The wet cream pooling between my legs just wouldn't stop coming. He turned my panties to mush without laying a finger on me. If I wanted to be brutally honest, the pleasure of him rubbing up against me on the ride in was just as responsible for the blackout as the exhaustion buzzing in my body.

Maybe plunging headfirst into this sick fantasy would finally get it out of my system. Maybe if I told enough lies to myself enough times, I'd believe them.

Anton glowered. He darted forward without warning, grabbing both my wrists, throwing me down on the mattress as he bent, pushing my body with him.

Determination wasn't worth a damned thing when he was on top of me. I kicked, I thrashed, I screamed, just like in the prison and the truck. He held me down, rubbing his rough body over mine. The power packed in his muscles was inevitable.

He reached down with one hand, squeezed my thigh, pushed the gown up above my belly. "Let's get one thing straight, Sabrina. This shit's no joke. I laugh about it, sure, laugh at your fiery ignorance. But there's nothing fucking funny here. Nothing at all. You think you can challenge me? Control me? You think you've got a single shred of fucking leverage here at all?"

He squeezed my inner thigh. *Holy shit!*

Desire pierced through my explosive rage. My blood, my skin, my eyes burned hot. I hated him and needed him at the same time, split down the middle by the violent storms turning my blood molten.

Anton grunted, satisfied with the way I'd melted in his arms. He pushed my legs apart and his fingers went for the waistband to my black panties before I realized what was happening.

"What's the fucking matter? Too scared to answer? Too fucked up already with how bad you want this dick hammering some hot wet truth outta that tight cunt?" I shook my head, denying it, terrified to let him find out I was too sopping wet for words.

Of course, he found out a second later. His fingers brushed over my folds, wet and slick and swollen. My pussy craved his touch, a rough primal magnetism stronger than the hate surging through my heart. I thrashed one more time, mostly against myself, abhorring my body's betrayal.

"I'm gonna make you come, babe, and you're gonna love it. Come on. Fuck my fingers. Show me how you'd ride my cock."

If I could've imagined this was the way my first time would be with a man's fingers there, I would've whored myself out to some cheap high school kid years ago. Now, I had this brute stroking me, slathering his fingers in my wetness, grinding his fist against my pussy, slowly zeroing his circles in on my clit.

Each time his tips brushed me there, my whole body jerked. Electrified wasn't half of it. No, lightning struck deep again and again, rolling me against him, making me come undone.

My fragile will and virgin ignorance collapsed against his power, his years of experience. He stroked me like he already knew my body, listening carefully to the moans spilling from my tortured throat. I couldn't stop myself.

A single shot of sickness pulsed through my stomach once, and then I was sinking into his pleasure. Into his control. He locked his thumb on my clit and began to rock, circle, and jerk, a steady rhythm taking me over the edge.

My hips turned. They rocked against his hand, and my thighs clenched around him, drawing him to me. I wouldn't let myself look at him. The devilish satisfaction on his face burned without even seeing it, almost as hot as the hand between my legs.

Pushing. Pleasuring. Owning.

My head slipped back and I caught a quick blur of his lips moving. "Shit, you're beautiful when you come, aren't you? Let go, Sabrina. Enjoy these hands. They're just the very tip of the way I'm gonna fuck you when I'm balls deep in that tight pussy. Think about that. And don't you *dare* stop grinding that clit against me."

His breath was hot, hurried, the same as my breathing. I was turning him on, turning him mad with lust, and for some sick reason I loved it. I tried to resist the burning coal constricting everything in my womb for as long as I could. But all at once, it exploded, sending hot shards up and down my waist.

I clenched my jaw, smashed my thighs together, and rode his fingers for all I was worth.

I came like it was the end of the world. And for me, it probably was. Everything I knew was swept up in the roaring tide that passed through me with the pleasure, hurricane force ecstasy. It promised to leave me wet, exhausted, and destroyed.

I thought it would go on forever. Fiery pulse after pulse ripped through me, curling my toes each time muscles I didn't know I had convulsed. They hadn't ever been worked like this. Self-pleasure was a pathetic substitute for this man's touch, driving me apart with his tireless fingers, forcing me to understand.

When I started to come down from the high, I finally did.

He was in control. All the happy thoughts about resistance died right there in the bed. He was going to lead me to my demise or else my freedom some dark day. One thing was for sure: it was going to happen on his schedule, and there wasn't a single thing I could do about it.

I collapsed with half my sanity, spent and confused. It wasn't until I closed my sweat drenched thighs that I realized his hand was gone. Planting my palms on the bed, I forced myself up, pulling down the gown's hem, hiding the soft, leaking slit he'd ravaged.

The curtain was open. I saw him near a huge fireplace, going through some kind of large cabinet. I was still staring at him when he turned and saw me. My eyes shot to the small box in his hands.

Condoms. Fuck.

There was no putting the brakes on anything, was there? He was going to finish what he'd started, completely chisel out the last flimsy stones I had to hold onto for dear sanity.

Jesus, what were they again? What did I have left?

I tried to think about the article, the blog, my budding career. Everything I'd ever hoped to write and throw on a resume. I tried to think about the Silver Pear, about Uncle

Gioulio, the honorable and ruthless blood that led me to his place.

Blood and family. Sophistication and sin.

I was a prisoner of war, wasn't I? Then why the hell was I giving everything to the enemy?

Maybe this was my fate, to pay the price for what my father and his brother had done. I swallowed hard, feeling the dryness in my throat. I tried to brace myself for what was about to come, but I couldn't.

Having his hand seizing me like that, forcing me to come on his fingers, was one thing. Having him deep inside me...shit. Losing my sanity wasn't just a figure of speech if that happened. I didn't know who I'd be, or if I'd ever be a functioning person again if he took me tonight.

I glanced up. Our eyes met, sharing new dark and light. His were strangely calmer – the exact opposite of what I'd expected after he'd taken me, after I'd seen the erection raging in his pants.

"Here." He dropped the box he was holding on my lap. "This shit doesn't mean anything's changed. We're fucking, Sabrina. But not today."

My hand was shaking as I gripped the box and turned it over. No, not condoms after all, but birth control pills. Why?

"I'm a bastard on a one way mission. I'm not the fucking monster you think I am." He paused, reaching softly for my face, making sure I didn't break his gaze by holding up my chin. "I'll give you a few days to settle in.

Give that shit some time to work if you're not already on it. Take it. Or don't, for all I care. I got no problem blowing off if you think you're gonna fuck me over not taking it. I'll put a kid in you without hesitation. Shit, I'll need a son or two to take over all the new business we'll be dealing with once your family's outta it."

"What? What is this?" Blood throbbed in my ears, and I wasn't sure if I was understanding his bizarre threats mixed with reprieve.

"Your chance to get ready for the rest of your life. Your time to get your pretty little head screwed on straight. Your opportunity to figure out that doing what I'm telling you isn't half bad." He cocked his head. "Neither is fucking me. I know you enjoyed that shit just as much as I did. Next time you open your legs for me, don't fucking fight it. Enjoy it."

Red heat settled in my cheeks. I flushed like this was a stupid prom date, rather than a ravishing by the heartless tattooed Russian beast before me.

Had he done this to me? All of it? Or was I just born with crossed wires meant to burn me down twenty two years later?

"I'm gonna leave you here to get some sleep. It's been a big day. Don't do anything stupid. We're upstate and there's no way out for miles, even if you managed to get past the guards. You need anything, you knock on the door to the room where I'll be sleeping." He pointed to the adjoining door on the other side of the room, between two immense bookcases.

He started to walk. I watched the dark shapes on his back shifting as he moved, huge like the tiger I'd seen the first time we came face to face behind glass. And yet, he seemed just as conflicted, like he was still caged.

I didn't understand. He turned, brought his palm to his lips, and – honest to God – blew me a kiss.

I almost threw up. Almost laughed hysterically too. The urges collided, obliterating them both. I sat and stared like the rattled dove I was.

"Goodnight, babe. I'll be by to check on you real fucking soon."

He tapped a few keys on a panel next to the door, swung it open, and then disappeared, leaving a resounding thud behind him when it swung shut. I waited a minute. Then I collapsed backwards on the bed, feeling the cool, wet ache between my legs where his fingers had been.

Was this what it felt like to be buried alive?

IV: Promises to Keep (Anton)

I took a long shower and an even longer walk through the estate's corridors after the brush with Sabrina. Fuck, I could still smell her on my fingers.

Scared, sexy, and so damned tempting. I inhaled her scent until the shower washed it all away, wishing I could get rid of the ridiculous hard-on pulling at my skin just as easy.

I should've fucked her. I wanted to. Temptation clung to my gut like an angry dog, hounding me to march back there and put my dick where it belonged.

She'd be the best fuck of my life. I knew it. And if it wasn't for those big dark doe eyes drilling into my soul, I would've already found out how hard her pussy clenched around my cock when she came.

Shit, let's be honest. Any pussy would've been divine after three hundred and ninety days in Correctional. But hers tapped buttons no other bitch would ever reach because she was so innocent, so taboo, so fucking wrong for me. My dick begged me to jerk it off the entire time I washed my hair.

I resisted. I wasn't taking my nut until I blew it all over that girl locked in the chamber attached to mine. I'd give her a few days, maybe two or three, to settle in. All the time I had left before my cock overrode everything else in my skull and fucking her was as much a need as sucking oxygen.

Also about the time I estimated I'd need to get her on my side, to make her want it and want me without hesitation.

Lev and Daniel were waiting for my plan. I knew I'd have to explain what good the girl was now that I'd busted out, and why we shouldn't just shoot her dead and dump her carcass in the closest landfill.

I dried my hair, dressed, and took the long way through the big house. It used to be my old man's, a vacation ranch spun off to a family friend after papa's murder. The cops would be too busy the next week or two combing Chicago for my escaped ass. They'd go after all the obvious places first, and there were a lot of them with all the warehouses, bars, and lounges under our name. They'd never look here, or not when it mattered.

By the time I was back in the city, it was gonna be for a quick hit and run. If it went off as smoothly as my jailbreak, the Ligiotti clan would be decapitated, and I'd be on my merry way to blow this country and leave Uncle Sam hanging with his dick in his hand.

Clear your fucking head, man, I told myself. The tension rolled through my body like a razor blade riding my bones. There were about ten reasons why my fists were hard as hammers at my sides, and they all had to do with *her*. Shaking off the adrenaline rush of fucking my way out never felt like this.

I took an extra lap down the hall, shaking off my wood. I pinched my teeth together. The only thing my brothers would find funnier than my weird obsession with this chick was walking into the dining room sporting dick like a goddamned horny teenager. I shook off my erection before the meeting.

I rounded my way back, opened the door, and saw them sitting at the long dining table. My seat was at the head of the table. An honorable gesture from both those beautiful bastards.

No sooner than I was in my chair, Lev looked at me with his eyebrows up. "Did you fuck her yet?"

"You think that's really my first thought after breaking out of prison? Jesus Christ. It's been boring as fuck behind bars, but I'm still man enough to put business first."

A smile spread across his broad face. "Brother, we both know what's on your mind. I can't fucking imagine being denied pussy for a year. You're a braver man than me."

I suppressed a growl and turned my chair, looking at Daniel. He was all business, same as usual, his attention on some paper in front of him.

"Well, what's the fucking story? Have we got the guys in place for this ambush before old man Ligiotti hears I'm a free man?"

"Financials aren't a problem. Neither is manpower." Daniel looked up. His face looked like a smoother, slightly younger mirror of my own. "Only problem is getting close to him. If he'd showed up last time, like we planned, we wouldn't be having this fucking do-over right now."

I slammed my fists on the table. "Like I don't know that! It wasn't my fault. We all signed off on the intel that said he was supposed to be at Club Duce. Gioulio was due to be greeting those sick fucks before he turned his new girls loose. Somebody tipped him off."

"Got a feeling all our asses would be in jail if you'd triggered the blast a minute or two later," Lev said, wagging his finger. "The girls were on their way. Just them and their handlers. Gioulio changed plans at the last minute."

I shrugged. "Might've been a mercy if they'd died there. You guys got me out of prison, quick and easy. Those girls he's got chained up? They're the ones who're really suffering. The bastards keep them in cages like dogs 'til they're brought out to suck and fuck."

"Yeah. If only that was the only thing going on at Gioulio's parties." Daniel stopped short of listing the sadistic shit we'd discovered.

It nailed me in the fucking chest to this day. No, we weren't out to play hero. Killing the head of the Ligiotti family and taking their business was priority number one. It was a selfish goal to enrich our family, secure ourselves. But just between us brothers, we'd hoped killing those fucks with a well timed explosion would set the women free too.

We'd slaughtered their asses before the women showed up, so that was something. None of the girls died that night. It even gave the bastard pause from everything we'd heard, rattled him so bad he let the sex ring languish for a couple months. Too bad it didn't last. Gioulio started pimping them out to a new line of Chicago scum the day after I went behind bars. The city's filled with fucking rats, always ready to come outta the woodwork and do favors for anyone willing to satisfy their psycho needs.

"Look, Anton, we've been working on the logistics of a follow up hit the whole time you've been behind bars," Daniel said, reaching across the table to freshen his mug with more hot water from the samovar in the center. "Hell, we would've taken that bastard out ourselves by now if we didn't have to worry about somebody killing you dead on the inside in retaliation."

"You should've done it anyway. I could've handled myself in there."

A white lie. Yeah, I knew how to fight. I'd broken the bones of any fuck who tried to get smart or slip their dick into my ass in jail. But there were other tortures I didn't handle so well.

Solitary was hell. All three times I'd been there, my mind went crazy, wondering if I'd ever see a human face again. It was worse being caged with a cellmate, which was fucking plenty to deal with by itself.

I had to be out in the world. I was too used to business and play, killing and fucking, laughing with my brothers and looking for a chick worthy of expanding our family with my wild seed.

Never again. I'd never let those fuckers drag me back to that place for defending my family and butchering some dirty bastards with lived like angels and pleasured themselves like pigs. I'd do this shit with my brothers, accomplish the mission ahead, or die trying.

"Whatever. What happened – or didn't happen – is all done. We're here tonight to figure out how we're gonna dig Gioulio's grave."

"Right," Lev agreed. "Is that where the sweet ass hanging out in your bedroom comes in?"

"We should've drugged her and dumped her on the way here. Bitch is Ligiotti trash. I'm glad she was there to help you out, but I don't understand why the fuck you wanted to keep her here. She's a risk."

"Because she's gonna be our Trojan Horse," I growled, half a heartbeat away from slamming my fists on the table again. Couldn't believe how callously my brothers were talking about that girl. Vengeance is some poisonous shit.

"Yeah? And have you got a plan, or are you just bullshitting as you go along?" Daniel quirked an eyebrow.

"Nobody knows what we're up against like I do, D. I read about her old man and his asshole brother. I know what happened. And I definitely know the right questions to ask to get her on board."

Lev shook his head, downing the shot of vodka waiting in his glass. "You think she'll turn that easy? Especially when the hard questions are coming from you? Why the fuck should she trust anything coming outta your mouth?"

I nodded, anger bristling in my veins. "She will. You forget I've already sat down a time or two with this girl. She knows me."

Not to mention laid her down, pinched her ass, made her gush and twitch on my hands, I thought. Fuck, what I would've given to do a whole lot more with her that instant.

"I know what makes her tick. She's not complicated. Her uncle never told her shit about the family business. Fucker tried to keep her outta it. Not outta kindness neither. He's got plenty to hide to keep his ass whole, prevent any shakeups in his crew. It's up to me to show her all the dirty laundry that's been stuffed in her closet all these years."

"Just remember we're trusting you on this, brother," Lev said. "You're trying to turn blood against blood, and history tells us you've got stiff fucking odds of pulling it off."

His hand moved for the vodka bottle again, but I was faster, pulling it towards my chest. My brother glared jealously.

"You think the odds weren't total shit for me breaking outta prison? We made it work, Lev. We always do. We owned those fucking odds and bent them to our favor. Division of labor. You boys keep figuring out the best way to drop that fucker, and leave the rest to me. I'll have

Sabrina Ligiotti begging me to help kill her uncle in a week."

Just as much as she'll be begging for my dick, I thought, feeling more hellfire churning in my balls.

It was a short, fitful sleep. The only kind I'd expect my first night as a free man.

Knowing she was right next door, ripe and ready for the plucking...fuck. I woke up six or seven hours later with my dick beating beneath the sheets like a second heart. Took a few minutes to clear my head, get the hard-on under control, and then dress.

Shit. Light streamed in through the enormous window overlooking the countryside, a pale October sun peaking over the horizon.

I waited an extra minute for my cock to stop straining in my pants before I went to the door joining my room with Sabrina's. Hoped to hell she'd have a talk with me on peaceful terms. Pinning her to the nearest wall and pinching her swollen little clit between my fingers would be fun, sure, but I didn't think I'd be able to control myself again.

Next time I got my skin on her pussy, I wasn't gonna be able to hold back 'til I conquered every inch of her. I had to fill a hole, and my dick would have his pick. I'd fuck her mouth 'til she gagged, take her ass 'til she screamed, fill her sweet fucking pussy up 'til she –

No. Stop it, you bastard.

You gotta treat this just like the prison break. This is business. This is a job. You can get your dick as wet as rain after Gioulio Ligiotti's choking on his own blood.

There are hundreds of chicks who'll be glad to fuck and suck. There always are.

I steadied one hand on the cherry wood door, feeling for the silver knob with the other. The thoughts weren't much comfort.

Yeah, pussy always came fresh and easy ever since I'd been old enough to pump lava outta my balls. But there wasn't much to admire about the girls who sank to their knees right away, wet and moaning before they even felt my fingers, my hands, my lips.

I liked it rough. Challenging. I liked to fuck the girls who didn't admit how bad they wanted it – and the dark haired Italian thing behind the door had every reason in the world to hate my guts.

Too fucking bad. Ready or not, here I come.

I didn't knock. It was my fucking house, my rules, and nobody matched my dominion here except Lev and Daniel.

My dick started throbbing against my zipper again. So much for settling the fuck down.

The curtains were still drawn around her bed. I quick stepped my way over there and ripped the partition at the base open, hoping I'd see her naked.

"Goddammit. What the fuck?" The bed was empty.

For a second, I rushed out, stalking the room like a wolf who'd caught a rabbit's scent. My brothers had this room cleansed of anything heavy and sharp she could pick up and use against us before she arrived.

Where the fuck could she go? There was no place to hide, nowhere to roost for an ambush.

A low growl slipped out my throat. Then I noticed the big vanity, where she'd shed her gown, an empty glass of water next to it.

Of course. I felt like a fucking idiot. Old Grigor, the family servant, had been through already, or else had one of his underlings take her down to breakfast. I'd overslept.

Snarling, I stepped out and punched the code into the panel, opening the locked door and stepping into the hall. It was a quick march down to the dining room, all while I wondered how long I'd been off in la-la land dreaming about all the dirty shit I wanted to do to this chick.

The double doors to the big dining room swung open. There she was – right next to my two brothers near the head of the table – a nice spread of food, juices, and coffee laid out for the trio.

"Good morning, Anton." Daniel smiled coolly.

I stepped over and took the seat next to her, glancing at her face as I sat. She was red eyed, frustrated, like she was holding in tears or volcanic rage. Maybe both.

"What the fuck's going on here? Somebody should've woke my ass up so we could all sit down together."

"You needed your beauty sleep, brother." Lev grinned. "We thought we'd better let you rest while we met the house guest ourselves. It's only been twenty minutes or so. You came down sooner than we expected."

I looked at her. "What did they say to you?"

"Your brothers…they're complete *assholes,*" she said, a hateful glint in her eye. "Just like you."

The anger stabbed deep. But what really got to me was seeing the little plate beneath her, a few orange slices and a muffin sitting on it. All untouched.

I bolted up and slammed my fists on the wood. "Breakfast time's over for you two fucks. Go work on the shit we discussed last night. I told you I'd handle the rest – and it's gonna get handled a helluva lot easier without you fucks rubbing your noses in this shit."

Daniel stood first, crumpling his tablecloth and throwing it on his empty plate. He took a couple steps away from the table, passing me on his way out, and paused.

"I trust that's the old attitude talking, the one you developed wearing orange. I get it. Going behind bars makes a man angry and a little crazy."

I growled, giving my brother the evilest eye I'd produced in my whole fucking life. "Shut up. Do what I say. Leave her to me."

"We will, brother. We will. I just wanted her to know how lucky she is being here."

Before I could grab him by the neck and throw him against the wall, he was on his way out. Lev was smart enough to keep his distance, heading for the door with the table between us.

He looked at Sabrina. "Remember what we discussed, love. You do everything Anton says. Everything we ask.

That's the price for keeping you alive and breathing. Any other Ligiotti would've gotten their head popped and dumped in the nearest ditch on our way home after breaking out Anton."

She shook once. No fear, but rage. The door shut and he was gone.

Fucking assholes. It was in their nature. I didn't expect anything different – especially because they sure as shit didn't have the same weird connection with this chick I did. But fuck, sworn enemy or not, when did my brothers forget how to treat a woman with basic civility?

When did I?

Obviously when we looked at her. Their blood roared with hate, venom, vengeance. Mine stormed pure lust, a barbaric need to fuck her, more than I wanted her uncle dead.

I walked to the other side of the table and sat down with her, still pondering that shit. I tapped the table several times with my fingers 'til she took her face outta her hands.

"Look at me, Sabrina. We've got shit to discuss. Before we do that, I wanna give you a chance to eat to your satisfaction."

"I'm not hungry," she snapped.

"I don't give a fuck. You're gonna keep up your strength because we both have jobs to do. Pick something up off that table and take it bite-by-bite. I don't wanna have to force anything down your throat."

Bullshit. There was one thing I wanted to force through her lips more than anything else. Cold, stoic war crept back in my heart, but it hadn't turned me to total ice. I wasn't so far gone I'd throw the food off this table if she disobeyed, throw her down flat, and fuck her right there.

No. Not yet.

"Do it for me, babe. Do it for yourself. Let's go. I want you talking to me with a full stomach. You'll be way more pissed and irrational if your belly's running on empty."

She stared at me for a good long while with the same hateful eyes she'd aimed at my brothers. Finally, she moved her hand to the plate, took the muffin, and chewed an angry bite outta it. I would've laughed if she wasn't seeing red and I didn't have a deadly serious mission here.

"I overslept," I said, watching as she swallowed and took another bite. Good. "If I'd been down here on time, I wouldn't have let them get away with that disrespect. They give you any trouble in the future, Sabrina, you let me know. Promise me."

My fists tightened, and I leaned forward on the table. She set her half eaten breakfast down and took a gulp of tea before answering. "Why bother? Stop acting like you're here to do me any favors. I know a good cop, bad cop thing when I see one. It's how you tricked me to come back for that followup."

Fuck. The girl was smarter than I'd given her credit for, at least in hindsight.

"Fine. You wanna play rough instead of treating this like a civilized business arrangement, I can do that."

She snorted. "Civilized? I don't think violating at least ten Federal laws and keeping me hostage fits the definition. Neither does blowing up my uncle's nightclub downtown and killing twenty well respected men."

It was my turn to laugh, letting the derision roll out. Incredible. She still had no clue – no fucking idea – what I'd really done.

"Come on, babe. You wanna be a part of the media, I get it. Just thought you'd know by now half the stuff you read about's pure bullshit."

She narrowed her eyes. "What? Are you going to tell me the bombing didn't happen and it wasn't you? I never figured you for the tinfoil hat type."

"No. I didn't tell you a single lie during our other talks, except for the fact that my Uncle Volodya's place wasn't really called the Red Eagle, and he never died on a Wednesday. That was code for Lev and Daniel to break me out." I paused, reached over to the coffee pot, and poured myself a tall mug. "I blew that fucking place to kingdom come, and the only regret I've got about it is not having your asshole uncle there to die with the rest of those freaks."

She shook her head. "Great. So you admit you're a killer."

"Admit it?" I blinked. "I've never denied that shit once. I *own* the fuckers I kill. What you don't get is that every asshole I'd knifed or burned or shot has always had it coming. You really don't know shit about the underside of your family's business, do you? If you did, you'd know the guests Gioulio has at his parties are some of the most sadistic, twisted motherfuckers in the entire city."

She looked at me like I'd just spat out a tall fucking tale. Okay, maybe I had, but this one was all true.

"What are you talking about? Don't tell me this is some kinda *Eyes Wide Shut* crap. You killed them in cold blood. All because my uncle was your target."

"No. I wanted to make sure I killed all those fucks. I just missed a couple when Gioulio and his guards didn't show up on schedule. You're missing the point – none of them were collateral damage. All twenty of those assholes deserved to be executed. You don't know them. I do."

Another shake of the head. Another flick of that dark, smooth hair. Fuck, how good would it feel to just grab it while I shoved my cock between her legs? I'd hold on and rock her, pluck it like reigns, just short of ripping it out while we fucked.

"If you want me to even consider a word you're saying, you'd better tell me what's going on."

I folded my arms. "Not 'til you eat some more breakfast. Go on. I'll fucking wait."

She glared. At first, I didn't think it was gonna work. But then her small hands reached for more muffins in the center of the table and another orange. I watched and waited as she ate, sipping my coffee, trying not to admire the cleavage peeking through her top too close.

Grigor and his maids did a good job picking out her wardrobe. Shit, she was dressed a lot like the Latvian girls I'd fucked a couple years ago, two dark haired, blue eyed chicks straight from the old world. They barely understood a word of English and even less Russian, but their cunts understood my dick pounding them to blubbering pieces. One of them tore stripes in my back when she clawed me, and a few warm streams of blood poured down my ass.

It was the roughest, craziest fuck of my life. And I had a damned certain feeling it wasn't half as intense as what I'd feel unloading my balls inside the Italian girl playing bitch across from me.

Sabrina's fork clanged on the ceramic plate when she was done. She blotted her mouth dry and then looked at me.

"There. Is there anything else you'd like before you can trust me with an adult conversation, instead of treating me like some little girl you've got locked up in your tower?"

The poison on her tongue made me grin. "Babe, you're gonna stay locked up for a good long while. Even when I tell you the crazy fucking truth, it's gonna take you time to chew on it. Digest it. But you'll turn on that fucker. You'll help me kill your uncle. I know you will."

She waited. I swore I heard her foot tapping on the tile underneath the table.

Impatient. I liked that.

All right. Enough fucking around. It was time to let her know what really happened that night.

"It was an assassination, plain and simple. My brothers and I had enough intel to know how Gioulio ran these parties. Shit, he'd been doing them since your old man died and there was nobody left in the windy city to stand in his way. Drugs and guns are the bulk of this business. Always have been, always will be.

"But that shit's hard money. Your uncle wanted to diversify into something easier. Nothing like trafficking with some rich, well oiled assholes to bring in a few easy million more."

I watched her jump and squirm in her seat. Heard her swallow before she spoke.

"Trafficking? Like...women?"

I nodded. "Yeah. Seems like no matter where you go, powerful fucks like to play devil when they're done pretending to be angels all day in front of the public. It's not all about the money either. By giving the high and mighty an outlet for their depraved desires, your uncle gave himself something sweet to hold over their fucked up heads if this city ever gets a mayor who wants to go tough on crime. Probably part of the reason Ligiotti business has been smooth as ice since your old man died.

"Gioulio's got himself a stable of girls he keeps for his boys. Slaves who have to do anything and everything short of holding out their throats to get cut.

"Not that there's a helluva lot of difference sometimes. You should've seen what that banker, Wilkins, did to this Sicilian girl your uncle imported...left her bleeding and infected for weeks with the chunks he tore outta her with his teeth. Then there was that fuck on the city council. Bastard liked to put out his stogies on fresh young skin. My boys told me the last chick he had needed plastic surgery after the fucker was done with her. Gioulio charged his ass a hefty damage fee and an extra premium for the night I blew him straight to hell.

"Then there was that real estate mogul, Chuck Winston Mayhar. You know you're dealing with a bastard when a man flaunts three fucking names. Too many business trips to Japan for that boy, where he got into some really sick stuff he saw in his comic books. He couldn't even get your uncle to say yes to half the twisted shit he wanted, but damn if he didn't keep trying. The boy picked this pretty little blonde from a shelter in Rome, had her shipped back here by Gioulio, and –"

She'd been reaching for the tea, and the half-empty cup crashed on the table. Sabrina was red in the face, bunched up like her seat turned into needles. She almost leaped halfway to the ceiling when the china smashed.

"Enough," she said weakly. "You made your point. Please, I don't want to hear anything else."

Fuck. I kinda felt bad for her. But only a little bit.

I'd done my fucking job. I'd planted the seed of doubt by shining the bitter truth right in her eyes. And shit, that wasn't even half of it. I'd read the files my brothers collected before we put the bombing together.

Every one of those sick motherfuckers was the kinda stomach turning shit no sane prostitute would ever do. All the money in the world wouldn't buy them what they needed to get off from any regular escort service. That's why they went to Gioulio, the magic man who could fulfill their depraved desires, all because the girls he pimped didn't have a choice.

I'd stopped trying to figure out why some dudes needed to torture and kill to get their nut. All I needed was right across the table, staring at me with huge, tormented eyes, and a pussy that would rocket me to heaven when I finally got it wrapped around my dick.

I reached across the table and grabbed her hand with both of mine. I held her, refusing to let go, lacing my fingers through hers and stroking up her arm.

"Don't worry about the mess. Housekeeping will take care of it. Look, I'm not saying this shit to hurt you, Sabrina. I'm trying to make you understand there's more to every story than what you read. I've done terrible things to terrible people. I don't regret a goddamned thing."

She took a long, ragged breath. Her lips opened, like she wanted to say something, but she couldn't get it out. A fast moving tear swept down her red right cheek.

"I need you to help me because you're different, babe. Your asshole uncle knew that. It's why he kept you sheltered. If you were remotely like him and his crew, you wouldn't be crying over this shit. You'd be feeding me excuses."

"I don't…I don't know what to believe," she forced out.

I tightened my grip on her. "You will. Very soon. It's been a long morning for both of us, and yesterday was even longer. Come on. Lemme walk you back upstairs so you can get some rest."

I wasn't gonna drop the rest on her when she was like this. That was for later. I had to chisel away every evil piece of Ligiotti bullshit left in her, everything Gioulio had hidden and twisted inside her.

She walked limply in my arms as we headed up the stairs, back to the big bedroom. I got her into the chamber and laid her on the bed, pulling off her shoes.

Two black heels with straps. Didn't know the girls in charge allowed her such luxuries. Didn't know she'd choose that kinda shit to wear around here either.

Maybe she was hoping to use them as a weapon – whack me in the head or take out an eye when I wasn't looking. Whatever the case, she wasn't gonna do a damned thing now.

I let her smash her face into the pillow while I stroked her back. Soon, her breathing grew slower, more normal, and I lightened my caresses.

It wasn't easy to walk away while she slept, but I fucking had to.

This job was far from over. And if I'd stayed there another minute, I knew my dick would rip right through my pants and plunge into what she had underneath that sleek purple skirt, pulling me into her like a fucking magnet.

I'd hurt her enough for one day. I did what I had to. The only screaming I wanted her to do was the kind she made when her mind was exploding with a good, deep fuck.

God willing, we'd get there soon.

I headed for the gym. I needed some time to think, something to distract me from the lust boiling my blood. I walked into the spacious exercise room, stripped off my shirt, and went to work on the punching bag.

Everything Sabrina stirred up came ripping out in my punches. The ceiling rattled with my blows, angry and hot, filled with all the obligations and vows I had left to fulfill.

Too many promises were piled on my back. Heavy, heavy promises, one-ton obligations, ready to snap my fucking spine like a brittle twig if I took a single step outta line.

Oaths to my family, oaths to my brothers, oaths of seething vengeance.

Vows to my flesh, my blood, my heart.

I had no guilt, despite the way I'd stolen her and blown apart the only world she'd ever known. Dealing with Gioulio and his boys was the first priority, yeah, but fuck if I wasn't gonna make her whole.

If I could make her work with me, see me for the man I really was, then I'd remake everything she knew. I'd push my dick in that hot, wet space between her thighs, that pink slit I craved worse than freedom itself when I was behind bars. I'd fucking brand her, own her, fuck her 'til she opened her eyes and saw exactly what I wanted her to see.

This girl was gonna see the stone cold truth soon, the truth about me and everything else.

I hit the floor, sweating and shaking, totally spent. The black leather punching bag bobbed in the air, the impressions from my fists fading like evening shadows.

This was my chance to start over, living like a free man, and no fucking way was I gonna squander it. I wouldn't let Sabrina waste a minute more of her life without a good man, hiding in the dark from her fucked up family.

I couldn't make any promises about being good. But I sure as shit was the man she needed, and soon she'd see it, plain and pure as the sweat sliding down my chest.

V: Captive Trust (Sabrina)

I expected him to throw me down and fuck me, leave me locked up, subject my body to the craziest tortures until I gave all three psychopaths what they wanted.

But the bomb he dropped on me that morning was worse than anything I could've imagined.

I trailed him limply to my room, slow and blasted like a zombie, my brain melting in my head.

The 'truth' he'd told me about the bombing at Club Duce defied everything I thought I knew. It was sick, wrong, insane – and just terrible enough to be true.

No, I wasn't ready to give in and believe him yet. But if I totally doubted what he'd said, I wouldn't have spent the evening cramped up in bed, feeling my stomach twisting in bows.

I used the intercom to hail the servants after a couple of hours. Thank God they actually came, an old woman with a thick accent carrying a silver tray. Toast, a carafe of mineral water, and lots of Pepto Bismol.

I was sick right down to my soul. I didn't know what to believe, didn't know where I was, didn't know what I'd really left behind anymore.

Uncle Gioulio always scared me when I was growing up. His personal thugs were always around at dinners and birthdays, menacing as well trained wolves.

Once, he took me out to get a prom dress, a strangely touching attempt to make me feel better about the fact that no boy had the balls to ask me out. When we came out of the shop, he opened his trunk and I saw the black bags inside.

"Fucking shit. Can't believe I forgot to unload my lamb from the butcher," he'd said with a grin.

I couldn't unsee the very mangled, but human shapes beneath the plastic. A man's limbs, torso, and head, clearly dismembered, folded neatly into the trunk and forgotten. The faint stink of rotting flesh didn't lie either.

He rushed me home and then waited with the servants while his men came to deal with it.

He was a brute, a killer, and seriously intimidating.

Still, he took me under his wing after papa died. He protected me, even when he wasn't around, sending steady checks and fleshing out the already sizable accounts I'd inherited. I lived like a spoiled brat during my teens and put the richest sorority girls at college to shame.

Good old Uncle Gioulio was always there for Christmas or New Year's, my last real blood relative. Even when he had two drunk, slutty bombshells half his age draped around his neck, he brushed them off for a couple hours to have a glass of limoncello or good wine with me.

Now, I wondered if those bombshells were just well paid whores with a taste for older men, or well trained slaves ready to suck his cock because they had a well concealed gun to their heads.

Later, I got up and took a nice, long bath. I had to hand it to Anton – this little prison he'd chosen had all the amenities I was used to, and maybe a few that were even nicer than the condos and suites I'd grown up in. The hug jacuzzi in the adjoining bathroom helped work out the creases in my skin.

But it didn't stop me from cursing my captor and all the Ivankovs at least a dozen times in the space of two hours. Yes, he'd rattled me, but he hadn't broken me.

I didn't know what kinda help he wanted either – probably something to do with handing me a knife to gut my own family. I wasn't going to do that. I promised myself I wouldn't do a damned thing until I had absolute proof he wasn't bullshitting me. Even then, I wasn't about to commit to helping him.

I had to know. A bland, but filling dinner laid out by the old servant helped calm my nerves. Tea, bread, and some kind of broth. I fell asleep quicker than I expected, saving my energy for tomorrow, when I expected to lay into him.

The dreams came, harsher and more fragmented than before. Bastard.

Bastard. Brute. Demon.

He'd abused me with cruel knowledge and captivity as much as seduction. My psyche let me know that night how messed up I really was. I *still* wanted him in all his awful glory.

My virgin pussy burned, clenched, and ached in my sleep. I rolled over, wrapping my wrists around the sheets, imagining how good it would feel to shove my fingernails through his hair. He'd made me come so hard with just his hands.

Jesus, what would his mouth or that huge ridge I'd felt between his legs do?

Would his tattoos come alive and dance on his skin when he held me down, pushed inside me, and fucked me until I shook and whimpered? Would I lose myself in the dark ink or his Neptune blue eyes first?

One way or another, I knew he wouldn't hold out forever. He *would* take me, whether I was ready for it or not, whether I wanted it or not – and, of course, I did. I could only choose how I was going to come up for air after he held me down, filled me, drowned me in his scent and strength and sex.

A rap on the door woke me up late morning. I yanked down my nightgown, shamed awake by the sopping wet heat between my legs.

I threw my legs over the bed and waited, sliding my cold feet into the burgundy slippers they'd given me. Another bang.

"Coming! Just hold on."

I had exactly twenty seconds to collect all my wits. When I flung open the door and saw him, I was ready to demand answers. I'd give it to him point blank, tell him I wasn't just going to be his wind up toy, marching in whatever direction he sent me.

"Anton, I –"

I threw open the door and stopped. The thick, blue eyed devil named Lev was standing there, a smile spreading across his lips. Before I could think about stopping him, he pushed his way in and shoved a small black box into my hands.

"Gift from Anton. My brother's very busy today, and he won't be by personally." He stopped, one hand on the wall. His sleeve rose just enough to see he had black stripes of his own going up one arm.

"I see you've settled in much more nicely today" His eyes moved up and down my body, making my skin crawl. "Hm. Perhaps I regret thinking about putting you down after all. Has he fucked you yet, or is there still room for an Ivankov to lay first claim?"

He started coming towards me. I dropped the box, ready to lunge, scratch at his eyes. He was almost as big and strong as Anton, and my odds against him weren't any better. But he caused me to feel repulsed in a way Anton didn't.

When he was just a couple inches away, I threw my hand out and raked his face. He fell back, stunned. He exhaled painfully through clenched teeth, and I saw the neat red rows I'd left on one cheek, quickly covered by his searching fingers.

"Bitch! I should throw you down and fuck your little ass for that." I didn't move. My knees were like steel, running on fear and hate.

"Go ahead and try," I spat.

He stood up, circling me at a distance, the same mischievous sparkle in his baby blues that I recognized in Anton. "You're a fighter. I like that. I respect it. You would've gotten off easy with me. I'm the more tender one, or so the ladies say. My brother's going to fuck you sooner or later, you know."

"Yeah? Not you?" It felt good to taunt him, dangerous as it was.

He growled, shook his head, and widened the distance between us. It looked like he couldn't decide whether to make good on his crude threat or get the hell away from me. I swallowed hard, praying he'd finally leave me alone.

"I like rough and hard to get like any red blooded man. But I'm not about to ruin Anton's little prize before he gets a crack at it. We're brothers, after all. What's his is his. I was just having my fun."

I stuck my tongue out. So risky to keep pressing him, but he was backing off. I couldn't resist. I'd officially had it up to *here* with these intrusions, all the sadistic extras that came with being Anton Ivankov's hostage.

"Stay here like a naughty *devotchka* then. Anton always liked them beautiful and completely at his mercy." I watched him fish a silky red handkerchief out of his pocket and press it to the scratch I'd left on his cheek, soaking up the blood. "You're very lucky he's got big plans for you, babe. If it was up to me and Daniel, you'd be dead. We can't see the sense in sparing *any* Ligiotti."

He pointed at the box and turned. Then he threw the door open and slammed it behind him, leaving me to collapse, grabbing my knees, listening to the lock click shut behind him.

When I'd caught my breath, I crawled to the black box. It opened easily enough. There was something rectangular and electronic inside, a brand new tablet. Except it wasn't packaged like anything I'd ever seen before.

I dragged it out of its container and found a little note taped to the back. The big, sharp script could only belong to Anton, a penmanship as imposing as the rest of him.

You've got a lot of questions, and I'll be back to answer them soon. Until then, do your own research. Find out everything you can. Don't take my word for it. And don't you fucking think about calling for help – it's read only. Nothing gets past this house's encryption. – A. Ivankov

I shrugged and complied. It wasn't like I had anything better to do, and how the hell could I help it when he'd dropped such a juicy invitation in front of me?

I sat on the bed with the little device, wondering if the encryption was really as tight as he'd claimed.

Yup. Email, apps, and all the chat sites I knew were off limits. The browser wouldn't let me move through the web fluidly. There seemed to be a list of bookmarks, and nothing else.

The first page I pulled up was an old profile on a fetish site. The face belonged to Michael Wilkins, the investment banker killed in the attack. I recognized his smug face from the obituaries I'd read for my piece.

I only browsed a few lines of his interests. It was enough.

Not a fucking game...real pain...I like to leave permanent marks.

Another page opened up a large PDF. It was an account statement from a dead city councilman with monstrous amounts marked gratuity for the Club Duce. The last transaction was just an hour or two before the bombing, about what you'd expect a multi-millionaire to tip for exceptional service.

On and on the evidence ran.

Sick profiles. Financials he'd gotten by some black magic. A carefully suppressed draft of a story that was never published in a major paper about one of the dead businessmen breaking his wife's jaw when she confronted him about his depraved affairs. The reporter's boss was on the dead man's payroll.

Over and over, I saw GIOULIO LIGIOTTI in big letters whenever the owning party was named for Club Duce. Anton left it there, as if to shove it in my face, constant reminders saying, *you see this shit, babe? You see who's responsible? Fucking look!*

Oh, I did. I saw it all.

I took the longest, harshest look I could until my eyes wouldn't work anymore and my fingers went numb on the little device. Then I picked it up, stood on the bed, and hurled it through the opening in the curtain.

The thing went flying towards the vanity and smashed with a clatter like fireworks. I collapsed, clawing at my face, sick to death and shaking.

I was beyond fucked. Only, I didn't know who to blame. I didn't know whether I should hate my own dirty blood or the bastard who'd made me think my Uncle was the filthiest man on earth. Maybe both.

The truth wasn't necessarily any clearer. There were a million ways he could've doctored everything on the screen.

The man seized me, and he was holding me prisoner right now, after all. How far would he really go to get his way, to get me to help him destroy the only man who'd ever offered me his protective hand?

I was still wondering when I crashed, exhausted, stuffing my face in the pillow to dry my hot tears.

At some point, I must've fallen asleep. Next thing I heard was the door swinging open. I sat up in the darkness. Didn't need to make out the dark silhouette near the entrance to know who it was.

A piece of busted plastic from the tablet crunched under one of his shoes. He stopped, ground his foot into the tile, and whistled.

I glared as he looked at me through the dimness, folding his arms. "Fucking shit, babe. I knew you'd get upset when I confronted you with what was on that thing…never knew you were the smashing type."

"I wish I'd saved it for later. I'd have held it and waited until you came in."

God, it would've felt so fucking good to belt him in his stupid handsome face with that thing.

A smile pulled at his lips. An instant later, he was on me like a wolf, pinning me to the bed with ease.

"I'm gonna let you up, and you're gonna get dressed. We got shit to talk about. But not here. I'm not comfortable keeping you cooped up in this room forever."

Something about the icy, commanding tone in his voice tasted extra bitter. I narrowed my eyes, pouring heat through his dark blue gaze.

"No."

One of his eyebrows twitched. "Don't fucking make me stuff you into a dress. I'll do it with my own bare hands if I have to. It's been a rough few days. That's why I'm gonna go easy on your sweet ass. Work with me. Don't make the rest of your week hell, babe."

"I don't care anymore. It's not like I have a choice. I never did."

"What the fuck are you talking about?" He growled.

"I don't believe a word of what I saw on that tablet. Did you really think I'd buy it when I couldn't connect to the web on my own? How was I supposed to fact check anything?"

"I was doing you a goddamned favor." More thunder in his voice. "I laid it *all* out. You wouldn't have found shit anywhere that wasn't already in those documents."

His muscles tightened around me. His hands had slid behind my back. It took all my energy not to flinch, not to let the heat smoldering beneath my skin reach an inferno.

Bastard! Even when I wanted to hate him, bite him, kick and scratch, being this close activated more primal instincts that weren't ruled by sane emotions.

"I don't need anything from you. I'm done with this. Let me go or kill me."

He took a good, long look at me. His eyes were glowing like the devilishly powerful, sexy predator he was. He scared me, but the current running through my nerves was far more fearsome.

If this was my fate, a prisoner to this insane attraction, I hoped he'd put me out of my misery.

"Get. Dressed." This time, his growl was barely human.

It almost made me move. Almost. But I held my ground, planted my hands on his chest, and pushed against him.

Resistance. It taunted him, and he responded.

In a flash, he flipped me over and ripped at my gown. I yelped when I heard the thin fabric tearing in his hands. Then he was pulling at me as one shredded strap fell across my shoulder, lifting me up into his arms.

I thrashed and yelled, trying to fight him, but he held on. He pulled me over to the huge closet and pushed me inside. I caught myself against one of the large mirrors just as he kicked the door shut.

He turned his back to me, rifling through the outfits overhead. I watched him stop on a sleek red cocktail dress. He spun, threw it at me, and I somehow caught it in my flailing arms.

"Put that fucking thing on and come out when you're done." The second my mouth popped open, he closed the two steps between us and pushed his hand over my lips. "Think real, real carefully, babe. If the next answer outta your sweet mouth isn't 'okay' or 'yes, sir,' then I'm gonna dress you up myself. Don't fucking make me, Sabrina. I'm gonna get a good, long view of you naked real soon, but I don't want it like this. I don't wanna ruin my surprise."

His hand tightened over my mouth, and then it was gone. I fell backwards, holding the dress out in front of me, shielding the bare shoulder he'd revealed by tearing at my gown. Any inch of me exposed to this bastard was too much, too vulnerable.

"Go," I said softly. "I'll do it."

He nodded, satisfied, and stepped out, closing the door behind him more gently than I expected.

What else was there to do but listen? If he was really taking me outside this room, maybe there'd be another chance to calculate my flimsy odds of escape. Assuming he wasn't dragging me out into the thick woods I'd seen through the window to shoot me, of course.

I didn't think so. He wouldn't be dressing me for that. By some sick miracle, he still needed me. Probably the only reason he put up with my crap.

Not that I cared. I wasn't going to stop flinging it his way. If I couldn't get away from him, then I'd make his life as miserable as I could.

The dress was weirdly calming against my skin. It was quality fabric, something familiar, the sort of thing I was used to wearing out on my girls' nights back in college.

The lights were on in the bedroom when I stepped out. Anton was waiting.

"Fucking shit," he said, moving his eyes up my body, admiring me from head to toe. "Follow me."

We took a different direction in the hall, heading for what seemed like the house's west wing. He took a fork to a staircase leading up, banishing my hopes of an easy escape path on the ground. I kept my legs moving, up the long stairway with three different landings.

A narrower floor waited up top. He opened the first door and pulled me in after him when I took the last step.

It was another bedroom – but not quite like anything I'd seen before.

All the luxurious trappings were there: a bed, fine stained dressers, a dark blue rug. The window and the walls were completely encased in glass like it was some kinda sun room or observatory.

He motioned to a small silver telescope in the corner. "I like to come here to think and gaze at the stars. Not that we'll be doing much of that tonight. I picked this room because being under the night sky has a way of settling my brain the fuck down."

I looked up. He wasn't kidding.

My jaw dropped. I'd spent so much time in Chicago with its light pollution that I wasn't used to a country sky. Stars, galaxies, and a fat harvest moon hung above us like bright ornaments, so breathtaking I forgot I was here as a prisoner, not a guest. The heady illusion lasted about five seconds.

"Take a good long look," he said. "It's fucking beautiful up here at night."

When my captivity came back, it was twice as bitter. I pursed my lips and looked at him. "You can't control how I think or feel. I'm smarter than you give me credit for."

"You really think I believe you're a fucking bimbo, babe?" Anton snorted. "I know a thing or two about the blood that's in your veins. Even if I believed you were a spoiled little bitch, totally ignorant about everything your family's done, no fucking way would I call you stupid or gullible. Your clan's always been cunning. Smart. Sophisticated in a way us Russian bastards aren't."

I rolled my eyes. Was this really supposed to be flattering?

Big mistake. The instant the eye roll was over, Anton was on me, grabbing me by the wrist and pulling me into him. I squirmed for a few molten seconds in his arms, and then settled, surrendering to the huge, hot, heavily tattooed chest hiding beneath his button shirt.

"I showed you the shit on that tablet because I want to earn your trust the honest way. I can't force you to do shit if every part of you wants to sabotage me. I want *you* to want the same shit I do, babe. I want it pumping in your own heart because it's meant to, not because some other bastard's bullying you. I want you on my side. Right down to the second we shovel your asshole uncle into his grave."

That did it. The dreamy heat swirling through me broke apart in his icy eyes. I tried to pull away, but he tightened his grip, holding me so I couldn't.

"I *don't* trust you, Anton. I don't trust anything here, anything you've said. I don't think I ever will."

"Sit down with me." Without giving me a choice, he pulled me towards a little table with two chairs next to the starry sky.

I sat and instantly gave him another glare. I hated what he was doing to me with every touch. I felt so empty without his fingers on my skin, and I didn't understand why, couldn't understand anything except that it was so wrong.

"Tell me about the night your old man died."

I blinked in surprise. *Another manipulation. Has to be. He wants me to talk about something upsetting so he can come swooping in like the big, bad hero.*

I promised myself I wouldn't crack. I wouldn't flinch about it either. I stiffened my heels on the floor and leaned forward.

"What? You haven't read up on it yourself?"

"Of course I have," he snapped. "You see the kinda shit we Ivankovs dig into to confirm our own intel. It was all there on the fucking tablet. Documents and second hand stories never compare to the shit you see first hand. It can't capture what raw emotion can. It can't tell me what you saw with your own two eyes. Tell me what you remember."

Five years melted before my eyes. I took a deep breath, remembering that night, when I walked in on my dead father at our condo. It was worse than when mama died because at least I'd never seen her broken, crumpled up body on the street.

No matter how many years passed, every time the memory came flooding back, it hurt.

"He was slumped on the sofa. I'd been out late with a couple friends when I came home," I said quietly. "Papa was a mess since my mother died, but it was getting really bad that winter. Uncle Gioulio came by the week before it happened. They were arguing so loud I heard it from my room upstairs. I think he slapped my father around, trying to knock some sense into him – anything he could do short of forcing him into rehab..."

Anton's face tightened when I mentioned my uncle. "Go on."

"He was already cold when I rushed over and touched him. I knew he was dead the second my fingertips brushed his cold brow. Didn't want to believe it, of course. I was only seventeen. I don't care if I was basically a grown woman by that point. It's never easy becoming an orphan at any age."

Slow, thick heartbeats pulsed blood through my ears. Anton's eyes were darker, calmer, almost understanding. Both his parents were dead too.

Great. I caught myself. The last thing I wanted was any understanding, any common link with this man, but there it was.

He reached across the table and grasped my hand. Of course, my skin melted all over again, and I leaned back in the chair and sighed, letting him draw the sadness away with his touch.

"You've gotta give me more. Was there anything coming out of his mouth? Did he vomit?"

What the fuck? I jerked my hand away, wrinkling my nose.

"Why do you care? He ODed just like I told you. I'm not an expert on what happens to junkies when they...yeah, I think there was some foam. Lots of blood dried around his nostrils, his lips...a few splashes hit his white shirt and stained it red. It was awful. I got the hell away from him as soon as I could and called Uncle Gioulio. He was there right away. He helped me through the whole thing."

Ouch. No matter how hard I tried to keep a lid on the pain, it started overflowing. I broke the death gaze with Anton and looked out the window, staring over the high trees into the stars.

"Blood?" He paused, waiting for me. "You'd better look at me right now, babe, because you just confirmed it's as fucked up as I thought."

I did, right as he reached for my hand. This time, there was no pulling away. His grip was so tight. Anton stood and circled his way over, scooping me up into his arms as I fought tears.

"What're you talking about? How could you know anything about papa's death?"

"I know junkie's don't die spewing blood like that. They don't bruise black around the eyes neither."

"His eyes? They were open when I found him. There weren't any circles, nothing noticeably broken or bruised…"

Anton walked me over to the little nightstand. I watched him pull open the drawer and fish out a manila folder. He held me, eased me onto the bed to sit, while I opened it.

"Autopsy report. Only fucking copy of that record without a buncha shit blacked out and redacted in the official record. Your Uncle did a helluva job pulling his strings and hiding the proof in the official shit. Guess he didn't know everything about your family runs through mine first."

I opened it and rifled through the pages. They were old, crisp, like they'd sat in a musty vault for a long time.

If this was another elaborate fabrication, he'd done an incredible job.

Anton pushed his hands over mine, planted his fingers on the pages, and opened to the one he wanted. His finger stabbed down on a long line – some medical term. "Says right here they found poison in his system. There's another tucked back here that says the syringe at the crime scene was half full. Your old man didn't even shoot himself up with a full dose of that fucking trash he was hooked to. He didn't kill himself on bad coke – somebody else gave him this shit I can't pronounce."

For a minute, I was frozen. He held me, taking my whole fucking world into his hands, all while everything I knew before splintered and fractured into pieces.

I was too stunned to cry. Too sick to choke. Too furious to know who the hell my anger should be pointed at. I tried to jerk away, but he wouldn't let me.

The folder dropped from my shaking hands and the pages went spilling across the floor. "Anton, I can't –"

"You don't fucking have to. You can look at that shit tomorrow. There's no rush."

Asshole. I shook my head, more vigorously when one of his hands began sliding up my thigh. He knew how to press buttons I didn't understand.

No way was I coming unraveled like this. Not here. Not now.

"Whatever. I still don't trust you." I hissed it through my teeth.

"I don't need you to, babe. I just need you to listen to what I'm saying and cooperate. You want to work with me, Sabrina. Stop acting like you don't." His chest shook as he took a deep, long breath. "Fuck. You can keep spitting nothing but lies and doubts outta those lips. But your body doesn't lie. There's no bullshit here. Just want. *Need.*"

His fingers pinched my bare thigh, higher than I thought he'd climbed, dangerously close to my panties. Tremors shot through me. The starry void behind me opened up and came through the glass, circled my head, drowned my senses in its glowing lights.

When I sucked in oxygen and tried to steady myself, I smelled him. It was all Anton Ivankov, that evilly masculine scent singeing my nostrils, leaving me pleading for more.

His hand wasn't stopping. His fingers slipped up, brushed my stomach, and then dove down the waistband to my panties. There was no stopping him from feeling how ruined I was, how soaked he'd made me without even knowing it.

"Tonight's the night, babe. You fucking know it, and so do I." He rubbed lower, spreading his fingers in my folds, holding his fingers apart so near my clit. I started shaking all over again. "I'm gonna lay you down and fuck you. That'll clear both our heads. That'll wreck walls. And if it doesn't, tough shit, because I don't think all the brick in the world could hold my dick back from your pussy right now."

"Anton…"

Stop. But please don't stop.

I'm dying. Losing my mind. Drowning in my own slick pool of fire.

What the hell's happening to me? Really?

My mind wouldn't work. The questions and sensations were coming so fast. He must've sensed the unease crawling through my skin because the next thing I felt was his stubble. It brushed my cheek as he pulled away from my ear, dragging his hot breath across my face, centering himself just right.

His kiss came before I could say another word.

I wondered if I'd ever speak again. Our lips locked in a fury, captured a black energy burning through my skin, straight down to my bones. Muscles clenched so hard deep inside me my entire body rocked.

My ass jerked through the red dress, unintentionally grinding against him, hitting the sweet spot raging between his legs. His next kiss came a whole lot harder, barely breaking for air. He smothered me, caught my lower lip between his teeth, and ripped me open for his tongue.

He was in me. One part of him, at least, and it was only a fraction as intense as it would be to have him inside me somewhere else.

The same tongue that barked endless filth and orders at me for the first week wasn't any less commanding on my flesh. He swirled laps around my tongue, caught it, and led it in a hypnotic dance. He sucked the air right out of my lungs in one long, hungry, panty wetting kiss.

Jesus. I wondered if I still had anything on underneath the dress at all when he finally let me rest.

His eyes glowed brighter than the stars, drawing me into the maelstrom. He kept looking at me while his hands circled my ass, pinched it tight, and pulled me harder against his dick.

"Fuck, babe. You know what's happening here?" Another push. Another jerk of my hips.

My clit throbbed so hard it *hurt*. I would've given anything for a good pair of shears. And no, I wouldn't even jam them into his throat like I should – I'd use them to tear off the clothes between us.

"No, Anton." My voice sounded so distant, smothered in the ocean of lust. "I don't understand. You're scaring me."

He let out a low, deep laugh. "Good. Because I'm a little afraid of how you're gonna be after I throw you down and fuck you. It's okay to be scared shitless. You think you're scared now? You'd pass right out in my arms if you knew the kinda shit rampaging through my skull since that first talk we had at the prison."

My hand was shaking. I couldn't stand being held like this any longer without touching him. I ran my uneasy fingernails down his chest, following the buttons, feeling his heat underneath the fabric.

Holy shit. I could practically sense his heartbeat, banging away like pure bass behind his ribs.

"Fear doesn't matter here. I know that. I'm ready. I can take you."

Was I out of my fucking mind? Had I really said it? The surprised, challenged look on his face said I had.

Shit.

He took a longer, sharper breath before he said anything. "I'll leave you screaming and sore, baby girl. Shit, I'll make you feel me for the next fucking week, inside and out, every time you move. Your little cunt'll burn, and you'll still want more. The bruises I'll leave on your ass and suck around your tits will remind you that you'll never fuck like the old Sabrina again."

"Like there's anything there to ruin and change. You'll be the first to show me anything."

My face heated, burned fiercer than I expected when the words left my mouth. Time froze. Anton looked at me like I'd just told him I was seeing pink elephants.

"What?" His hand clapped over my mouth before I could say anything else.

"We're done talking, babe. If you're telling me you're a virgin…" He closed his eyes. "Fuck! You realize there's no turning back now, right? I could've tied my dick down and walked away if you started to whimper your regrets. Now? No fucking way. I'm not walking outta here 'til you're thoroughly fucked and dripping come down your legs. You're not leaving this bed anything less than a beautiful fucking woman."

The tremors were crawling through both of us now. He spun me around, threw me down, flattened me on the bed. His huge bulk hung over me, and he smashed my legs around his torso, then zipped one hand up between my thighs.

I listened to him inhale sharply when he found the wetness there. He grabbed my panties and pulled, jerked them all the way off. I barely lost my heels on the floor in time to feel them skip along my ankles.

"Fuck," he growled again. "Hope you're ready to suck and fuck, 'cause there's no stopping it. Hope you remembered to take that pill too. If you didn't, tough shit. We'd be fucking tonight on a bed of angry cobras before I'd think about stopping. Nothing'll stop me from shooting up inside that sweet little cunt – not even if some fuck busts in here and puts a gun to my head. Nothing, Sabrina, do you hear me?"

I heard him, all right, but the raging fire in my pussy was the only thing reaching my brain now. He ground his hips into me, forcing my dress up my belly, rocking his swollen erection into the bare slit he'd exposed.

I saw it. This was how I was going to die: heat stroke, underneath this brutal animal who'd taken me prisoner, this man I should've been fighting with everything I had instead of melting all over him in a position that was way past compromised.

"Nothing!" He growled it again, pumping more rough friction against my pussy.

My thighs shook, involuntarily trying to close against the shock. Anton felt one ripple and took them in both hands, spreading me apart. He dropped lower, sucking one breast through my dress and bra on his way down.

It happened like lightning. When I opened my eyes and tried to breathe, his face was between my legs, rough stubble skating up my tender inner thighs. The kisses he'd leveled against my lips, my tongue, my neck were all turned on my drenched center.

Anton held me down. He had to when his tongue started flicking my pussy over and over again, a relentless motion filled with such gusto it would've shamed a man dying of thirst. He licked me, sucked me, fucked me with his mouth, cursing more dirty words I couldn't quite make out while I gurgled up above.

No orgasm ever came like this. I thought I'd lost a piece of myself when he forced me to come with his hands, but now my soul was being shredded with every merciless lick.

I couldn't help myself. I pushed against his face, locked my thighs around his face. He seemed to enjoy it, grabbing the outer edges and pushing both legs harder against his head. He worked like a madman, growling as he fucked me with his tongue, never losing a single precious second to come up for air.

Nothing! The last thing he said echoed in my head. Rampant in every lick. *Absolutely fucking nothing.*

Whatever doubts and fears I had were banished by his tongue and the forceful fingers pressed into my skin. His raw fury turned me to stone, throttling more pleasure through my body.

Anton found my clit, pulled it into his mouth. He held it gently between his teeth, a prisoner for his quaking tongue, gliding over its overloaded surface.

Nothing, nothing, nothing!

I had nothing left to hold back. Fire erupted from my core and spread through my body in one long awesome blooming sensation. My pussy jerked, and he increased his suction. I ruptured, felt like I was coming undone from the bottom up, creaming myself through the racing fire.

"Anton!" I shrieked, clawing at the sheets overhead, anchoring myself to the bed so I didn't jump right through the ceiling.

It was the last thing I said before climax took over. Then there was nothing but that choppy, insatiable fire licking me all over, especially my tender nipples and everything below my waist. His tongue was all over me, tingling through my sweat, mirrored on my skin when he was really still fused to my pussy.

My eyes rolled back and I surrendered. There was no way left to resist, nothing left to do but lay and let the tide carry me away.

Ecstasy carried me far from the mansion, away to some distant, hot corner of the universe before I slammed back into my own body. I regained consciousness with my face turned to the side, staring at the stars. When I turned my head, he was over me, bowed up between my legs. Anton's fingers pulled at the straps on my dress.

"What happened?" I whispered. As if the nascent tingle in my body didn't tell the story my brain couldn't process.

"You came your fucking brains out, babe. You came beautiful. I'd eat that sweet cunt all day and make you scream with just my tongue. But I gotta do something to shut my dick up now. I *need* to be inside you."

Holy, holy shit. The way his voice rumbled like an avalanche when he said the last part left no doubt about what was happening.

He was going to split me open and take my virginity. And I wasn't even going to regret it.

At last, it was happening. I would've preferred a few dates, some good food and wine before he took me like this. So I'd told myself for years. I never imagined I'd be offering myself to a criminal who wasn't really giving me a choice, but there it was.

He wasn't asking. And I wasn't saying no.

He'd picked me up, lit me on fire, and scorched away every shred of my resistance. I hated him when he was ordering me around, keeping me prisoner – but I didn't despise a single thing about him when his tongue smothered my tender flesh.

Did that make us both equally fucked up lovers in this...this...whatever the hell *this* freaky thing was?

The shuffle of his clothes interrupted my racing thoughts. My dress was already gone, tugged off my body sometime when I was deep in my own head.

He shed his shirt with superhuman speed. He yanked off his shoes and then his trousers, losing them on the floor, snapping the boxers down his muscular legs next.

A huge red bird adorned his chest. It was dark like blood, a shade brighter than the stripes and wild patterns running up his arms, flying down his back. Everything inked to this man looked like it was meant to fly, lift him right off the ground and carry him out the window into the silvery night.

I reached out, brushing the huge predator with my hand. "Is this an eagle?"

Anton smiled. "Firebird. You've heard of it, right?" I hadn't.

"This motherfucker's legend," he said, bowing out his chest so I could get a better look. "Every feather it sheds is a blessing or a curse, guaranteed to smother everything it touches in flames. The firebird gets to the true heart of people and things. My nana always used to tell me the myths. Guess it stuck after all these years."

Fitting. And way more thoughtful than anything I wanted to give him credit for. Maybe Anton wasn't just a hard headed thug after all.

Not that his bare, muscular body wanted me to think anything different. He flexed, pushed his hands together, lowering his face. I followed his stare and gasped when I saw what he had between his legs.

His dick was *huge*. I mean, I'd seen big men with large packages on modeling sites before – some of them just as sinister looking and inked up as him. But what he had waiting for me, throbbing between his cedar sized thighs...

I closed my eyes and swallowed. Would it even fit inside me? If average guys were like five inches, then this was twice that, maybe more.

He shifted, stepped forward, rubbing it against my belly, giving his hips a good pump to make me feel how thick and long and hard he was. I shuddered. It might tear me to hell, but damn if I didn't want to try to ride it, push it all the way to my womb.

I did a double take when the dim moonlight caught a flash of something metal on his cock. There was something like a small bullet, a stud attached to his tip.

"What's the matter, babe? Every chick I've ever fucked loves what she sees. Don't tell me you're scared of a pierced dick?" He grinned. "I get it. This is your first. You're nervous. Don't be. Stuff that shit down and meet the only dick you're ever gonna have filling your holes. I'm gonna rock your fucking world so hard you'll never think about what another man feels like. Just me. *Only* me. You're mine, Sabrina."

Our eyes met. His glacial blue seas were on fire.

Bastard. I'd never stop saying it, thinking it, feeling it. He was always so confident, even when we were both naked. Would he wipe that murderous smug off his face when he finally came?

My pussy ached at the thought. I wondered if he'd really burn me from the inside out when he unloaded. Jesus, then there was the birth control. I'd been taking the pill through all this, just like he'd asked, but I seriously wondered if it would do a damned thing to stop him from getting me pregnant.

"I just need a second," I whispered, fighting a stupid smile twisting my lips. "This is crazy. It's all happening like –"

"Just like it's meant to, babe. I knew we'd be fucking the moment I saw you. Just didn't know I'd want it this bad."

He pushed his hips against me and grunted. Up and down, up and down, his dick glided over my skin in a wide arc, slathering him in the cream I couldn't stop oozing. It made the next jerks smoother, but I still jumped in his arms when he brushed over my clit.

"You're so damned responsive," he said. "Maybe I should hold you down. Make you jerk me off with just your squirming when I'm balls deep inside you."

"Yes!" I hissed, a needy sound so sharp I barely recognized it as my own.

He must've decided the time for talk and teasing was over. Suddenly, he swept lower, manhandling my breasts, pulling the nipples taut between his fingers for his mouth. He sucked one for a good long while and then moved to the next, all while I buckled underneath him, keeping my sanity by brushing my sleek legs against his.

He was growing warmer by the second. When I ran my hands up his spine, it was like touching volcanic rock, something rough and hot the earth had heaved up, chiseled to freak perfection in the mantle.

"Please!" I whimpered when he pulled away from my nipple, now sucked to sweet softness. "I need this, Anton. I want it bad."

There. He had my confession. Now, I wanted him to push between my legs and take all twenty-two years I'd lived as a stupid virgin in my family's shadow away.

He read my mind. Next thing I knew, the hardness between my legs slipped lower. He raised his hips, pulling my legs tight to his hips, getting his dick in the perfect position.

Growling, he sank into me.

It was slow at first, gradual and just a little bit painful. Good thing my pussy was so damned wet, still dripping with the need he'd stirred. I buckled, jerked up, steeling myself to take every beautiful inch of him.

He grabbed me, helped me take him deep. My eyes were pinched shut tight when he was finally all the way in, pressing his swollen head somewhere near my womb.

"You good, babe?" He stopped, held himself there, and clasped my chin.

I opened my eyes and nodded. Even if I wasn't, there was no stopping the lunatic need churning in our veins, pulling us together, calling us to fuck at all costs.

"Good. 'cause now I'm gonna hammer this pussy to heaven. Hold on and let it all go. The more you come, the better it'll be."

Like I had any choice.

I had to rough out the first few strokes when he pulled backwards and slammed into me, clinging to the mad desire while his thrusts stretched me to my limits. But every thrust kindled a little more fire, feeding the frenzy building in my core. Muscles sucked, clenched, and relaxed with his rhythm.

My pussy knew what it wanted, and it quickly adapted to get its greedy way.

Another climax hit me out of nowhere, so fast and unexpected it was almost blinding. It scorched away the rest of the pain and discomfort, leaving only ecstasy in its wake. And it was just one more wave of the long storm he carried through my body, howling into every nerve.

He was fucking me faster when I opened my eyes and stopped screaming.

My fingers ached from clawing at the sheets. I was surprised they were intact. My grip wasn't so good after coming on his dick, especially with the way he was pounding me into the bed.

Grunts spilled out of his mouth. He panted and fucked like the huge Russian animal he was. He shook so hard it looked like the firebird tattoo was flapping its wings, scattering its mythic fire, this time all over me.

What little sense of time and self I had left came apart on his thrusts. I came for the third time, breathless and hoarse, feeling his trim hair grinding on my clit. And he wasn't done fucking me.

He pulled out, flipped me over, holding me by the shoulders. He positioned me on all fours and took me like the mindless, desperate bitch-in-heat I'd become in that moment. Even the beautiful night sky above was nothing.

There was nothing, nothing, nothing except him and I, nothing except this pleasure, nothing except his incredible cock strumming inside me.

"Oh, shit. Shit. Motherfuck! I hope you're close to blowing again for me, babe, 'cause I'm gonna fill this pussy up," he panted. "I'm gonna make you remember my dick throbbing inside you all damned day. You want me to come hard, don't you?"

I nodded. He reached up, fisted my hair, and gave it another good shake.

"Really? I can't fucking hear you. Listen, if you're not screaming, I'll just fuck you straight through the next hour. You wanna rest? You better work for it. Make me come by brains out. Beg for my fucking seed."

That was when my hips took on a life of their own. I clenched him with my aching muscles so hard my vision blurred. I wanted to milk his dick dry. I wanted to make him break.

I wanted him to lose this demonic control he'd had over me from the moment we'd met – if only for a few glorious seconds.

I bucked wild onto his full, pierced length, meeting his thrusts as hard as I could. Of course, it only quickened the latest climax, the explosions that seemed like they'd never stop as long as he was inside me. That little bead sitting on his tip scratched me in places no woman could resist, and I was no exception.

My body tensed and I screamed, pushing my hair into his fingers. He nearly ripped it out when his fist tightened.

"Shit! Fuck!" He took another deep breath and threw his hips forward so hard he impaled me on the bed. "Sabrina!"

Hearing my name on his orgasmic lips did it. I came so hard I nearly tore in two, rocking against his dick, losing my mind as he unloaded pure fire into me. I felt it shoot to my womb, fill me, and then flow out of me, spilling out around us.

So much fire. So much of his essence. So fucking much.

Feeling him let loose satisfied me at a level I could barely comprehend. We rocked and came together for what felt like half the night. When my muscles stopped pulsing and I could finally breathe again, I crashed flat, sliding off his dick and feeling lava leaking out of me, running down my thighs.

"God damn it. Fuck…just fuck, babe." It took him a full minute to collect his breath. "For a virgin girl, you fuck like you were built for it."

The bed wobbled one more time as he rolled, falling down next to me hard.

We didn't rest for long.

I curled up against his chest, loving his heat, his closeness. My nerves vibrated, confused and alive with heat and a pleasant sleepiness that wouldn't drag me under until he was ready to let me go.

Before I said anything, Anton pushed his hand between my legs. He found my clit in the slick lubrication we'd both left behind. His fingers pinched it, and then they started to fuck me for the second time, reaching up inside me and stroking me just right.

"Anton, it's too soon," I whimpered. "I don't think I can –"

"Shut it. We're fucking 'til I'm good and spent. I got at least four more rounds before that happens. So do you, Sabrina. When you realize you can keep coming your brains out if I make you, then we can rest."

His mouth smothered mine before I could protest. More kisses. More fire.

His fingers quickened, rubbing me faster, deeper, and infinitely right. I pushed my thighs together and bucked against his hand, taken to the precipice. When he abruptly pulled away, my face contorted, reminding me of all the conflicting emotions I still had for this man.

But we weren't in this bed beneath the stars to think. Anton spread my legs apart and mounted me a second later, pushing hard and deep, using his dick where his fingers left off.

I came so fast. It would've been embarrassing if it didn't feel so fucking good.

Clenching around his cock just encouraged him to go full throttle. I gushed and thrashed and came on his pistoning erection, loving the way his heavy balls slapped my ass. Anton fisted my hair and brushed his stubble on my cheek, stamping rampant kisses down my neck, focused on my throat.

He fucked me until I thought I'd faint. The stars seemed to move across the sky above and behind him, swallowing up the bed, the house, and this whole ridiculous situation.

Everything was devoured except me, him, and the beautiful silvery void around us.

My fingernails raked hard down his back. The sensation must've struck a nerve because he started to fuck faster still, riding like an animal in heat.

He pulled out, lifted a leg, and got behind me. His huge tattooed muscle held me down while he entered me from the side. My legs flopped like loose scissor blades as he thrust deeper, guiding that metal stud across my velvet like a precision missile.

Dizzying in his strength. Coarse in his whispers. Brutally masculine.

He fucked me like he owned me, and in bed, he finally did.

I reached for the pillows and tangled them in my hands just as the brimstone in my belly went off. Anton jerked my hair so hard I thought he'd tear a clump out, ramming his cock inside me again and again.

He threw his head back and bellowed. "Fuck, fuck, fuck! I'm filling this fucking pussy, babe. Filling you up the way you were meant to be filled. Filling you with the only dick that's ever gonna own this beautiful tight cunt."

His free hand pinched my thigh, holding me open for him, squeezing deep into my tender flesh. The heady mix of pain and pleasure collided and went nova. The stars became fireworks all over again, smeared across my vision, blinded by silver pleasure.

Tempo. Sweat. Spice. Fire.

All my senses fired on maximum as he drove deep and emptied himself inside me. My pussy instantly came when it took his come, pulsing and burning so fierce it shook every inch of me, threatened to collapse me into his world forever.

Everything became a total blur after that. I think he fucked me a couple more times, holding me by the hair on all fours, pulling it and slapping my ass to keep me conscious whenever my body tried to shut down.

He rocketed my body right to the stars and hauled me back to earth, always pressing his mouth to my ear when he wasn't kissing or biting or tormenting my nipples with his wicked tongue.

"I fuck deep enough to feel your pulse, babe. Don't ever forget it. I'll take your heart. I'll take your soul. I'll take your body. And I'll never, ever wanna let go. Don't get any fucked up ideas, Sabrina. You're bound to me by flesh and blood and sex. Especially the fucking." He sucked in a hot breath. "You're goddamned delectable, and I'm fucking insatiable. I'll never get tired of shooting off in this hot little cunt. Do you hear me, babe? No? Then I'll drill it in loud and clear 'til it echoes in your body forever."

I'd never been so…so *drained* by the time it was over. And I mean that in every sense of the word.

I remember him pulling me into his arms and finally listening to his drumming heartbeat guiding me to sleep. We both slept like the dead.

He rose before me, escaped the bed, and left nothing behind. When I got up, he was gone. It was early morning, and a cold one too. I reached for the sheet and pulled it around me, missing his warmth.

As I slid my hand over the empty impression his body left on the bed, I marveled at how quickly I'd fallen. The old Sabrina Ligiotti was hanging by a thread, about to slip into – what, exactly?

His control? Forever?

His presence was awesome. The sex was amazing. But I wasn't ready to submit and serve him on nothing more than powerful suggestions he'd made about my family.

I thought about Uncle Gioulio. If I gave in and let the Ivankov brothers have their way – or, God forbid, *helped them* – my only close flesh and blood would die a horrible death. The Russians wouldn't make it quick and easy.

Whatever I still had to learn about this world, I understood that much. I also knew my Uncle would burn for what he was being accused of. If he'd actually done it, he deserved to.

The proof hadn't sunk in yet because it wasn't total. I needed more than Anton's imposing speeches and a tightly controlled computer to show me what the hell was going on. It wasn't like I could just come out and ask either.

If this was an elaborate trick or an exaggeration to get me on his side, then the answers would always be twisted one way or another. More questions wouldn't tell me anything.

Escape wasn't any less appealing than it was the day before. And maybe it was one step closer now that I'd had an unforgettable romp with Anton. If this night meant as much to him as it did to me, the trust between us had grown.

Maybe I was stupid and naive. I *wanted* to believe he needed my help to do the right thing, even if it was making moves that would twist my heart in tourniquets. But I couldn't know until I lied to him and got my freedom.

I wasn't sold on anything yet. It was my job to make him believe I was. I'd say anything and everything to make him trust me, set me free, send me back to where I came from.

If I could return to the outside world, I'd be able to confront my uncle and all this insane history face-to-face, without anything suspect in the way.

Bowing my head in the early morning light, I licked my lips and tasted him. It felt so good when he was owning my body last night. Still, I'd never let him have everything else until I was sure he deserved it.

Things had taken a truly crazy turn, and now there was nothing left to do but follow the crooked path. It wasn't about old blood feuds and wars between mobsters anymore.

It was about him and I.

If the fiery gravity I felt here on the bed was real, more than just mind blowing sex, then I had to get to the truth. That's what they always say sets a person free, right?

Too bad they never tell you it's bipolar, a split revelation with the power to enslave, liberate, or destroy. Much like the firebird branded on Anton's body. I was ready to discover what it would do here, even when every possibility offered death or triumph.

VI: Spellbound (Anton)

I wasn't the only one who'd spent the entire fucking night blowing off steam. Shit, I wasn't sure what the hell I hadn't blown last night with her. Felt like I got hit by a semi when I dragged my ass downstairs the next morning, tasting her sleepy lips one last time before I left. The kiss reminded me the marathon night of fucking must've taken a year off my life, and it was so damned worth it.

Daniel was passed out in a chair by the window, an empty bottle of good vodka at his side. In the master office, Lev's naked ass was pressed against the glass, his big arms wrapped around the slim blonde I'd seen taking care of shit around the house.

Jesus Christ. None of us had time for this shit. Party time was over with planning to do.

When I ripped open the door, the girl woke his ass screaming. I pretended I wasn't the world's biggest, most thoroughly fucked hypocrite.

"What the fuck are you doing?! This is what I left you down here to work on all night while I did all the important shit? Look at this! Goddamn, brother. Now we'll have to find a new maid too."

They never lasted long when somebody's appetite got the better of them. If she was lucky, she'd get a fat payout and a one way ticket back to her old country, cold cash and a hard warning to forget all about America and working for the Ivankov brothers.

Lev stood up and covered the girl with his naked body, shielding her from me. Fuck. Way too early for the sight of my brother's naked body. He looked like an overgrown tiger standing on two legs.

"Asshole! Why can't you knock first?" He stepped up and slapped my chest.

I stumbled backwards, fully ready to send my fist into his jaw. Then I heard the footsteps behind me, fast and uneven. Daniel tackled both of us, knocked us onto the floor, all while the blonde bitch squealed and grabbed for her clothes.

She was out the door, running somewhere more discrete to dress while we all grappled with each other. I got in a couple punches and blooded Lev's nose. I was about to bust his fucking lip – best way to show him I was serious – when Daniel started laughing like an idiot.

"What's so damned funny?" I growled, wrapping my free hand around his throat.

"Just realized this is what it's come to. You and the Ligiotti bitch upstairs. Lev, burying himself in housekeeper pussy."

"And you with your fucking bottle," I snarled, tightening my fingers around his throat.

He moved surprisingly fast for a man with a hangover, jerking his head to break the lock I had on him. "Yeah. Point is, we're all procrastinating now. No more lying, brothers. We're afraid to do this fucking job, aren't we? What happened before killed us. Sucked the wind right out of our sails. We screwed up We let that bastard get away, and almost killed some innocent girls on top of it. Thank God somebody was looking out for them."

My fists weakened. Lev took the opportunity to throw me off him, roaring as he stood and marched across the room, finding his clothes.

I got back on my feet and contemplated a re-match while his back was turned. Forget it. Both my brothers were being total cocks, but Daniel had a point. He'd also just spat out the shit that used to keep me up all night behind bars, the guilt and amazement that things hadn't gone off worse when Gioulio escaped our bomb.

We'd killed a bunch of twisted fucks and almost bagged him, yeah. But we could've just as easily killed the slave girls. Nobody wanted to fuck up and miss him again, and getting clean blood on our hands was worse than spilling our own.

Fuck.

I pointed to Lev. "Soon as this jackoff is dressed, let's get some breakfast and talk business. No more drinks or fucking. It's time to be adults and get our shit in order."

Lev turned, buttoning his shirt, giving me a demon glare. "Don't act so damned high and mighty, dear *brat*. I know you were fucking the night away like me. Least I know how to stick my dick in a place that's only gonna cause us a *little* drama."

I suppressed a growl. Hearing him let Russian slip, the harsher foreign tone we'd been raised with from our father reminded me these fucks weren't my enemies. Not by a long shot. These boys were all I had. All I'd get to help me do what I came to do. All I had on my side to wrap this shit up and find out if there was more to Sabrina than discovering how many nasty noises she could make underneath me while I fucked her into the mattress.

Daniel smoothed a hand across his face, wiping at his hangover's afterglow. He looked at me with the same bright blue eyes set in my own head, only his were duller from the binge drinking.

"Breakfast it is. Bring the girl down. We'll all interview her to make sure she's truly ready to go out on her own."

Frowning, I pushed myself well into his personal bubble. Daniel stumbled back a couple steps and then caught himself, ready to fight if he had to. He lacked some of the brawn Lev and I had, but the boy made up for it in brains instead, and he was a sneaky motherfucker when push came to shove.

"No. What happens today is between the three of us. I'm not letting your bullshit undo all the fucking progress I've made this past week. She's ready to go. *I* opened her eyes. She's a believer after seeing all the fucked up shit her bastard uncle's been hiding. I didn't have to twist her arm an inch."

Thank fuck for that. If Sabrina hadn't cracked, my brothers would've been riding my ass to resort to darker means, longer captivity, and all the pitch black bullshit that came with making a hostage work with us.

We weren't the good guys. I'd never had any illusions about that. Sure, there were lines the Ligiotti bastards crossed that we never would, but it didn't mean we were exempt from using blades and cages and brutal threats when there was a damned good reason.

Daniel sniffed. Lev came up behind him, and I was the first one out. My brothers followed behind me to the dining hall, where I called the servants over the intercom and told them to get the morning grub going.

Ten minutes later, after some coffee and half a plate of good eggs and salami, I was in my right mind to work this shit out. Hopefully without putting a few more bruises on the boys at my side.

"We're gonna need that interview, Anton," Daniel said, forking food into his mouth. "Let us talk to her. Unless you can convince us she's done a full one-eighty in a week's time, we need to hear your girl with our own ears."

Lev chuckled, taking a big bite out of a green pear. "We all have a way with women, brothers. But, tell me, Anton, since when does fucking a bitch turn her against the only family she's ever known?"

My fists hit the table hard. My brothers both jumped, and then settled back into their seats with a glare.

"The dicking didn't do shit. She wanted it. It's not goddamned mind control, and you boys are smart enough to know it," I growled. "Sabrina's changed her mind because I showed her the fucking truth, cold and up close. I told her that all the upstanding citizens I blew to kingdom come were gutter feeding rats, and I backed it up with proof. She's gonna help us get to Gioulio one way or another."

"Yeah? What's that? Radio collar?" The tone in Daniel's voice said he was only half-serious. We'd done the wire thing before with a few other fucks under our care.

Of course, none of those fucks were one hundredth as pretty as Sabrina. I'd never fucked any of them 'til the point of collapse. They never clawed underneath my skin neither, making me fly into a chest thumping rage whenever I thought about 'em getting skinned alive by our enemies.

Shit. I grabbed my forehead and steadied myself, wondering what the fuck she'd done to me.

No joke. If she hadn't felt so fucking good last night, virgin and all mine, I would've believed she had something up her pussy to poison a man's mind.

"What the fuck? Are you okay?" Lev took another bite, his big blue eyes showing brotherly concern.

"I'm fine. Look, I'm telling you she's gonna work with us. If she doesn't, you can take me out to the courtyard and put a fucking bullet in my head. And I'd deserve a whole lot worse for fucking over this family on a gut feeling."

Daniel held out a hand. "Stop right there. I'm willing to give this crazy shit a chance because we've got no better way to get to the Italian, but you're gonna need more than guts backing this up. I've been wanting to try out my new gear anyway."

"The bug?" I exhaled slowly. "What good's it gonna do? Yeah, we'll be able to see where she's at and what the fuck she's doing. But really, if she wants to fuck us over as soon as she's outta our grasp, it's not like we can come roaring in to deal with it. Not when she's in family territory."

Lev folded his arms and Daniel glared at me like I'd flipped my fucking lid. Maybe I truly had. I'd fucked and unloaded in that sweet thing six or seven times last night, mere hours ago, and my cock was already throbbing the more I ate, hungry for more.

"She's not going anywhere unless D does his thing, brother. I'm not gonna fucking allow it. You know I'm right. Papa would start kindling a fire in his fucking grave from the spin if we let that bitch walk home without something on her. You believe your hunch is right. We want to believe it too. Keeping tabs on her will prove everybody's sincere. Maybe we'll even let her go without that friendly talk."

I swallowed. Fuck, much as I didn't want to admit it, he was right. And this time, the gut feeling about sending

Sabrina back had damned well *better* be right. If she turned tail and fucked us over, betrayed me…

She'd die. And I'd probably die in the process putting her and her twisted uncle down.

No, damn it, this *had* to work.

"Okay," I said at last. "I'll slip it on her tonight before I tell her the news. She'll be ready to go tomorrow."

"Make sure she is," Lev said, ripping down to his pear's core with his teeth. "We've already taken some serious delays. You know the state's bringing the Feds in to hunt your ass, right?"

Daniel nodded. "It's a small miracle they haven't dropped in on us yet. Keeping the family name off this place will give us shelter for awhile, but it's only a matter of time before some badge comes sniffing here, looking for Anton."

I didn't say anything. I wasn't a fucking fool. I knew damned well my chances to help end the war with the Italians were ticking away by the second.

Tick-tick-fucking-tock.

The big clock beneath our grandfather's portrait clicked behind me, a real world reminder of everything around me narrowing like a goddamned noose.

I'd make this shit work. Sabrina would waltz in, work with Gioulio to get us his location, and then I'd swoop in and carry her away after putting lead in that fucker. I'd carry her away like a caveman if I had to. No fucking way was I leaving her behind to rot.

And next time, I'd take my girl away from this shit for good. Far, far away. Somewhere we'd be safe from being separated. Anywhere we could both put this dark shit behind us and get down to what really mattered.

She was in the bath when I found her that evening, probably soaking her sore muscles after the night we'd had. I couldn't help but suppress a grin that I'd done that to her.

Her hands sloshed through water when I pushed open the door. "Don't you ever knock?"

"Not necessary, babe. It's not like there's anything in here I haven't seen before – and I'm gonna see it all again up close real fucking soon."

She quirked an eyebrow. "You're very sure of yourself."

I shrugged. "It's easy to know my odds after the way you screamed on this dick last night. You gonna bathe here all night or have you worked up an appetite yet?"

"I'm starving."

"Then let's get you dressed and have some dinner. I got the chef to set us up in a special spot. I think we can dine outside tonight. You won't run off."

I stuck a hand in my pocket and fingered the bug. Fuck, slipping that little black chip into her shit tonight felt wrong. But it was the only sane thing to do before I sent her on her merry way, the only way my brothers were gonna let her go back to Chicago at all.

There was still a damned good chance everything could go wrong once she was outta here too. Who knew when

I'd get to run my hands through that soft black hair again? What if it was months before I tasted her sweet cunt, or felt the way it jerked around me when I slammed my cock to the hilt?

Fuck, fuck fuck. I was already missing her, and she wasn't even gone yet.

"Let's go," I growled, stepping up to the tub and pulling her up with one hand.

She looked so damned delectable I wanted to rip off my clothes, push her back into the water, and fuck her right there. I'd make the water in the tub rain all over the fucking bathroom with how bad I *needed* to be inside her, raw and desperate, fevered as the way my skin burned a few degrees higher just looking up and down her sleek, naked body.

"Okay, okay! I'm coming," she said, flopping over the little step against my chest.

I reluctantly let her go and handed her a towel. Then I tugged her back into my grasp while I dried her off. Any excuse to get my rough hands on her was a good one. Something about the bath made her skin smoother than ever, exquisite in a special, feminine way.

My dick wanted to rip right through my trousers and push between her legs. The fiery pull between us was magnetic, pleading, do-or-fucking-die.

Goddamned it. I had to get her dressed now before I forgot all about the shit I had planned in the gardens. If I didn't, my appetite for anything besides serious fucking would be wiped.

"Pick something warm," I said, dropping the towel and walking her over to the closet. "It's a chilly night out there. There's a little jacket in there if you really need it."

She disappeared into the big walk-in closet. I waited outside it, re-thinking my dumbass encouragement for dressing in layers. Well, fuck. It's not like whatever she picked would be staying on all night anyway.

We'd all wind up naked, whether it was in the grass or in this bed. I was gonna fuck her like it was our last time tonight – and if God was cruel, it might be. My heart pounded lava through my veins, and it all went straight to my dick, hammering away in my pants 'til she finally stepped out.

Christ. Even when she was dressed in a cool cashmere sweater and a nice thick skirt flowing down to her ankles, she was beautiful. My fingers twitched at my sides, aching to grab her silky black hair and shove her to the wall, rip that shit off, and get inside her right now.

Control yourself, asshole, a voice rumbled in my head. *You've done it before and it always pays dividends when you finally get your dick wet.*

Yeah, but not like this. Not with *anyone* like her. I still had a lot to learn about this chick, but she'd become a fucking obsession I couldn't banish from my head. Morning, noon, or night, *everything* revolved around her, and not just because she was the master key to putting Gioulio Ligiotti in his grave.

"Well? Are we going? I'm anxious to see what this big secret is."

I swallowed. Fucking idiot. Felt just like a kid again about to go off to prom. Of course, that night I'd discovered I was a natural animal in bed. The little girl who rode my dick must've squirted three times for every load I popped.

I used a condom then, same as ninety percent of the chicks I ever fucked. But not with Sabrina.

I'd never, ever keep rubber between that sweet pussy and me. I'd fill her the fuck up and watch it run outta her pink slit with pride, one of many ways her perfect body smoked when it was done burning, trembling, and screaming on my flesh.

We got outside and headed downstairs, down the fork in the hall leading to the back gardens. Good thing Daniel was drowning his ass in the bar downstairs again. He would've given me shit over spending the night outside, even though the back gardens were totally enclosed.

Fucker worried too much about the Feds. Too much about her escaping too. What good was freedom if I couldn't do the shit I wanted because I was too busy looking over my shoulder for bastards eager to drag me back to prison?

No way. No how. I wasn't letting anything get in the way of tonight, and right now I wanted her warmth more than I loved the cool Fall breeze brushing against my skin.

When we stepped through the big glass door leading out back, she stopped and stared. The garden was lit with torches stretching all the way to the gazebo with the table, where dinner and wine waited for us.

I normally preferred something harder to go with my steak, but for her, I'd go classy as fuck. If I was hoping to knock her panties off, I'd done the job too well.

I had to grab her and pull her along the soft lit path to get the girl moving again. She couldn't stop gawking at the display, marveling at all the vines and flowers we passed on our way in. Old Grigor gave a respectful nod as we walked by him.

I nodded back, letting him know he was dismissed. He wanted to make sure everything was cool. Of course it was because the family kept the right man in charge of this shit. And if something was fucked, he'd come roaring back when I called to fix it.

Pulling out a chair next to me for Sabrina, I waved. "Sit down, babe. This is a special night."

She sat down, and then I took the chair across from her, trying to switch my brain off sex for one microsecond. Dinner helped with that.

Sabrina talked all about her life in the windy city while we ate. After her mom died, her old man got fucked up on all sorts of junk and put her in bastard Gioulio's orbit. The fuck kept her close like a caged dove – without her even realizing it.

"Uncle always wanted me to be a good girl. He saved me from getting in too deep with the family business, steered me into journalism instead," she said. "I guess he hoped I'd end up growing up and traveling the world for stories. He never counted on a burning interest in the local stuff — especially the roots my family's helped lay down here. Living history, you know."

I nodded, popping a perfect piece of steak in my mouth. Goddamn, it was good. Not so good it took any attention off fucking her, though.

"Don't you think he was trying to control you? He knew you'd break if you found out what he was into. You'd want no part of it."

She stared at her plate thoughtfully. "Yeah, I suppose. After what you've showed me...I wonder if I know who he is at all. Uncle Gioulio's not the man I thought he was. I knew bad things were happening in the drug world to keep the money and the lifestyle coming. I just never thought he was trafficking women. I never thought he'd go that far."

Her angry eyes darted up. If she was pissed at me for ripping back the curtain, fine. It didn't matter as long as most of that rage was directed at her own flesh and blood, the asshole who deserved to be taken out swiftly, ending a decades old cat and mouse game.

"He did," I reminded her, driving it fucking home. "And you're gonna help us make him fucking pay. Tomorrow. I trust you, Sabrina."

I reached for her hand. Dinner was just about over as far as I was concerned. I'd waited 'til she'd plowed through most of her food and was onto her second glass of wine.

"What do you mean?"

"Our boy Misha's gonna drive you home to the city tomorrow. Don't know if your uncle's sealed up your place or not, but we'll let you off at his night club, that pear place you're always hanging out at. The sooner he finds you, the sooner we can get this shit over with."

She tensed up. Her fingers smoothed their way over mine, and I tightened my hold. "I'm not your asshole uncle. I'm being open, frank with you in a way no man's been before. I want your help with offing his ass not just because we've got a blood vendetta. I need you to help me put him down so we can be together, babe. That's what you want, right?"

Her dark eyes met mine. Pale white cheeks flushed red, like she was afraid to admit it. Yeah, the world knew it was wrong to have us coming together. Warring blood wasn't meant to love. And it sure as shit wasn't meant to fuck so good, so natural.

"Don't play shy," I growled, pushing my chair out and coming over to her. "You wanna see how bright this future burns, don't you?"

"Yeah," she finally said, breath storming out her soft lips. "It's just happening so fast. I can't kill him myself. I can't be there when –"

I jerked her up and smashed her to my chest. My fingers caught her chin, gently twisted her face to mine, making her look at me. My dick knew damned well what it wanted, but for once my heart overpowered his greedy hunger.

"You won't have to. All you gotta do is figure out where he's gonna be and when. We'll give you a burner phone, and you'll call me as soon as you know. Give us a time, a place, something you'll know with certainty. I'll have you picked up and gone before he shows. My brothers and I'll corner him and finish the shit we should've wrapped up months ago. It'll be over fast. We'll be free to figure out the rest, babe. Everything we're gonna do with the rest of our lives."

My hands slipped down her back, and then trailed lower. My palm stopped on her ass and my fingers tightened, feeling her, rocking her hips into mine. I wasn't shy about showing her exactly what that future was gonna be.

Honestly, I didn't give two shits about the rest, as long as she was happy.

We'd have to flee the States for awhile, yeah. Maybe she'd finally get that foreign writer career after all, or else she'd learn to bake and paint if she wanted. We had the money to do it all, and with the Ligiotti clan neutered, there was nothing stopping us from making whole continents our bitch.

Even the Feds would get off my trail with time. We could come back to the States, home to Chicago. You'd be amazed what a lotta bribes in the right places plus a few years can do for any crime.

"Is it really that easy, Anton?" She lowered her head, looking strained, conflicted.

"Long as I'm in charge here, fuck yeah, it is. I can't stand you doubting me." I let my other hand glide down her ass, and when both were firmly there, I squeezed. She gasped.

Perfect. I wasn't gonna let her walk outta here thinking this shit wouldn't work. And if she couldn't get it through her head by words alone, then I'd give her body the best damned distraction in the world.

"Look at me, Sabrina. We're gonna wrap this shit up and get on with our lives. We don't have to spend the best years we've got wrapped up in this twisted underworld. I've already given my family plenty. After this, I'm done. I'm taking a well deserved break. I wanna travel with a girl and figure out all the shit I haven't yet."

She smiled, and I knew I was speaking to the same needs inside her. Warring blood or not, we were brother and sister in crime and death. We'd been shaped by the roughest edges in life a human being could know.

Could we smooth shit out? I didn't fucking know, but damn if I wasn't gonna try. I'd be the one to set her free, give her what her wicked uncle never could.

"What do I need before you send me out to play secret agent?" She asked.

I almost laughed. Now, she was in such a rush she wanted to get right down to brass tacks. I wasn't having it.

"I'll show you. Walk with me." I reluctantly pulled my hands off her ass and we moved down the long, winding path plunging deeper into the the gardens, towards a long crop of big trees in the flat Illinois landscape.

"It's beautiful out here," she said, smiling at the stars. "Almost makes me believe we can really do this."

"Good. You stay out here and look at this shit as long as it takes for you to know we can." I stopped by a big row of vines curling up a stone bear statue, pulling her to my chest. "Take a good long fucking look, babe. I can take you razzing me with that sweet tongue or fighting tooth and nail. But I'll never have you doubting shit. Not now. Not ever. Understand?"

She blinked. What the hell was that unease still tugging at her face?

I was starting to get pissed, wondering why my best words were falling deaf. Fuck, if words weren't gonna do the job, then I'd tear her clothes off and fuck her right here on the ground. There was another gazebo further out, some shit my old man installed when he brought his girlfriends out here.

"I gave you a chance," I said, shaking my head. "Looks like you're not gonna believe anything I say."

"No! No, it's not that. It's just that I'm trying to digest all this. Please, Anton, it's hard. I'm not used to playing these spy games and killing like you are."

I stopped mid-step and my arm tightened around her neck. "You don't need to get used to it. You only gotta do your job and scope your uncle's shit out once, feed it back to us. I told you to stop doubting me, babe. Now we're done talking."

Her eyes widened, full of wonder at what I was gonna do. Pushing her up the single step to the gazebo, I walked her inside it, straight to the smooth marble bench near the back. I sat on it, spinning her around, never letting her outta my grasp.

"Anton! It's so cold here…"

She tried to resist as I yanked off her skirt. Cold or not, I wasn't stopping. I was gonna give her one helluva send off 'til we met again. One last wild night to make damned sure she did what I said and came back, to make her forget about her fear, to make her trust and believe me.

I'd make her come so fucking hard it blew her brains out, and then I'd stuff whatever the fuck I wanted in her head. This girl was mine, dammit, and I wanted everything – body, mind, and soul.

She whimpered and stiffened up in the cool night air, bracing her bare legs against me. I'd let her keep the sweater on for this part, long as she buckled up and came for me like a good girl.

Sabrina moaned softly as I reached up her skirt and fisted her panties. They came down her sleek legs in one jerk. She stepped out of them and turned.

However conflicted she'd been a couple of minutes ago, her pussy sure didn't show it. She was swollen, wet, and waiting for me. When I saw the pearly slickness between her legs, my dick thumped hard in my pants, bouncing with thick, hot blood pumping through it.

Shit, I needed her. Needed her taste, her smell, the sweet fucking music she made when I nailed her clit.

"Anton!" She called my name once and I silenced her with a jerk forward.

My face dove between her legs and I pinched her ass tight, giving her no way to go but into my mouth. My tongue found what it was looking for. I smiled as I opened my lips, digging into her sweetness, teasing her lower lips with slow, sensual licks.

The girl deserved a little warm up before I caused her whole body to quake with my tongue.

Her nipples must've been hard as fuck beneath the sweater. I'd get to sucking them a little later, but fuck if I didn't treat her clit the same way. I found it with my teeth and pinched tight, letting her roll her hips, slowly working on my mouth just perfect.

My fingers pinched her ass harder. She'd show me how bad she wanted this, or I'd drag out this orgasm 'til dawn.

It didn't take long. Sabrina became a rocking, moaning, oozing mess, grinding her pussy into my lips, circling her clit against my tongue. When she least suspected it, I took her, opened her, sucked her tenderest target into my mouth.

That little nub got sucked deep and smothered with licks. Fucking incredible. My assault was too ferocious and she tried to squirm outta my grip, but I held on for dear life. No fucking way was she getting away before her body seized like lightning.

Fuck, she tasted good. Her cream drove me on, licking deeper, faster. My fingers helped her pussy slide back and forth on my lips. I was fucking coated in her juices by the time she came.

The girl went off like a seething volcano, running her fingers through my hair and screaming like a banshee. I made sure she didn't topple to the ground when her knees went weak. Her little clit throbbed between my lips as she lost control, giving it all up, giving me everything I wanted.

I knew right then I'd never get tired of tormenting her like this. No woman would ever compare to making this one come. Nobody else would ever start a fire in my guts that wouldn't stop burning 'til she was owned, branded, under my control.

She was shaking when she came down from the orgasmic high. I helped her onto the stone bench. Her little ass jerked, too cool for comfort.

Too damned bad. She'd be full of fire again soon enough. My dick thumped against my trousers like a fucking battery ram, and now was the perfect time to let it frolic.

Her legs were open, still trembling when I got on the bench and started taking off my clothes. She watched me undo my shirt and then the dark pants. Fuck, no use keeping the boxers on too. They slid down my strong thighs and hit the ground, and I joined her, naked in the cool, glorious dark.

"God. I'm freezing," she whispered, tucking her hands around her breasts, trying to tug her jacket lower to cover up what I'd exposed.

My lips quirked. Silly girl. Didn't she know the rest of what she had on was coming off right now?

Freezing or not, she didn't fight me as I drew off the jacket and then unzipped her dress, rolling it all the way off, then working on the lacy black bra underneath. My cock jerked when I saw her pink nipples pointing at the stars. I couldn't have stopped my mouth for anything in the world.

Her temperature flushed and overheated less than a minute after I sucked the first. She tasted so fucking good all over, every delicate part of her, curves upon curves begging to be conquered. Her back arched against me when I started on the other one, taking my sweet time, pinching the wet soft nip I'd already sucked between my fingers.

Her hips shifted against mine. We both knew damned well what she wanted, and her sneaky little body brushed against my cock, calling me home, calling me to fuck.

Just feeling her opening a couple inches from me turned my blood molten. She was melting underneath me, sure, but I was rattling apart, inch by savage inch.

Fuck me. Fuck her.

If I didn't take her right that second, I risked shooting off all over her belly like a goddamned teenager. Just the thought of wasting my come anywhere but inside her pissed me off royal.

I rose, giving my cock a good jerk to aim it right. Her wide dark eyes were all over me, marveling, as if she knew how bad her body teased me. If she did, then she was gonna find out right now how hard I fucked when I'd been teased too damned long.

I filled her in one thrust. Her sharp gasp made my ears bristle, and I swore I could hear her heartbeat too. The tempo thudded harder in her chest when I pulled my hips back and slammed into her again, grinding my dick so close to her womb, making her feel every fucking inch, smothering her clit with my pubic bone.

"Anton! Yes!" Her bones were shaking again, calling me to shake them harder. "Please…"

Her nails scraped my shoulders, begging me to fuck her. Request granted.

I plowed into her again and again, shook her entire body, didn't slow down once 'til I heard her ass bouncing on the slab underneath us. That was my cue to rear up and grab her ass, thrusting deeper still, feeling my balls start to boil when her legs got a death lock around my waist.

One look told me she was about to come. I pistoned faster, slapping my balls on her soft flesh so fucking hard it hurt. We fucked right through her second orgasm of the evening.

No lie, I almost lost it more than a couple times when her pussy sucked and clenched at my cock. But I wasn't done yet. I wasn't giving her shit 'til she was a totally ravaged incoherent mess.

I wanted her to burn with me, roast like a human torch in the gardens lightning up our path. I wanted to fuck her senseless and bring her back to life again. I wanted to fuck her so hard she forgot her own name.

It didn't fucking matter. Nothing did except her knowing exactly who I was: the man who owned every beautiful inch of her, the man who made her come so hard she forgot about all the bullshit waiting for us tomorrow.

Her eyes were wide, bleary, and insatiable when she started coming down from the climax. I held her ass, pushed her to me, and rolled her over.

"Get on my dick," I growled, pointing and pulling her onto my lap. "You want my come? Then you'll pump it outta me, riding this cock for all you're worth."

She blushed. Shy as usual, but that act wasn't fooling anybody. I watched her sweet cunt sink down on my length, grunting as her hips locked onto mine. Her legs pinched tight.

I tried not to grin. Fuck, this was gonna be good, just knew the girl was a natural rider.

She bobbed up and down, getting her footing at first, slowly picking up speed. She stopped every few seconds, throwing her head back, trying to keep going as the pleasure shot through her.

I grabbed both her hands and held them tight. "Come on. You can go harder than that. Fuck me like you mean it, babe. Make my balls melt."

A minute later, I realized what an animal I'd just turned loose. She went wild, bucking against me a little harder with every thrust, riding my full length like a champ, showing her little teeth as they dug into her bottom lip.

Oh, shit. Motherfuck.

Her nails raked my chest and those plump thighs slapped mine in a steady clap. It must've been forty degrees that night, but I was drenched, drowning in my own sweat the same as her. The approaching release took us both by the throats, a fever that wouldn't break 'til I spent everything I had.

I couldn't suppress my own beast anymore. I wrapped my fingers around her ass and power fucked her, slamming my cock so hard into her pussy she bounced in the air, rode me like I was running a hundred miles an hour. And I always yanked her back, right where she belonged, impaling her 'til her pussy squeezed my nuts.

"Oh…oh…oh. My. God!"

I'm sure he could hear her prayers as she threw her head up to the sky. Sabrina's pussy convulsed like a maniac. The hellfire churning in my balls wouldn't stay put anymore – not when her cunt was jerking me off like a vise wrapped in silk.

I exploded. My fingers dug into her ass so hard it had to hurt, but she just kept riding me, making me lose my mind buried inside her.

Fuck, fuck, fuck!

Coming never felt so good. Half my soul ripped out my cock in the jets I pumped inside her. Snarling, thrashing, grunting, I went full primal as our orgasm fused us together.

I could feel her in every pulse, just the same as she could feel me each time my cock twitched and spat fire up into her. Shit, we were completely toasty by the end, but on the way there I forgot we were fucking buck naked outside.

Thank fuck the cool night air blanketed us. For the first time since we'd started, I actually felt cold, listening to her make little sighs as she recovered her senses.

"You're one helluva fuck for being so new to it, babe," I said, tugging her to my chest.

She answered me with a long, hot kiss. The girl knew how to tease, even when my dick was so numb and zonked out it felt like it'd take a thousand years to recover.

More like a thousand milli-seconds at the rate we were going. I pulled out and kissed her again, rolling her on her back, letting more blood pool into my dick. I fisted her hair and held her down while we kissed, letting my teeth get into it when she moaned into my mouth.

Before I knew it, I was hard as stone again.

It was the start of two more sanity stripping fucks out in the old gazebo. If my old man could've seen the shit I did to her in his favorite spot, he probably would've jumped outta his grave and bought me a tall shot of good vodka.

When our fires burned cooler and we were both half-frozen, I gathered up our clothes and helped her dress. The servants asked no questions as I carried her inside. They got paid good money to keep their fucking mouths shut and treat every Ivankov brother like any other gold plated swinging dick.

A steady pay check and common blood rooted in Mother Russia did a lot to make sure we never got traitors in our house.

I carried her up to her room and laid her down, lighting a fire to warm us both up. Yeah, we fucked again, two or three more times. The last time my dick shot off inside her was bittersweet.

A couple more kisses, and she was out like a light, giving me ample opportunity to do what I needed. The little bag the servants left out for her was waiting by the door. I grabbed my pants off the floor and fished out the small circular plastic chip Daniel had pieced together.

How that boy came up with these fucked up inventions, I'd never understand. The CIA and FSB would've drooled their fucking hearts out at the size of this thing.

It easily hooked to the side of her purse like a little bead. GPS and a microphone. We'd be able to see everywhere she went, and hear her the second she started talking to her bastard uncle.

It's for her good and yours. Just turn her loose with this shit and bring it to a close. She never has to know.

Yeah. Yeah, fucking right.

If only I could've believed it would be that easy. Guilt jumped up and bit me in the ass, sinking its venom deep. Compromising with my brothers wasn't neat and pretty. In this case, it was downright fucked.

What's a man supposed to do when the only way to save the woman he loves and his only family was to betray her like this?

Shit. Did I just feel the L-word rattling around in my brain?

Too many questions for tonight. I slipped outta her room and stepped into mine, downing a few smooth shots of vodka from my liquor cabinet before I returned. I crashed down on the bed and she nuzzled her way to my chest.

The girl trusted me, wanted me. Mission accomplished. It was only for a week or so, and this would all be over, as soon as she was able to tell us where to corner Gioulio and put him down.

I'd been around long enough to know a fucking lot can happen in a week. The plan might go off perfect, or she might find the dirty secret in her purse and blow it all to hell.

There was nothing left to do but sleep through my doubts 'til morning. I held her so fucking tight I thought she'd wake up, but she didn't. My girl slept in my arms, murmuring like a kitten every few breaths, ticking down the seconds 'til fate called us both to the bench and decided whether we'd burn or live our lives in bliss.

I kissed her hard, just short of bruising her lips, in the entryway the next day. My brothers lurked in the background, not saying shit. Daniel gave me the evil eye, silently telling me I'd better have planted the bug on her like we agreed.

I tuned them out. This whole sick situation melted in my lips on hers, a kiss so savory it would soothe our time apart.

"Take care of yourself, babe. You know how to get me on that burner phone anytime. Keep it away from your dickhead uncle."

"You know I will," she said, brushing her lips over mine one last time. "I never thought all I'd want while leaving you would be to come straight back. I didn't think Stockholm Syndrome was real either..."

My brothers snickered. I turned, shot them an angry look, and pulled her to the porch outside. The chauffeur was down there waiting.

"We both do what we have to. Don't think for a second you're falling for me because of some fucked up glitch in your head, Sabrina. You know what we had the last two nights was real. No bullshit. No joke."

My greedy hands went around her and tugged her close. She gasped like a shock rolled through her when her nipples rubbed against me.

Goddamn. How the fuck was I gonna survive a week without her body tangled in mine?

My dick wanted her again. It didn't matter how many times we fucked in twenty-four hours, I still wanted more. And I wanted way more than just her pussy.

Then she finally said the words I needed like this fresh autumn air swirling around us. "I know. This thing is crazy, Anton. There's a lot I'm still trying to understand. Can't figure out if you're a scary lunatic or the best thing that ever happened to me."

My hands found her ass and squeezed. Yeah, the boy down by the car was getting a bit of a show, but fuck it. I didn't care who saw, or how it made them feel.

"A man can be both, babe. I don't give a shit what you think I am. Long as it makes you wanna come back and kiss these lips, we're good. Now, get the fuck outta here before I rip off your clothes and fuck you in the backseat of that car."

The chauffeur smirked. I watched him outta the corner of my eye rounding to the passenger door and opening it, waiting to take her away.

I gave her a gentle push and she went down the steps, her shiny new heels clicking the concrete. Damn, I was gonna miss that sound – almost as much as I'd miss having her legs wrapped around me while she screamed.

Sabrina turned around and bathed me in one more dark brown longing look before she slid into the car. The door closed, the driver got in, and soon the car was rolling down the long winding path towards the gate.

I watched 'til Lev came up behind me and slammed a hand on my shoulder. "You're really into this chick, yeah? Don't fucking fret. She'll be back as soon as her asshole uncle's gone."

"I know. We never miss our target twice. That's the easy part."

He stared at me as I turned, heading inside. I wasn't in the mood to enlighten him.

Gioulio Ligiotti and his crew were gonna die by our hands one way or another. That much was sure. What I didn't know was how I'd get a second chance with her heart if something got fucked up.

The world I was holding in my hands was like slippery, fragile glass. It was good as long as it was in my hands, but there were a million ways for it to roll away and break in the world beyond my grasp.

And once it did, there was no putting that shit back together.

VII: Twisted Truths (Sabrina)

It was beyond surreal being at the Silver Pear again after what felt like a lifetime away. The driver, Misha, let me off a few blocks from the place and then took off, flooring it as he turned a tight corner, heading away from enemy territory as fast as he could.

Honestly, I didn't know who the real wolves were anymore. I'd lied to Anton. Pretended to play along with his plan, the only way to get away and discover what was really going on.

Still, my body hadn't lied to him last night, or the night before that. He'd taken my virginity and come dangerously close to stealing my heart. Each time he made me come, I lost a piece of myself, offered it up to him on a quivering silver platter.

Fucking him felt good. Felt right. His body consoled me when everything I thought I knew about my family turned to ashes. The sex protected me, possessive and safe as it was pleasurable.

I just wasn't sure if it was enough. Even if I didn't have these terrifying truths up ahead, I needed space. I had to take my time away and figure out what the hell Anton Ivankov had done to me.

This thing between us went way beyond a family blood feud, and way beyond fiery loving too. He'd been the only man with the balls to treat me like a lady right before he fucked my brains out.

That had to count for something, didn't it?

I should've expected this freakish love-lust thing storming in the middle of our family war. But nothing prepared me for how much I loved feeling him pressed up against me, not to mention how much I missed him now that he was gone, separated by a divide far more vast than the country bleeding into Chicago's concrete jungle.

I sat down in the bar without a second look, ordering my favorite martini. It tasted bittersweet. I wasn't sure if I should linger there all day or try heading back to my condo.

Regardless, Uncle Gioulio wouldn't take long to find out about my return. The sooner he did, the better. It meant this would all be over that much quicker.

The burner phone in my purse blazed hot every time I reached inside it, fumbling for a tissue or a piece of gum. I had the power to betray my family and kill my uncle. It was a sick curse to have this justice weighing on my shoulders like a stone, but I refused to use it unless I knew there was total reason to.

I wouldn't do anything until I knew the truth. And even then, I had my doubts. If everything Anton showed me was real, and my uncle was really a disgusting sex trafficker who'd murdered papa, could I really pull the trigger by dialing the brothers?

I choked on the thoughts, coughing up the last uneven sip of my martini. I was still trying to stop when a big hand fell on my shoulder. I turned, blotting my mouth with a napkin, and looked up into Vitto's nervous eyes.

"My god! It's really you, Miss Ligiotti. Wonderful to see you again. I thought my waiter was mistaken." His lips twisted from side to side, as if he was chewing on the revelation. "I already placed a call, just in case. Your uncle will be here soon. He's been worried, looking all over for you since he heard about the breakout. It's been all over the news."

Panic shot through my chest. Almost set off a dry coughing spell, but I managed to keep it together, reaching for the glass of water on the table and guzzling it down.

"Are you okay? Please, just say the word if there's anything you need from us. Water, aspirin…ambulance?" The last word was strained. I knew my uncle told him not to involve the police.

I threw off his trembling hand, shaking my head, rising from the table and carrying my water with me, heading for the benches near the front. "I'm fine. I'll wait for him near the steps."

Vitto hesitated, but he didn't pursue me. Whatever. He'd played his lackey part too well.

I'm sure he would've been screaming after me if I'd taken a single step outside the restaurant. As long as I was waiting for my uncle to collect me, in a place where the manager could watch, he'd done his job.

I wished it were just as simple for me.

Waiting for Uncle Gioulio was worse than death row. He must've come racing from one end of Chicago to the other because the sleek black limo jerked up to the curb five minutes later. Rough, stoic men jumped out in their neat suits, opening the door in the back.

Uncle Gioulio wore the killer look I'd dreaded ever since I was a little girl. It was the look that transformed him from my favorite uncle, my protector, into the cold blooded mobster he truly was.

I shuddered. It wasn't so different from Anton's expression during the prison break, was it?

Ready to strike. Ready to kill. Ready to rip apart anything and anyone who got in his way.

My uncle slapped the door so hard it flew open, and then he was right in front of me, six feet of hard, balding judgment stuffed into a five thousand dollar suit.

"Niece!" He dropped on his knees, banging them on the floor hard enough to make me wince. He pulled me halfway off the bench into his arms, pressing his cool face to mine. "This reunion's nothing but a miracle. My God. What did they do to you?"

I tried to promise myself I wouldn't shake when he touched me the whole ride here. All those promises turned to ash, and I started to shudder in his arms, sick like death himself was holding onto me.

"Brina!" Uncle Gioulio pulled back, looking me in the face. "Talk to me right now! How did you get away? What the fuck did they do?"

I saw his hand fingering the switchblade he always kept near his pocket. His eyes were big, bright, churning like they were filled with tears.

God! God damn it.

He really cared. I couldn't ignore that. It wasn't just an act – he was ready to avenge me for every filthy touch, every torture, every insult raging in his mind. It took all my strength just to pry my lips open and make my tongue work.

"Uncle, they let me go. They wanted me to give you a message." I used the first of the lines Anton had given me.

"Stop, niece. Come with me. This isn't the place for this kind of business." He grabbed me by the hand and pulled me out the door.

Nobody spoke again until we were in the limo, heading for the big house he kept in the city proper. I watched him pour a tall glass of wine from the silvery dispenser in the car. He downed it in one gulp and wiped his mouth, folding his hands as he leaned forward.

"Something to warm my guts. It's been so cold without you, Brina. I was ready to raid every fucking Ivankov property when I heard he'd taken you…"

The guards at his side were as tough and serious looking as ever, but Uncle Gioulio's face was ten times darker. Meaner. Insistent in a way that told me I'd better start feeding him answers.

"Did they hurt you?"

"No." I prayed he'd believe it. I was prepared to lie a lot to make this go down like I wanted – hell, I'd already done enough pretending to make Anton let me go.

"I told you not to see the Russian again." Gioulio's face tightened and turned red. "Do you realize you could've been killed in that prison riot? I can't believe they didn't torture you on the outside, or worse. You're a lucky girl, niece. And a fucking *stupid* one."

I blinked. Uncle Gioulio had never insulted me like that before. Shame passed through me like a sickly current, and my eyes went to the floor. I hated him for what he'd supposedly done, especially if he'd killed papa on top of his crimes.

But it still hurt to be called out like that. When I looked up, the edge was off his face, if only a little.

"I'm sorry."

Yeah, I truly was. Sorry I'd ever gotten myself into this fucked up situation. Maybe sorry I'd been born.

"It's done, Brina. Let's not dwell on it. You're safe – that's what really matters. You understand, all that's left for us now is payback, *capisce?* No one takes my niece and treats her like a slave. I'll skin them all alive myself."

His hands moved in a whirl. Next thing I knew, the knife was out, extended and sharp, the dull edge sliding up his gray thigh.

"Uncle, please don't do anything too rash. We need to think this through."

"We?" The darkness curdled his features again. "My dear girl, we're going home and you're going to tell me absolutely everything you remember about the time you spent with those barbarians. And then you're going back to your condo under lock and key with permanent men assigned to protect you. I won't let you out until the city's free from the Ivankov bastards. I should've killed them all when they were still in diapers. If it wasn't for your old man and that fucking truce..."

He trailed off, smoothed his face, shot me an apologetic look. Strike two. He'd never bad mouthed my father. Uncle Gioulio was flustered, enraged, maybe even scared. I wondered if he was just going crazy from all the emotions, or if the mask was slipping.

My lips stayed sealed. I wasn't going to argue with him. Not now. We took the next few miles in silence, rumbling into the gated community where he had his Chicago mansion.

My lungs felt sharp tacks inside them every time I drew breath. It hurt just to breathe because it made me think about the complications burying me alive, suffocating the happy nights I'd had with Anton.

I hoped with all my might that there was still some way out of this without someone getting killed. But the chances were fading like the pale sun overhead slipping into its tomb-like clouds.

There was no stopping Uncle Gioulio once I spilled my guts. And there was no stopping Anton either. Kill or be killed. Inevitable as the day was long.

All I had was the power of life and death in my hands, and even that threatened to slip away from me with every volcanic breath.

Inside his sitting room, underneath the big chandelier, Uncle Gioulio fixed us drinks and sat down across from me.

The first sip burned before fading to sultry smoothness. Brandy.

"Tell me, why did they send you back? What's this message they were willing to forfeit their lives for? I'm going to kill them all, you know. Letting you go unharmed doesn't change that."

The two guards near the door shuffled uncomfortably. Who could blame them? This very second, my uncle's full hellfire was focused on me.

"They were trying to kill you when Anton blew up Club Duce –"

"Anton?" My uncle cut me off, narrowing his eyes.

Shit. I shouldn't have used his name like that. It was too familiar, too intimate. If only he knew *how* intimate.

"The oldest one, the man who took me hostage during the interview. Ivankov has a terrible grudge. He blames you for putting him behind bars. He suffered a lot in prison. These state facilities aren't so kind to men who pick up nicknames like Chicago Bomber."

"Ha!" Uncle Gioulio slapped the armrest so hard brandy sloshed out of his glass and stained the rug at his feet. "He killed twenty of my fucking partners. Twenty of

Chicago's finest men. Did you know fifteen of them had families? Young kids? They were cut down in their prime like dogs by that fucking coward."

I gulped my brandy. I'd need the extra buzz for this next part. I was going off script, departing from the cold, half-believable words Anton taught me to say.

"Yeah, about that…the Russians told me they weren't upstanding citizens. They said these men came to your club to indulge in some really depraved desires…sick crap I don't even want to say. Uncle, do you know anything about this?"

For a second, Uncle Gioulio paused, eyeing me like a hawk fixing on its prey. Then he shot out of his chair and stood, fists balled to iron at his sides.

"Come on! You don't believe that horseshit, do you, Brina?"

I swallowed. God help me. I didn't know *what* to believe. I'd been poisoned, tossed and turned until I couldn't make sense of anything. My belly tightened up in knots and sweat seeped out my pores like needles.

Why was this so hard? Why couldn't I see who was really pumping venom into my mind and soul?

"Sabrina…fuck. Having you looking at me like that's a dagger in the side." He sounded genuinely hurt, running one hand across his lower torso for effect. His eyes hardened, darkened, shaking in his head. "You know they'll tell you any lie to come between us, don't you? That's the way it is in this game. Brother against brother, father against daughter, a patriarch against his bright young stars."

He turned, staring at the fire. One of the guards coughed and immediately clapped a hand over his mouth. If I thought having his disgusted eyes on me was tough, the silence was worse.

It ended with Gioulio's fist banging on the masonry. That had to hurt.

The big painting of Florence above the hearth tumbled to the ground and splintered. I jumped, feeling the resounding crash echoing in the room for the next thirty seconds.

"Do you think I'd work with such diseased minds, Brina? Believe that I'd give them innocent girls to tear apart with their teeth? Is that what the Russians told you?" The smile creeping across his face was so nasty I struggled back in my chair. "What else did they tell you? They wanted to sow the seeds of my death in your own pretty head. I know their type. Cowards, who can't face me man-to-man. So, they send my own niece to do the dirty work for them."

He came close, circling me like a shark, stopping behind me. His suit shuffled. I heard something snap and skate up the fabric.

His blade appeared next to my right temple. I screamed, pressed myself into the chair, and only opened my eyes when he didn't start to shred my skin.

What kind of psychopath was he? Why was he just holding it there? Was he fucking terrorizing me?

Uncle Gioulio reached for my hand, pulled it up, and tucked my fingers around the handle. "There. On your feet, Brina. Stand up. Right the fuck now."

I clenched the knife and did it, turning toward him. The metal was so cold in my hand, heavier than I'd expected.

"What do you want?" I asked, barely a whisper. "Why are you making me do this?"

"If you believe anything those bastards told you, then I need you to drive that knife into my throat right now. Go on. Do it." He held his head up, stepping around the chair, until we were a couple feet apart. "I'd rather be killed by family on my feet than stabbed in the back on my fucking knees and tossed to my enemies."

My fingers clenched until they turned numb. The tingling spread. It felt like I'd left my body and I was observing the surreal scene from somewhere on high, adrift in total confusion.

"Go ahead, niece. Do it. Make your old man proud. He'd want you to rid this world of evil. It's what I deserve for pushing him into an early grave."

I snapped back into my body and gasped. Would've dropped the blade if I didn't have such a death grip on it. Did he really just say that – a confession I hadn't asked for?

So, at least one of his atrocities was true – the one that hurt me most. My own father, killed by the man in front of me, the man I'd always trusted.

"Why, uncle? Fucking why?" Hot tears stung my eyes.

For the first time in my life, Uncle Gioulio was shaking, alive with the same vicious current tearing through me. His savage offer was so fucking tempting just then. One push forward, one stab, and all my troubles would be over. Well, right until the guards fell on me and did who knew what for striking down their master.

"I did it for you," he whispered, grasping the edge of my empty chair and steadying himself. "Gio was outta control. He died the night that car ran down your mama. He turned to the needle, blew his brains out with that junk, wouldn't even look after his own fucking daughter! I had to do everything for you. Those men I sent by the house every week were there to make sure you were being fed. I had to know he hadn't fucked up and abandoned you. I thought it was just a phase at first, something he'd get over. But the fucking weeks turned into months, then into years...my brother was gone. That shell he left in the condo snorting and drinking until he passed out wasn't the man I grew up with, the man you called papa."

I turned the blade up in my hand, one good jab away from his neck. "You could've fucking saved him! He needed help! Rehab, treatment..."

Gioulio chuckled hoarsely and shook his head. "You know that's not the way this family does things. Yes, I could've shipped him off to see some quacks and get him clean. And then what? Watch him pick up some other terrible, reckless habit? Lose everything when he cracks and tell some pissant doctor all about the sins this family's done for money? You can't bring back a man's dead black heart, niece! I thought you could, at first, and I was dead wrong. Don't you get it? I loved him so much I saved you both the only way I knew how."

"You killed him! He drowned in his own blood. I saw him, uncle. He suffered."

"No!" Gioulio wiped his tears and held a finger up like steel. "I made it painless. The stuff I gave him did the job instantly. He never knew what hit him. He died blasted out of his damned skull, a high like none of us will ever know. And thank God we won't!"

Every part of me was shaking except the hand I had around the blade. That was cold, eager to kill, if only I weren't having my brains blasted out my ears by this horrible revelation.

Anton was right. He must've been right about everything.

But then, why did my uncle deny serving the twisted freaks at the club when he admitted to killing my own father? It didn't make sense. Or else Gioulio was playing one big fat mind game designed to make me clay in his hands. My heart was falling to pieces finding out Uncle Gioulio was this filthy, this damaged, this tormented. And I didn't even know how bad it truly was.

Who else was lying to me? If the men at Club Duce hadn't been demons torturing girls for their pleasure…then Anton was dirty too. He'd lied to me and gotten lucky about my uncle killing papa. He'd used me, wanted me to take the blade and kill my uncle in a fit of rage.

Fuck me.

I wanted to end it all right there. The urge to fall on him, tear out his throat, and then turn the knife on myself was overwhelming me. I held the knife out several times when he looked like he was about to come closer, warning him away.

"Don't." It was the only word I could manage, and it came out so hateful my mouth tasted like I'd bit into a strong pepper.

"Brina, please. You're fucking killing me. Either slit my throat and finish this, or else find some way to forgive me. I was gonna come clean, you know. I just didn't think it would have to be like this." He sighed sadly. "There's too much at stake. You're young. I kept you away from all this, and now the underworld's hurting you, bursting through my shield. You can't see through their lies the way I do."

God help me. My burning wrist made the decision for me. I let go. The switchblade dropped and rattled on the floor, and my fingers came off it like it was hot iron. The clatter on the ceramic tile drilled through the silence.

"The Ivankovs are never honest," my uncle growled, stepping up, jerking me into his embrace. This time, I didn't resist. "Remember that. I'm telling you the ugly truth. All of it."

His wrinkled fingers pushed their way through my hair. For some sick reason, it reminded me of Anton, and then I completely broke. I bawled like a baby, splashing his expensive suit with tears.

His confession about killing papa repulsed me. I should've jumped away and scratched him in the face if I didn't have the courage to slaughter him for what he'd done. But I was too weak, too utterly lost in his torturous confession.

Whatever plan there'd been when I came here, it was in total ruins now. I'd never see Anton Ivankov again. And I didn't know whether I ought to miss the bastard or not. I wasn't sure if he'd screwed me over just as bad as my asshole uncle.

Damn it. This whole fucking thing was supposed to bring clarity. Now, I was just drowning in confusion, burning every last bridge I ever had to the men I loved.

"You want the truth?" Uncle Gioulio whispered, giving my wavy hair another pull. "I can give you the rest. I put Gio out of his misery, and I deserve to burn for it. I know that. But I'm not the one who destroyed him. I know who killed your mama, little lamb."

My eyes burned harder. I turned my head up, hating him for offering another twisted truth.

God. Everything they said about honesty was a wretched lie, wasn't it? The truth never set anyone free. It condemned them to the darkest pits of hell, and whatever he was going to tell me offered no illusions about anything else.

"Marino! Gabriele!" He clapped his hands, calling to the guards. "Leave us. This talk's for family ears only."

Still holding me, Uncle Gioulio walked. We left the room with the blade still lying on the ground. The guards didn't follow, a first for any time I'd been in my uncle's presence. We headed downstairs through the concealed kitchen entrance, down past the wine cellar where we'd always stopped before.

There was a small, unfinished room next to the laundry I'd never seen before. He fished out a key and opened the door. Dust wafted up my nose and I sneezed, then did a double take when I saw the walls lined with filing cabinets.

My uncle motioned me over to the tiny desk with two chairs in the middle. As soon as I sat, he opened up a drawer and rifled through it until he found what he was searching for – a simple manilla folder like something you'd see stored in an old clinic.

He circled the table and slammed it on the table. "Everything's here about the night your mama died. It wasn't a simple car accident. You're a smart girl, Brina. How is it you've never doubted that before?"

A numb chill crept up my spine and bathed my brain. My emotional circuits were fried, and he was hellbent on piling more through them. I looked up, one hand squeezing my purse. I needed it to hurt, cramp my muscles so I could feel something.

"You've ripped my heart out plenty today. Whatever you're going to say about her, just tell me the truth. No more theatrics."

His eyes narrowed. Slowly, he nodded, licking one finger to pluck the folder open. Then he stopped in mid-turn. His eyes went to my purse, and he rose from his chair.

"What? What is it?"

"That bag. You brought it back with you, right? It was with you at the Russians' compound."

I tried to protect it, but Uncle Gioulio was too strong, too fast. He ripped it away from me in one swift motion and hauled it over to his side of the desk, tearing open a drawer with his free hand.

"Hey!" I screamed at him like he'd just stepped on my foot in a grocery line.

If only that was the least of his sins.

"Just a moment, Brina. This won't take long." He was more careful than I expected, pulling out my things and setting them on the table nearby.

My heart pounded when he plucked out the small plastic shell with my birth control. All those hours with Anton buried deep inside me came roaring back, hot and insane and totally wrong. Thank God for small favors – Uncle Gioulio passed it over without stopping to gawk.

"Damn, where is it..." He reached into the empty drawer next to him and held up a long, shiny blade, a sharp letter opener. Except this one looked thicker and sturdier than any commercial kind, like it would just as easily split someone's skull with a well placed jab.

Weapons were everywhere in this house, really nothing more than a luxurious fortress under siege.

How had I been so blind for so long? Jesus. And the truth wasn't even blinding me in its full ultraviolet light yet. I eyed the folder and then turned back to his hands, wondering what the hell he was doing slicing into my purse.

There was a *zzzt* sound, leather coming apart. A second later, he held up a small black circular thing with little perforations in the middle. I would've known it was a microphone of some sort even if I hadn't watched all those stupid spy things growing up.

"From your Russian friends." He tossed it like a pebble, and it bounced once in my lap before coming to a rest. "Typical Ivankov sloppiness. I knew there was something on you from the moment you walked in. I wanted to do the search myself – kinder and gentler than my boys would."

My teeth banged together. Jaw clenched, it felt like my head was about to explode and take the world with it. I pinched the cool plastic between my fingers and turned it around, over and over.

God! And to think I'd been feeling bad about the harmless white lies I'd used to get back, when he and his demented brothers were tracking me the whole fucking time!

How long had it been on me? The entire time I'd been in the house? For all I knew, the other two coarse men were listening in while he held me, mounted me, and fucked me into the dreamiest nights of my life.

My body jerked. Uncle Gioulio smiled and ducked as it whizzed past his head, slapping the concrete wall behind him.

I buried my face in my hands and screamed. The world dimmed, narrowed, swallowing me.

This wasn't supposed to be happening. The original plan was beyond derailed – it was a smoldering tangle of metal and fire, burning up the entire track.

"Don't cry, niece. Nothing's beneath the peasants we're dealing with. *Nothing.*"

That word. Whenever I heard it, my whole world shifted. With Anton, it burned hotter and brighter with a sweet excitement I couldn't shake. Now? All circling into a black hole as dark and imposing as the little microphone I'd hurled against the wall.

Uncle Gioulio's hand slid softly across my cheek. I felt the chip in his hand and winced, then turned on him, grabbing his arm with both hands and digging my nails into his suit.

"Get rid of that fucking thing. Please."

"That's the whole point." I watched him take a couple steps back.

He reached to the ground, set it down, and stood up. His foot crashed down on it, and it shattered with one stomp.

The thing was discrete, but it clearly wasn't designed to be durable. Not that it was much comfort.

Anton's betrayal lingered. My mind was spinning, questioning everything, once again feeling like both the bridges I had to the Ligiotti and Ivankov lives were dead flaps swinging in the wind.

"I hope they heard every fucking word we said before I killed it," Uncle Gioulio said, squeezing my shoulder. "We let them know we're aware this is the latest screw-over this family's had. It goes much further than that. For you, for me, the pain's deeper. Personal in a way that won't stop until the last drop of blood on one side or the other's gone."

He walked to the desk and picked up the folder. My uncle pushed it into my limp hands, and I struggled to take it, flipping through the fat documents.

He put his hands behind mine and helped me hold it open, navigate to the right spot. "There. She was out Christmas shopping, you know. We could still see the crushed bags next to her body and her lost white heel when your father and I rolled up."

Every breath I took became more like broken glass as he bypassed the police reports and got into the section with the pictures. Downtown Chicago's bright lights filled my eyes from all those years ago. Yellow police tape lined the zone where my mother died on the pavement.

I never saw her face. If there was a photo somewhere, then maybe Uncle Gioulio took it out when I wasn't looking to spare me. Seeing her small, soft body thrown on the dirty ground was enough. Both her shoes were knocked off, and the matching white coat she'd been wearing had black stripes going across it, like the bastard made a conscious decision to drive right over her after the fatal strike.

"These are surveillance photos from nearby businesses," he said, flipping through to some grainier black and white pictures. "When our contacts in the police brought them over, we couldn't believe it. Gio wanted to march out and kill every last one of those fucks. I wouldn't let him. It would've been suicide. The entire fucking incident was a sneak attack. We had a fucking truce with the Ivankovs when they struck. Same truce I warned him years before not to roll with because I knew it'd bite us in the ass, cause us to let our guard down.

"No, shit was never perfect. War was gonna come between our families sooner or later because we were running up against each other's business. But Christ, even in the old days, you *never* fucked with a man's family. Here's the piece of shit who ran your mama down, Brina. Take a good look."

He stabbed a slightly blurry photo of a car racing down the street. Two men sat in the front, but the one behind the wheel had the unmistakable, determined, icy blue eyes of an Ivankov. He was too old to be Anton or any of his brothers.

Seeing those features, wide and full of hate, were just as bad as if it was Anton himself. I ripped the file out of my uncle's hands and held it to my face, forcing my eyes open, letting seething tears fall down the sides of the old documents.

"That's Boris Vassarinivich Ivankov. First generation, first real thug here after the Soviet Union collapsed. Former head of their family. Every branch of the Russian mafia's infamous for letting their commanders fire the first shot when they go to war. Well, this boy did, and he decided to go after the most vulnerable, innocent target he could. He struck down poor Allison. The medical report at the back says she was dead before she hit the concrete, but I know the bastard ran her over twice just to be sure. He wasn't fucking around. He was gunning for her."

His hand slid down my shoulder, smoothing my back, just the way good old Uncle Gioulio used to do. I'd never forgive him for putting down my father, but I didn't turn his comfort away.

He held me when I dropped the file, rocked me until I stopped shaking.

I was drowning right there in his arms, suffocating in the invisible quicksand pulling me into its fierce undertow. I wanted to die. But first, I wanted to make sure the assholes who'd truly stabbed me in the back found their way to hell first.

My whole body felt dirty. To think I'd relished fucking an Ivankov man with such lust, such insatiable need...

I turned my head up to the ceiling as far as I could, anything to stop the vertigo, one wrong breath away from forcing me to throw up.

"You've seen enough. The rest is all history, as they say, my niece." His voice was soft and understanding. "Don't cry. We all spent months grieving her. That's behind us. Your old man couldn't ever put it behind him. He started killing himself recklessly, surely, pushing that shit into his veins every second he was awake."

"Then why? What's the point of all this? You just want to turn me back to you."

He blinked, looking strangely hurt. My uncle slipped away, rounded the desk, and plopped back down in front of me. "I want you to work for this family, Brina. Not me. I know I've lost your love doing what I had to do to my poor brother. Fucking kills me to this day. But I'd do it all over again if he was about to fuck you over in a junkie rage or drive you off a bridge some cold night."

"And how do I do that? I already helped the Ivankovs without even knowing it until you showed me what was really going on. They used me."

There. I said it.

I wanted to say *he* used me. I should've known the fucked up whirlwind romance was too good to be true, built on Stockholm Syndrome from the very beginning. Like a good little slave, I'd trusted him, worked for him.

Nothing else. Anton really had *used me*, taken me for his pleasure, and then threw me back at my uncle like a poisoned dart.

How could I believe anything else? My insides were too turned out and fried to even think about pressing Gioulio about Club Duce again. It was hard to care if the men Anton killed in that bombing were bastards or not. It wouldn't change a thing.

I *knew* – knew beyond all reasonable doubt – that he was a demon for doing this. The same as his brothers, the same as his father for murdering my innocent mother.

And, of course, the very same as the dark eyed man folding his hands and leaning in across from me.

"Brina, look at me. Don't make this about egos. I know I'm not. I'm going to keep loving you no matter how you feel about me, the same way Giovanni would've wanted. I hurt you. I kept secrets, hoping to keep you on my side. I know I can't do that anymore. I realize I fucked up."

"You're right," I said, pushing my heels together, getting ready to stand. "As soon as you tell me it's safe to leave this house, I'm gone. I'm taking every last penny he left me and going far, far away from all this. I'll send you a postcard from London or Paris or San Diego. I haven't decided yet. Or maybe I'll decide it's better we never speak again."

Uncle Gioulio's face darkened. He cracked his knuckles. "All within your rights, niece. If that's what you'd really like to do, then I won't stop you."

Too easy. Well, as easy as easy could be when my heart battered my ribcage, wanting to leap out, trying to kill the bitter, throbbing lump of pain it had become and take me with it.

"It's a shame. I can see the future laid out in front of me," he said quietly. "Everything's going to pieces, and there's nothing I can do to stop it. I'll send my boys after the Russians, but those bastards will have some idea what's coming when you don't pick up the burner phone I found in your purse and dial them up. We'll fight. We'll kill each other. I'll lose a few guys and kill more of theirs, maybe take out one of the brothers, if I'm lucky. Anton, that fucking roach, he'll get to me eventually. He's the most expendable one. The bastard's got a statewide manhunt on his ass, and he'll come screaming in for vengeance if I off Lev or Daniel first."

He paused, shook his head. "So much blood's waiting. It's not like I haven't lived through it all before, but fuck, a guy shouldn't be dealing with this in his old age. I ought to be retiring, passing this shit down to somebody younger."

The asshole looked at me. I knew exactly what he was thinking. No way.

Fuck no. I wanted absolutely no part of this insane business. I totally meant everything I said about packing up and putting as many miles between myself and Chicago as I could without heading all the way to Antarctica.

"You could make this easier, Brina."

"I'm not helping you," I snapped.

It was time to go, at least get out of this room and head upstairs. I stood, stomping my heels on the floor to relieve the pressure screaming through my body, heading for the door. My hand grabbed the cold steel handle and pulled.

The force nearly ripped my arm out of its socket. Uncle Gioulio was behind me, a gentle hand on my back.

"It's locked. Here, let me." He took his sweet time reaching for the keys in his pocket. "I'm not the one asking you for a favor, niece. Yeah, I'm the dirty bastard down here whispering in your ear, but these aren't my words."

What? I looked at him cautiously, wondering if reliving all this trauma had driven him insane. I couldn't be sure I was going to walk out of this room with all my marbles still intact.

"Who is it?" I asked, cringing as I did, knowing I didn't *really* want to know but couldn't help myself. "If it's not you talking, then who?"

Uncle Gioulio hesitated, jingling the keys in one hand. "Your parents."

Rage shot through me. He saw me twitch, broke eye contact, and pushed the key into the lock.

"Fuck you, uncle," I growled. "Mama and papa would've wanted me to get away from all this. Not bury myself deeper."

I was out. He didn't follow me, but the deep, dim lit staircase had some really strange acoustics. If I wasn't scared to death of falling backwards and breaking my neck, I would've taken my hands off the old railing and covered my ears when he yelled after me, drowning out his hateful voice.

"The only voices screaming at us here are *two* of our flesh and blood! I tried to be nice, I tried to show you, Brina. I tried to press on, even when you were breaking my heart, and you're still so fucking blind. You're going to let the Ivankov brothers walk with our blood on their hands. I see it now. I was wrong about you, niece — so wrong it's killing me. You're a coward!"

No! I couldn't listen to this anymore.

I ran like a madwoman up the stairs, snarling and climbing, punching through the door and clawing at the smooth floor when I was finally through. I ran past the two goons who looked up with concern when they saw me coming. They wouldn't pursue unless Uncle Gioulio told them to.

I headed straight for the guest room and turned the locks. Part of me wanted to get a driver and return to my condo, but I was just as much a prisoner there as I was here. I wouldn't be away from his evil influence until I was out of the city.

Even then, I wondered if I'd ever be free. The deafening beat in my head drummed me to sleep, echoing with the last shot he fired into me, showing me his true face.

Coward. Coward. Coward!

I hated him so much. But in the darkness, I hated Anton even more. Every time I closed my eyes, I saw myself bracing for his sickening touch. Sex brought us close, gave me an opportunity to use him the same way he'd used me.

The weapon I dreamed about was always different. Sometimes it was a handgun, which I picked up, pressed to his rock hard chest, and fired. Other times, it my uncle's switchblade, and I slid it across the Russian's throat when he tried to give me one of those heart stopping kisses.

Up until then, I'd never truly wanted to kill a human being with such gruesome need. Guess it ran in the blood.

When I woke up, something like a bad hangover fogged my brain, I told myself I'd never let my uncle call me a coward again. He'd never get to speak for my poor dead parents either.

He'd get his blood war, his vengance, and then he'd never get anything from me again. The bastard was right – there was no leaving and getting on with my life until I knew the men who'd used me and betrayed me were destroyed.

I was going to kill Anton Ivankov, and both his psycho brothers too, if luck was kind.

His goons gave me the evil eye the next day. Still, they didn't stop me from knocking at the door to his study.

Uncle Gioulio's kinder eyes met me as soon as he opened the door. Overnight, his Hyde retreated back into his inner Jekyll, and now he was playing the kindly old uncle again.

"Brina, listen, I've got to apologize for last –"

"No need. I'm not here for your sympathy." I pushed my way past him, taking a seat in the big leather chair across from his desk.

"I meant everything I said yesterday evening. I'm going to take my inheritance and leave this city. As uncle and niece, we're done. We're not family anymore."

Pain throbbed in my heart just to say it, but only for an instant. What little respect and love I had left for my uncle died last night. But you can't stop loving anyone completely all at once – unless you start hating them instead.

And right now, that's all that kept me moving.

Uncle Gioulio's face dropped to the ground as he sat. "What is it you want? You're facing me for a reason."

"Before I leave and try to forget about all this, I want to do right by this family, the ones who're gone. You're right. This isn't about you and I. This is about mama and papa. I want them avenged just as badly as you do."

We locked eyes. He never smiled, but I could see the satisfaction glowing in his face, a beacon in the darkness.

Uncle Gioulio stood, walked over to his liquor cabinet. Seriously? A celebratory drink this early was way too weird for my taste.

I was about to tell him to hold it right there while he was pushing bottles aside. Then he stopped, grabbed a small glass flask filled with some clear fluid, vodka or gin, and what looked like a silver needle inside, and walked back to me.

"This is the best way to kill them. The Ivankovs won't be able to resist a drink if they think you've got me by the balls." He pushed it into my outstretched hands.

The glass was cool. The transparent stuff inside it sloshed around like any other vodka I'd seen, clear and unassuming.

"One little drop of that and they won't know what hit 'em. It's a kinder, swifter death than the bastards ever gave Gio and Allison. It'll do the job just the same."

My fingers tightened around it, full of evil wonder. I carefully pushed it into my purse, making sure it found a safe spot.

"You'll always be a Ligiotti, niece. You can hate me until your last breath, and I won't blame you, but you know blood and heartache, just as I do. Take it. Slip it to them carefully. Cut the chains that'll try to hold you here forever. Avenge *them* the way I couldn't."

I couldn't stop him from embracing me one more time. There wasn't a hint of warmth and I almost shivered in his arms. When I pulled away, Uncle Gioulio was still looking at me with those sad, knowing eyes, a thousand thanks whirling in his dark pupils.

We'd never be family again in the proper sense, but we had ourselves an understanding.

I spent another twenty minutes with him and his guys, talking about the logistics of how I'd get back to the Ivankov's estate without drawing suspicion. He gave me a tattered white coat – the same rumpled one that belonged to mama the night she was struck down – and I was on my way.

Anton tricked me, used me, sent me to sabotage my uncle for nothing but his own disgusting gain. His poison was love and lust, and now it mutated in my veins, becoming as bitter and intoxicating as the toxin stowed in my bag.

I was returning to him as a weapon. I'd deceive him the same way he wrecked me with his lies.

It was time for the bastard to pay.

VIII: Disconnect (Anton)

It was nine o'clock. Second day since my girl went missing, and I was ready to wring Daniel's neck for the dozenth time.

The fucking bug hadn't lived up to expectations. Sabrina and Gioulio's voices were garbed, and the last thing we heard before it went dead was crashing and arguing. Fuck.

"Back off, Anton. Don't make me hit you again brother," Lev growled, putting up his fists in warning.

Asshole. We were roughly the same strength, but he wasn't fighting for her the way I was. Fuck, Daniel was pretty strong too, especially when he knew he'd be fighting for his own life if we didn't find out what the hell happened – and soon.

"Shut the fuck up! This is his fault, and you know it. You're a cocksucker for protecting him." I stormed to the other side of the great hall, pacing from end to end like a caged tiger.

"You're not in your right mind, *brat*. That bitch got underneath your skin. Fuck, for all we know, she was playing you the whole time. You let her go, she dumped the bug, and now she's probably given us up to the fucking Italians."

That did it. I spun, came pounding right at him. Our bodies slammed together like colliding trains and Daniel was dragged into the melee.

Too bad we'd all gotten that Ivankov gene for big muscles and fists of fury. Two against one. I didn't have a chance, but I fought like a goddamned devil.

All I knew was the sweet crunch of my knuckles slapping flesh and bone. I swung, kicked, and thrashed 'til my arms went numb, same as I always did in a brawl like this. Except it never got that far.

Daniel got a choke hold not long after I pounded his face, hard enough to leave a black eye. Lev tackled me while I was struggling to get my brother's arm off my throat. He slammed both fists into my stomach. The wind was right outta me like a ton of bricks landing on my chest.

I couldn't move. Couldn't breathe. Daniel maintained his death lock, leaned down, and whispered in my ear.

"Don't make us knock you unconscious, brother. Calm the fuck down. Stop taking this all so personally. She could've done it to anybody."

Damn if I didn't start struggling again with what little energy my body had left.

Sabrina hadn't stabbed me in the back – I wouldn't fucking believe it! There were a thousand reasons why that goddamned spy chip he put on her could've went dead, and these assholes were fixated on only one. Betrayal.

"Come on, Anton. Knock it the fuck off. We need you to save that shit for later if the Ligiotti's goons come storming in here."

"They won't!" I snarled, feeling my ribs creak when I spoke. "Your heads are so far up your asses you'd think your own guts were trying to strangle you. There's nobody coming. We're the fuckups for laying here like rats while they've taken her, taken my girl."

"Your girl?" Lev wiped his bloody nose. "Prison fucked you up, brother. Dunno why the hell you can't see it. You went head over heels for the first piece of pussy that landed in your bed, and she fucked you over. You should've let us handle her."

My fists slapped the floor. I fought like hell to get up and bust his fucking jaw for saying that, but Daniel held me down, giving the back of my skull a good crack against the hard floor.

"None of us are thinking rationally. That goes for you too, Lev." He looked up, as if trying to smooth shit over. "What we need here is patience. We've got to buckle down and wait instead of tearing each other to pieces, dammit. Just wait, brothers. The crew we sent out to the city will tell us *something* soon."

Bastard. Always the voice of reason, even when I'd just come within a hair trigger of fracturing his damned eye socket. My fists were still seething, ready to beat and blind and kill, when he finally let me up.

197

Breathing without his fat arm around my throat was amazing. But it still wouldn't come easy, not even twenty minutes later when I sat in the chair, rolling out the latest knots in my arm with the table's edge. I'd never breathe easy 'til she was back in these arms, safe and fucking sound.

She shouldn't have gone out with nothing more than a secret bug and a burner phone. And I was the asshole who sent her, the fuck who'd let my brothers get away with this bullshit compromise, tracking her like a goddamned animal.

All three of us eyed each other like hungry wolves hovering over a lone rabbit.

A knock at the door shattered the tense silence. I was the first one up, beating my brothers to the big door.

It swung open, revealing old Grigor in his prim suit. I nearly bowled him over heading for the small, broken looking thing behind him.

"She just showed up on our doorstep," I heard him say, and then I stopped listening to anything at all.

"Sabrina!" Her name bounced off the high ceiling as I scooped her up, threw my arms around her, and crushed her in my embrace.

Shit. She'd appeared outta the darkness right when I needed her like an honest-to-fuck angel. I squeezed her tight, forcing myself to understand she was real, wondering why the hell she wasn't grabbing me back.

"Damn it, babe, I thought you were a goner. What happened? They didn't hurt you?"

"I got away," she said coldly. "Uncle Gioulio welcomed me back at first, but he started to get suspicious pretty fast. He kept me in a room at his house, posted guards outside. I managed to sneak out, hail a taxi. Here I am."

She pulled away. Too cold, too tired, too defeated for my liking. Hearing her say that shit was like listening to a dull recording.

What the fuck's going on here? And where the hell did she get that mangled, ugly ass coat?

My eyes slid up and down the weird thing draped around her shoulders. It was an overstuffed winter coat that looked like it'd seen better days. I didn't like looking at it, and not just because it covered up that bitching body my cock was starting to pine for all over again. It was jagged, dirty, one shoulder coming apart at the seams.

"Babe." She flinched when I reached out and grabbed her chin.

My fingers dug in harder. I forced her to look at me, all while the voices behind me went dead silent. My brothers were watching the scene with Grigor.

Lev approached, fists balled at his sides. "You'd better sit her down. Make her start talking. If this bitch has betrayed us…"

I spun, dragging poor Sabrina with me. He stopped mid-sentence. Our cold eyes met, and he was the first to break, looking away with a loud snort.

That's right. Brother or not, I promised another beating if one more word came outta his mouth. And this time, they'd have to put me in a fucking coma to stop my fists.

"She's mine. I'll do the debriefing. Neither of you fucks is patient enough to do it right."

Patience. Motherfucking patience. I threw Daniel's word back at them and took off, leaving my brothers standing with our old head servant at the base of the stairs.

"My room. Let's go." Sabrina moved on a little ahead of me.

I watched her walk for telltale signs of pain, injury. Nothing. Her footsteps were slow, almost reluctant, and I couldn't figure out why.

Great. Not only did I have my brothers to shut up, I needed to dig the truth outta her. I made a promise right there that anybody who did her the least harm was gonna fucking suffer.

Soon as she was in the room, I slammed the door behind me. "Babe, what's going on? We're home. You can tell me without worrying about their ears on us."

She sat down at the edge of the big veiled bed where I'd fucked her half a dozen times. My cock stirred, and it took all my mental willpower to slap him down while I got to the bottom of this.

"My uncle's a traditional man," she said, reaching into her purse. After a second, she pulled out a little black book, not much thicker than my thumb. "He doesn't use tablets and phones to store his schedule. Less risky that way, I suppose. I managed to swipe this before he sent me up to my room – it's his planner for the next month. At least the stuff that's on the books. The rest is coded. I couldn't figure it out, but maybe you can. Catch."

The little book flew through the air. I slapped it between both hands and opened it.

Shit. It was Gioulio Ligiotti's handwriting, all right. I knew it from seeing our intel before, a small crabbed script in English with the odd Italian word sprinkled throughout. The black book must've been about fifty pages long, everything laid out in a calendar grid. Pretty standard for the kinda scheduling book you'd find at the drugstore or whatever.

"Holy fuck. You brought us gold, babe!" I tucked it in my pocket and walked over, hitting the bed next to her. "Christ. My brothers are gonna be so fucking happy. They'll lay off my ass and yours. We'll be able to hit him soon without the choppy doubts we had before."

"Better make it fast," she said, a quirky smile on her lips. "He'll realize it's gone within a few days, or else his guys will."

"Shit, you're right. We'll get cracking on it tonight. What about you?" My eyes rolled up and down her sweet body, trying to see past the heavy, ragged thing clinging to her shoulders. "What's this shit? Something you picked up on the street?"

Her lips pursed like she'd bitten something sour. "No. It's a family heirloom. Just happened to be in the room with me where I was staying. I needed something to stay warm, and it might be my last chance to get it out."

Hm. The girl sounded sad. Her little fingers clung to the opening, where it looked like it was missing several oversized buttons. It was the sorta jacket well off chicks were drooling over like ten years ago, if memory served. I'd hiked up a few black and purple ones in the same style and fucked the girls wearing them.

My cock jerked at the memories, but not half as hard as it lurched when I imagined doing the same thing here.

"Take that shit off. Or you want me to do it for you?"

She stiffened when I shifted, rolled on top of her, and pressed her into the mattress. She was soft and warm and sweet all over, calling me between her legs, begging me to fuck her. My body needed to show her how damned happy I was to have her back in all the way words failed to do.

I smashed my lips on hers, hungry as hell. My dick hammered in my pants, beating its way out, howling to get inside her. If I could've kissed her 'til the universe went cold and collapsed in on itself, I would've.

I wanted to tongue her, bite her, leave my lips on hers 'til we were nothing but this beautiful fucking kiss. But the primal lusts wouldn't let it be anything but a prelude to the insane storm whistling in my blood, bellowing to hold her down, rip her pants away, and fuck her and fuck her and fuck her.

Fuck!

Something's wrong. I kissed her hard enough and she moaned, but it sounded more like real pain than just rough lust talking. I reared up, fisted her hair, and held her in a ferocious grip.

"What the fuck happened out there, babe? What's wrong? Talk to me. I'm not gonna read your fucking mind. Did he hurt you?"

My veins were about to explode and collapse. All this lust was churning with pure rage now, confusion and frustration. I'd never seen her look like this – not even when I held her here the first night after the big break.

"Uncle Gioulio told me some things," she said, pulling away from my hand.

I had to let her go. It was either that or she'd tear out a huge clump of hair. Pissed, I darted up, stood over her, heartbeat thudding so damned hard I felt all the fresh bruises on my skin left by Lev and Daniel.

"What things? Don't tell me that piece of shit's got you all mixed up again. He's a manipulative fucking snake, the worst kind this city's ever seen. What did he say?" I got up in her face, trying not to scream.

Christ. God fucking damn it.

If that freak turned her against me, then I really had my work cut out. I was already gonna kill him the worst way I could, but this shit meant I had to think of something sicker, crueler, ten times more painful.

My hands landed on both her shoulders and shook her. A hot diamond tear drop slid down one of her beet red cheeks and she pinched her eyes shut.

"I can't help you if you don't fucking talk to me, babe! Come on! What did that bastard say? Whatever shit he's been shoveling into your pretty head, it isn't true!"

She coughed, sputtered, started to struggle like she was really hurt just by having my hands on her. Fuck!

I ripped myself away from her, stumbling over a shoe lace that had come loose. I caught my balance, crossed the entire room, and kicked the chair next to her vanity. It went flying across the fucking room and one leg smashed beneath the window.

Idiot.

Sabrina was bawling. This shit wasn't helping, but my anger and frustration was off the charts. When the waterworks stopped and she looked at me with open eyes, she stared at me like I'd killed her own mother.

What. The. Fuck.

"Just…just give me a minute. We need to have a drink," she sighed. "I'll calm down after that. We'll talk."

Fine. I'd play along, though the thought of pouring liquor down my throat right now was like dumping fuel on a roaring fire.

I marched to the cabinet and opened it. Grabbed two shot glasses and the finest vodka in there. When I got back to the bed, Sabrina was holding a little bottle in one hand, looking at it.

"What's this?" I ripped it outta her hands before she could protest.

No label. I opened the cap and sniffed. Didn't smell like any fine stuff I'd ever known. It was almost slightly sour, vinegary.

"Something else I swiped from the house – an ancient family recipe. We only bring it out on special occasions, and I think this qualifies. Let's have a little, maybe mix it with the other stuff." She pointed at the big bottle I was still holding.

I nodded. "I like your thinking. Hope to fuck whatever's got you in knots is good news."

Honestly, the stuff in the little bottle smelled like shit. I'd down it to humor her – whatever made this chick feel better. I'd do anything to pry the stone cold truth outta her.

I walked everything over to the small stand next to the bed. Poured out two tall shots with just a splash of the shit she'd brought on top. If it tasted as shitty as it smelled, dousing it in the good stuff would drown out the crap.

Sabrina had both her hands clenched tight in her lap when I came back with our drinks. I passed her the shot glass and raised mine.

"To better times, babe. They're coming. Sure as you uncle's bones are going into the fucking ground."

I was about to knock the shit back when she reached for my thigh. Her fingernails pinched so hard into my skin it was like a goddamned miniature bear trap. The surprise almost caused me to drop the shit on the floor.

"What the fuck?" I growled.

"Wait. Not yet. There's something I need to know before we do this…something Uncle Gioulio told me. Don't drink yet."

I looked at her without saying shit. The girl was rattled, couldn't make up her damned mind. Long as she started talking, I'd let her. Maybe the horse piss in my glass would taste an iota better when she threw off whatever was on her chest.

"You keep looking at my coat. It's more than a family heirloom." She looked down, staring at the crap in her own glass, giving it a little stir, collecting her words. "My Uncle showed me some pictures. It was from the night my mother died. She got run over – somebody flattened her to the ground. Until the other night, he let me think it was an accident, even though I suspected something more all along. He showed me the man who ran her down and killed her in cold blood."

Oh, fuck. My mind started spinning a million miles an hour, ready to split right through my skull and launch to the fucking moon. I knew who she was gonna name before it was outta her wicked fucking mouth.

"It was your father, Boris Ivankov. Don't deny it wasn't," she said coldly. "Uncle showed me the pictures. He…he had your eyes. I know Gioulio wasn't lying about this."

She looked at me like my baby blues were gonna turn her to stone. Fuck!

I turned away in disgust, throwing my shot glass on the floor. It shattered and sent a million little shards in all directions. I wished like hell that sound was enough to wring the neck of whatever demon fate cooked up in our pasts to fuck up our present.

The whole damned cosmos wanted to keep us apart. It was a travesty, a fucking atrocity, when we were *so* fucking good together. No, I wasn't just talking about being balls deep inside her, throttling her perfect pussy 'til she shook from head to toe. We worked because we were one and the goddamned same, two lost worlds who'd been fucked over by their own blood too many times to count.

No, dammit. If this was what had her all knotted up, I'd untie everything, every dark rope keeping us apart. I turned around, ready to reach up to the ceiling and salute the entire universe with both my middle fingers.

"My old man fucked up. He told me it was the worst mistake of his life, running that poor woman down. He had bad intel – same shit I did when I tried to blow your uncle to kingdom come with all his degenerate buddies. Your mother wasn't the fucking target." Volcanic air pumped through my lungs. I stepped closer, grabbing for her hands, forcing her to set the small shot glass between her knees.

"Christ, babe. Don't tell me you believe that motherfucker if he told you my old man ran down your ma on purpose?" Shit. One look at her eyes said that was exactly what she believed. "Fuck. You gotta be kidding me! He had no reason for targeting your mother – none. It's not the way we do shit, and we never will. We go after the bastards who fuck us over, the demons who deserve to die. Nobody else."

"Why should I believe you!?" She cracked. She tried to rip her hands away from me, but I held on like an ogre, unwilling to let her go 'til I took a wrecking ball to the bastard's lies. "God damn it! Every time I hear something from one side, the other's always got another version. I wanted to believe you, Anton. I trusted you. Then my Uncle took out the bug you left in my fucking purse, and I couldn't."

Fuck, fuck, fuck...

The confession went through my eardrum and blew my brain apart. If it wasn't for seeing hate and confusion flashing in her eyes right in front of me, I would've marched out, tracked down my damned brothers, and finished the ass kicking we'd started earlier in the great hall.

"It wasn't my idea, babe. I fought the fucking thing tooth and nail. Daniel and Lev...they wouldn't let you leave without having some way to see what was going on. D told me it'd only help keep tabs on you in case something bad happened. Well, we both know it didn't do shit – and now I know why!"

Fuck. This time, my brother's wise ideas had screwed us hard. They'd fucked over the trust I'd built with this girl, stained this crazy thing we had with blood and venom.

"You're not even sorry," she said, lowering her eyes. Why the hell wouldn't she stop looking at that fucking drink?

"You're dead wrong. There's a lot of shit I regret because without it sticking to me, everything would be ten times easier for everybody. I regret being hitched to this family, son of a bastard just like me. He killed for cred and money and – yeah – he made mistakes. I regret coming along years later and using you to get to the last Italian motherfucker we've got to take down in the windy city. Fuck, you can believe me or not, but I *really* regret compromising with my asshole brothers and letting them slip that shit into your luggage. If it was up to me, it never would've fucking happened. I'm sorry."

Her eyes flitted up, distrusting and dark. I didn't give a shit right then if she hated my ass worse than her dickhead uncle. I wasn't gonna let her.

I'd spun her around and made her fall for me before, and I could do it again. I'd never been the kinda bastard to talk about love in words. All the red hot fucking we'd squeezed into those days did the talking for me before, but now I had to make my damned tongue work, make her realize I wasn't a total dipshit.

I *knew* how bad I'd fucked up by going along with my brothers' plan. It wrecked what we'd built as well as taking Gioulio down.

"My old man died with regrets too. I already told you, he never stopped beating himself bloody over that night. I remember it then. I was just getting deeper into the biz.

He stumbled through the door all fucked up on pills and drink, screaming about the woman who wasn't supposed to be there.

"It was supposed to be some bitch named Mercedes. This French whore with a love for good shoes and riding your uncle's dick back before he needed the blue shit to get it up. She was his partner for awhile before she fucked off back to Paris. Built one helluva gun trade on our turf, and my old man was ready to break the truce to tear her down.

"She was supposed to be there. Bitch was a creature of habit. She'd have her drinks and hit the outlets, harder with Christmas coming. Guess your uncle introduced her to the good old American holiday frenzy, and my old man was determined to make it a fatal weakness.

"Thing is, the sly bitch must've seen it coming. She was still in the bar after my old man did the dirty deed. He fucking saw her smiling at him through the window, right before he sped off and rolled over the woman he'd just crushed into the ground. He panicked. He fucked up *bad*."

Sabrina swallowed. Hard. Neither of us were there, but I could only imagine how bad it hurt to imagine her mother's bones cracking underneath the tires.

"Don't," she whispered, harsh, holding back tears.

"I'm done talking about that night. We never found the French bitch. She set your ma up, and my old man died with a stinking suspicion Gioulio knew about it too.

They had some kinda fallout not long after that sent her scurrying overseas like a fucking rat in flight.

"I'm telling you the truth, Sabrina. I know, you've got all the reason in the world to wonder whether or not I'm feeding you more bullshit. I could offer to trot out more files. Whatever the fuck your uncle showed you, we got our records too. I'm not gonna bother because I need you to hear me out. I need you to listen, babe."

"What do you think I'm doing?" She sassed. Her cheeks were red, flush with shame and anger.

She was still talking, responding to me. That was something.

I hit the floor and kneeled. I didn't even feel my balls tighten up and try to crawl up my guts. This girl was the first one who'd put me on my knees, and I didn't feel bad about it because she was worth it.

Had to have her. *Had to.*

Letting her spit in my face and walk away wasn't an option if I wanted to keep my sanity intact, regardless of whatever the hell happened with finishing her uncle. Shit, I'd let her slam those long nails into my fucking eyeballs and rip them outta my sockets if it would make this better. I'd bleed for her, bleed myself dry.

I was obsessed. A totally whacked out junkie for her voice, her laugh, her touch. A frothing, craven jackal for claiming her, mounting her, fucking her. Hearing how she screamed with my tongue between her legs, or clenching around my dick was like rock and roll blasting from the heavens.

I couldn't live without that music. Couldn't live without her.

Growling, I grabbed her by the knees, sloshing out a little bit of that shot she was holding. She quickly snatched it up, held it higher on her lap, just looking and looking, waiting for me to convince her.

Fuck. Okay.

"Just keep your mouth shut and listen to me for a fucking minute. I gotta say this. I already told you about all the shit I regret, all the things my old man died with hanging onto his black heart. All the danger, all the killing, all the assholes I've broken apart with my own bare hands…"

I sucked in a deep breath, remembering fifty different fuckers I'd killed one way or another over the years, including the twenty bastards who'd died in the blast at Club Duce. Their blood was sacrificial. It brought me here, step by ugly step, straight towards the greatest beauty of my life. My missing piece.

"They're all worth it 'cause they led me to the one thing I've ever crashed into that I'll never regret. It's right here in front of me. It's you, babe. You, you, only *you*."

I grabbed her legs and squeezed them tight. Fuck, I wanted to hold on forever, cling to what was mine and always would be.

Love or hate, heaven or hell, sin or sweetness.

I had to look up. Had to find out right fucking now if ripping out my heart and offering it up was enough, or if her bastard uncle had truly poisoned her against me forever.

Her eyes were softer. There was love there, heat bouncing through a sadness I couldn't understand. Maybe she was overwhelmed.

I stood up, pulling her with me. My brain analyzed every little syllable and cadence when she spoke.

"Anton, please…"

"Please what? Kiss and make up the way we should've the second you got here?" I pressed my lips to hers, testing and urgent, craving her to kiss me back and really want it.

She did. Fuck, she melted, twining her tongue with mine, and it was absolutely beautiful. My hands ran up and down the mangled fabric wrapped around her, a relic of the dirty secret that almost cost us this forever.

"Babe, come on. I love you, and that's enough. You shouldn't be wearing this thing." I pulled.

She absentmindedly passed the liquor carefully back and forth in her hands, turning while I gently drew the coat off around her. There was that hot fucking body again. My dick saw red and wanted to nest right against the crack of her sweet ass, rubbing 'til her pants came off, but I checked his greedy shit.

This was our moment to right wrongs and put the bloody, evil shit behind us. There'd be plenty of time for fucking her brains out soon, and when we did it was gonna be dynamite.

"Take it off," I said. We both paused and listened as it fell to the ground in a heavy lump. "Your uncle's gonna pay for what he fucking did to you. He killed your old man and your ma, and he tried to make you kill me too, didn't he?"

She shuddered when I said the last part, almost like it was true. What the fuck? She hadn't really come here to put a dagger in my throat, had she?

I turned her around. She was melting again, her face cracking and breaking. With one arm, I slammed her against my chest, pulling her arms around me.

"It's gonna be okay. Soon as the motherfucker who caused this shit's dealt with, we're gonna give that thing a proper burial. Frame it or make something outta it. A reminder that all the death and hell that's come between us is *over*, babe. It's past. It's done because I say it is. I'm gonna fill that hole in your heart the same fucking way I love filling up your body."

She kissed me, smiling as our lips pressed.

Finally. There she was. The Sabrina I'd been looking for all along, the dark haired babe I missed who lit my blood on fire and turned my dick to steel.

Oh, fuck. She tasted so soft, so wet, so warm. So irrevocably *mine.*

I couldn't hold the lust storm off forever. Soon as she was breathing regularly again and drying those eyes, I'd throw her down on the bed just a few feet away and fuck her seven ways to Sunday. And then seven more after that.

Shit, we'd go seven hundred fucking ways 'til the end of time with all the ways I needed her body hitched to mine.

A happy growl tore my throat like thunder. I broke away, sweeping one hand low to her ass, rubbing my stubble over her snowy neck.

"God damn, you're hot. I'm gonna blow the fuck up if I don't get something in me to cool off." I reached for the little shot still dangling in her fingers.

Had the fucking thing pressed to my lips before she let out an earsplitting scream. Both her hands clawed at my arm, trying to force it down.

"Stop it, Anton! No, no, no, no, no…you can't drink, you can't drink that stuff!"

Was this some kinda fucked up game? Smiling, I fought her, wheeling her around. We crashed down on the bed in chaos, and I was laughing as she tried to fight that shitty alcohol outta my hand. By some miracle, I hadn't spilled the damned thing.

Now, Sabrina was right on top of me. Right where I fucking wanted her, except with a lot less clothing.

I fought her and she went at me like a mad dog. The whole thing only lasted ten seconds before I had the cool glass pressed to my lips.

"Anton!" She screamed my name, twisted in my arms, and then rammed her little face against mine.

Fuck!

The shot broke away from my lips and I saw it go spiraling to the bed with Sabrina over my shoulder, face first. She was wide eyed and wiping furiously at her lips a second later.

That was when I realized this wasn't just a stupid game.

My girl's chest jerked unnaturally. She couldn't breathe. Her throat was closing.

I pulled her up in my arms roaring, thumping on her back, holding her close 'til I smelled that nasty vinegar shit on her lips.

Shit, shit, shit! The shot glass lay right next to where her face had hit. She must've downed half of whatever hadn't soaked into the sheets.

I went ape, jumped off the bed, and dragged her to the bathroom. She was coughing and struggling against me like mad, but now it was because she really couldn't breathe. I had one arm around her and my other on the phone, howling into it as fast as I could when Grigor answered.

"Get the fuck up here right now! Call a doctor – I don't care how fuckin' much you've got to pay the shit to keep his quack mouth shut. Move your ass!" The phone snapped shut and I hurled it into the tub.

Oh, fuck. This was bad. Her gem-like eyes were bugging and starting to get glassed. I didn't have a fucking clue what that shit really was, or how fast it worked. There was nothing I could do about the unknown poison right now except try to get it outta her system this second.

"Hang on, babe! This won't be pretty. Just remember I'm trying to save your ass!" I didn't know if she could hear me.

She looked panicked, half-blastd outta her mind. I held her over the toilet and reached into her mouth, jamming my fingers against her throat, anything to make her heave that shit up.

It took a few tries to get her to retch. She coughed and let it all out, and I kept going, holding her while she spasmed and expelled what little was in her stomach. Of course, the deadly shit was indistinguishable from everything else.

There was no way to know if I'd gotten it. I held her, shaking like a fucking fool while she kicked and thrashed, one hand on her little belly going through its spasms.

She went limp. I barely jerked her away from the bowl in time before she dove in. Laying her out carefully on the floor, I pushed my hand against her chest, checking her breath.

Somebody was knocking at the door out in the bedroom, but fuck if I was getting up to answer it.

Her breathing was still choppy, shallow, and difficult. The bluish tinge in her lips told me she wasn't getting enough oxygen.

Fuck, fuck, fuck!

I wiped her lips on my shirt and dove, pushing all the air from my lungs into hers, pounding on her chest to get her to suck it in.

Don't die on me, Sabrina. Don't you fucking die on me!
Breathe, baby, breathe.
Come. The. Fuck. On.

My brain was right off its rails by the time old Grigor came bursting in, belting loud Russian orders at the servants. Incomprehensible grief and desperation and terror turned me into a fucking maniac, but I wouldn't let myself do anything but breathe, pouring as much air as I could into her lungs.

"Master Anton, you need to let us through. We have steroids to help. Doctor is on his way."

I pulled myself away from her just long enough to jabber a few words about poisons and fuck ups to Grigor. I think the old man got the message. He never let a damned line of emotion show in his face.

Exactly like he'd been trained. A last line of defense for reason when all the Ivankovs were flipping their shit.

I wouldn't fucking leave her. Lev and Daniel grabbed underneath my arms and carried me away, kicking and screaming. Last glimpse of her I had was Grigor and two of the maids with First Aid shit piling in around her.

"Brother, please! Calm your ass down before you tear the whole house apart!" Lev leaned down and screamed in my face when we were outside.

The second they let me go, I lunged for them, grabbing both their necks and throwing them to the ground with superhuman strength.

"This is your fucking fault! Bastards! Both of you!"

Daniel's nose cracked beneath my fist and I felt blood come running out. Lev sank his teeth into my arm, but damned if I didn't stop moving it, snarling like a lion on crack while I pounded his head into the floor.

"Fuck! Just tell us what happened, Anton. Anton!" Daniel's words gurgled with the blood pouring down his throat and my continued punches. "Gonna fucking kill us…"

Fuck. I had them both by the balls. If they were any other men, they'd already be dead, their skulls fractured and their nose bones driven up their brains.

Damn it.

My brothers deserved the ass kicking, but they didn't deserve to die. They were only partially responsible for my woman laid out on the cold floor, fighting for her fucking life.

The real culprit was the sonofabitch we all wanted dead. And if I let my emotions boil over into murdering my own kin, I'd never get Gioulio. Not when it'd take a small miracle to show my face in Chicago without getting picked up and thrown back behind bars by the first fat cop looking to play hero.

I let them go. They crawled, putting some distance between us. Daniel grunted, wiped his face with his sleeve. I'd bloodied his nose and busted his lip bad.

"You gotta learn to talk to us without using your fists," Lev snarled. "What's this shit about poison? Did that bitch seriously try to kill you in our own house?"

It took everything I had to stay put instead of marching over and planting my fist in his broad fucking face again. "It was an accident. She was trying to take it back and prevent my dumbass from taking it. Change of heart. And none of it would've happened if I'd thrown the goddamned bug in the trash instead of planting it in her purse like Daniel said!"

D coughed, flashing me the angry eyes in his shattered face. "You fucking turncoat! We all agreed, and her pulling this shit just shows I was right all along. She stabbed you in the back, turned us on each other."

"Wrong answer!" I beat my fists on the floor, all I could do to avoid breaking his nose, or else breaking it a second time if the fucking thing was already snapped. "She poisoned herself because she stopped trusting me! Asshole Gioulio found your stupid bug and used it to open up her head and pour his crap into it. She was already poisoned way before she got here, before she swallowed that shit he gave her to kill me."

My brothers lowered their eyes. They were pissed, disappointed, and neither had a damned thing to say to my accusations because they knew it was all true.

"She found out, you know. Both you shits. Uncle fuckface told her about the night our old man ran down her ma, going after that French bitch, Mercedes."

"Shit!" Daniel's curse was extra shrill through the blood. "No wonder."

The heavy silence was interrupted by Grigor and the women carrying Sabrina. I heard my girl groan, stood up, and screamed after them, following as quickly as I could.

"What's going on? Is she gonna make it?"

"Still breathing!" Grigor yelled back. "Doctor is on his way. We need to lay her out in your bed, sir. Somewhere away from the toxin on the sheets."

Fuck. We moved to the adjoining chamber, and I watched them lay her out in the only bed where she'd belonged from the very start.

Her breaths were coming, slow and steady, an obvious struggle in her chest every time her lungs pumped. My brothers followed us in, but they kept their distance against the wall.

Lev was braver, the first to come over. His hand fell on my shoulder. By some insane miracle, I didn't instantly spin around and break his fucking jaw.

"Patience, brother. We're gonna make sure she's all right. This whole thing has been an epic clusterfuck."

I turned, shaking off his fingers. "Tell me something I don't already know, asshole."

"We're sorry. We're gonna make it right. Come on, Anton, you've gotta give us another chance."

Jackass. I thought it, but I didn't say it, because he was actually trying to help.

My chances for living like a sane man were all flashing before my eyes, spinning and vanishing with every rough breath I watched her take. God damn. Where was that asswipe doctor?

We stayed with her 'til the quack came in. He got to work right away and surprisingly kept his calm, even with all three of our hell hungry eyes on him.

He pierced her in the arm with a syringe. I watched him push some shit into her. The stethoscope came out, and he listened to her chest. Irrational jealousy raged in my veins while I watched him touch her, feel her.

I suppressed a growl. Yeah, it was insane, but fuck it. I never wanted another man's hands on her for any fucking reason. Nobody got to touch what was mine.

The doc stepped away just before I went off like a warhead. He murmured a few words to Grigor, something about needing a sample of the shit making her sick. Good thing there was still a whole fucking bottle of it in the other room.

I watched the doc grab his things and head for the door. My hands flew to my mouth and I screamed, loud enough to echo through the whole house.

"Well? What the fuck? Is she gonna be okay?"

The doctor spun, looked at me, clearly jarred. Good. Fuck him.

"She's stable. If you hadn't gotten it out of her right away, she'd be dead right now. I think she'll be okay – I just need to test the toxin to be sure." He shrugged. "Patience, please. I'm doing exactly what I was brought here for."

Arrogant little shit. I saw the recognition flash in his eyes. He certainly knew who I was from all the big stories in the media. Good thing I trusted Grigor to bring us a corruptible, but capable man. He always did, somebody who'd take the green and shut their fucking mouth instead of ratting to the Feds.

I shot my brothers a look that told them we were done. Grigor and his women stepped back to the other side of the room.

I sat down on the empty chair next to her, reached for her hand, and squeezed. She was like ice. I rubbed her fingers in mine, anything to make them warmer.

There was nothing left to do but watch and wait.

My girl stirred softly in her sleep. She wasn't conscious, but the danger had gone. Took me a good long while observing her before I believed the fuck with the stethoscope.

"It's done, brother. The call went out on the streets an hour ago." Lev leaned down to me while I perched at Sabrina's bedside. "We've got to move fast. You know how fast info travels down this bastard's pipeline and –"

"Let's go. I'll be back in time to see her wake up. That's a promise."

My knees bent reluctantly. I didn't want to leave her there 'til I saw her eyes shining at me again and I heard her sweet voice. But we'd just put all our fucking chips on the table to flush the rat out.

It was the only way. Daniel leaked a rumor to the media that we were all sick and dying in Chicago, both the notorious Ivankov brothers plus yours truly, target of the biggest manhunt in recent history.

We had to move our asses. The cops would raid all our properties in the city first, looking for a secret penthouse. I hoped that would keep them distracted while we went roaring after our target, the only fuck who *needed* to hear the reports.

I knew he had. Gioulio Ligiotti would be all over that shit like a bee starved for honey. Hell, he was probably celebrating this second, not giving a shit that there was no word from his niece.

He used her – fucking *used* her against me.

Little did he know the cannon was pointing his way now, and I'd only offer my woman the final shot. She was never, ever gonna find herself fucked up in the crossfire again, and everybody who'd put her there was about to pay big.

My brothers looked freaked out by the time our black van parked near Gioulio's Chicago estate. Their nerves were fucked, frayed, about to combust. Still, when the war went hot and bullets started flying, I knew I could count on them.

We were synchronized killers. We never let each other down. We never failed – not in any way that would get us killed.

Me? I was all ice. I couldn't imagine fucking this up after the promise I'd made.

No way. No fucking how. Gioulio and his men were gonna pay for decades of blood, plus a monstrous premium for hurting my girl too.

We all had black hoods on our faces. We hunkered in our seats and waited. Soon, we'd be out like hounds, gunning for the house. While we ran, the van was scheduled to plow through the gate, a fierce, noisy diversion to let us inside the mansion with minimal resistance.

The three men crammed in front of us were the best guys we had without Ivankov blood. I had total faith. Brother or not, nobody in this vehicle would let us down and blow the operation.

One more turn. The vehicle wheeled around, and I stood up, got in front of Lev and D, next to the back door. They lined up behind me, ready for the jump. My hands fisted the handles like they were swords, ready to hack through anything and anyone who stood in my way.

Vlad was the first to start screaming from the driver's seat. A good, hearty, very Russian *oooraaah* roared like thunder from his throat. The van jerked forward faster, making its final run at the gate.

"Now!" I screamed, throwing open the doors.

We threw ourselves out and hit the pavement hard. I saw my brothers right behind me as I stood up. We threw ourselves against the gate and began to climb, heading for good bush cover. A second later, the whole world exploded behind us as the van battered down the gate.

All hell broke loose. Screams in English and Italian rang out while we found our footing, going for a service entrance near Gioulio's garages. The bastard had twelve cars, and right now there'd be no one guarding them while they were pouring out to deal with my guys.

Six dark shapes went flying towards the van. Fuck. My boys were outnumbered, but we knew that from the beginning.

They'd put up a good fight, stall as long as they possibly could, trading fire from inside the van. I estimated we had about ten minutes to get our asses inside and hunt down the kingpin before police choppers and cruisers surrounded this fucking place.

By then, the Ligiotti crew had to be dead or wounded. Our crew in the van needed to be gone, waiting for us in the empty SUV we'd parked behind this place to make our escape.

The garages were near, and crawling with cameras. Whatever. They wouldn't do the fuckers inside much good when they'd spent their manpower fighting my boys in the van. I raised my nine millimeter and blinded one of the little black lenses with a bullet. Lights out.

Lev threw himself at the side door to the garages, hurling his boulder-like weight into it. Three good slams and it collapsed. Daniel and I were right behind him, running like hell, heading for the door leading into the house. We had to maneuver our way through all the shit in the huge garage, perfectly polished collectibles and sports cars from Gioulio's younger dick waving days, before he became an old mob boss with a lower profile.

I stuck out my hand and ripped a golden hood ornament off a sleek black shark on wheels – why the fuck not? I whipped it at the ceiling and heard it fall. The gold shape bounced on the concrete loudly as we started working on the door.

The loud, harsh jingle reminded me of bones rattling. I grinned behind my mask. Sweet music, reminding us what we'd come here for – death and judgment, vengeance for my baby girl, payment for every second she suffered in my bed from the poison in her blood.

Shit. This was really it. Do or die time. The blood hissing through my veins turned my whole body into a foundry, ready to melt from the inside out.

It was a relief when we burst inside and the first goon found us.

He fired at me and missed twice. Guess I stunned the fucker charging right at him. It was a stupid thing to do, but I was gonna get a lot more reckless if I didn't feed my bloodlust now.

I tackled the fuck to the ground, grabbed the back of his head like a ripe melon, and slammed him into the staircase over and over again. His forehead was a bloody mess by the time I was done. By then, the servants had inevitably heard us and come running.

"Freeze! You move your fucking asses an inch, you're dead!" Lev roared, flatting two old maids and a wiry butler against the wall with his rifle.

"Radio your friends outside and play stupid. Act like everything's okay in here. The real fight's out there. This doesn't have to end with your blood added to theirs. We're just here to pay your master a friendly visit." Daniel sounded surprisingly dark and dangerous when he had assholes under his thumb.

Had to be the Ivankov way. Even the smart ones turn into stone cold killers in the thick of it.

I took off while they secured the entrance. Flipped corners like a maniac spy, gun ready to spit death at any assholes who popped out in front of me.

Shit. Nothing. The whole place seemed like it was deserted.

I kicked down the door to every guest room and the big master suite upstairs. Nothing except the neat, tidy luxury rooms I expected a man like Gioulio to have – all empty.

Motherfuck. Panic shot through my chest for the first time. This wasn't the only time the demon managed to slither away before we hit him where he lived, but now the clock was ticking like never before. I couldn't stand here like a dumb fuck and piss away the *only* chance I'd ever have to win what my girl deserved.

I took off, mentally guessing we had about six minutes left. Flew down the stairs, crashed through my brothers, and grabbed the asshole butler. He shook like a fucking scarecrow in my lock.

"Where the fuck is he? Where!?" I growled it over and over again, dragging him headfirst through the house.

I checked every little twitch in the bastard's face, listened to every note in his voice when he begged for his life. His eyes were bulging, but I wasn't choking him so bad they wouldn't work. The butler just flailed around like any asshole screaming for mercy when I dragged him through the kitchen, the big sitting room, the dining room, and then back to where we'd started. He didn't reveal shit.

Fuck! Where the fuck is he, asshole? Lead me home.

Lev and Daniel looked at me impatiently. They were just as pissed as I was Gioulio hadn't turned up yet, and this latest stunt looked like fucking insanity. I thought I'd lost my mind too until I absentmindedly shoved the human scarecrow against the banister.

He stomped his feet, looking over my shoulder nervously a couple times. What the fuck was back there? I couldn't believe we'd missed the ratty looking wooden door, something narrow and old, straight outta the fifties.

Bingo. I dropped him on the floor and listened to him struggle for breath while I tore open the mystery door. It led down deep, branching off at one level into the house's basement, and then going deeper.

The air was too warm and dry for a boring old wine cellar. The old door popped open with a jerk. Inside, it looked like a total rat hole lined with linoleum and sleek metal filing cabinets.

A shadow moved between them and fired my way. Fuck!

I ducked, rolled on the floor, and returned fire. Some fucker screamed when one bullet found its mark on his calf. I quickly checked to make sure I was in one piece – sometimes when you're shot and hopped up on this much adrenaline, you don't realize it 'til you keel over.

Everything was still in one piece. Perfect. I stayed low to the ground and ran, diving for the legs in the gray trousers when I swept around the corner.

Gioulio got about two more shots off before I beat the gun outta his hands. They both went wild, embedded themselves in the old decrepit wall. Then I nearly did the same to him, slamming him so fucking hard on the old concrete his bones clacked like the hood ornament I'd bounced in the garage.

Our eyes locked. Bastard looked smug as the devil I expected, smiling through the pain from the hole I'd torn in his leg. Nobody ever looked like that when they were well and truly fucked.

Shit. He wasn't alone.

In one movement, I swung him around, using his pale body like a human shield. My gun lined up with the side of his head and I fired, careful not to graze his skull – not just yet. He had a bullet with his name on it for later.

The goon who'd had his gun trained on me dropped. Now, for the first time, the fuckhead in my arms began shaking. We moved, and I flattened him against the filing cabinets, satisfied with the way his spine crunched when I slammed him on the metal.

Fuck. Only about three minutes left, the clock in my head reminded me. We had to make this fast.

Gioulio didn't say a word. His dark, hateful, arrogant eyes said enough. I watched his jaw working, realizing he had one more surprise to take care of.

"Oh, no, motherfucker. No. You. Don't."

I reached into his wretched mouth and held his jaw open like a dog. He tried to bite my fingers off as I wrestled around for five obscene seconds, pulling the little glass capsule outta his mouth. It rolled on the floor next to my foot and I slammed my heel down on it.

He hadn't bitten into the cyanide, or else he'd be seizing in my arms. Good. The asshole howled, screamed, despair setting in as he realized I'd just slammed his last escape hatch shut.

My fists went to work. I pistol whipped him near the temple for my old man, remembering the way the fucked up hit tore papa up, reliving the night I found his body bloodied and dead.

Three more blows on both sides of his head for the girls he'd enslaved and pimped to those sick motherfuckers. Didn't know how the fuck we'd set them free, but we'd find a way once his crew was in chaos. Daniel and Lev promised me they'd do it.

I didn't know how many women he'd trafficked. Probably dozens. Unfortunately, those three blows had to make do for all of them. Anything more, and his old skull might shatter underneath my fists.

I clenched my gun like a heavy rock, and stopped just short of pounding it right through the top of his head, into his sadistic brain.

Shit, shit. Hold on. Just a little while longer.

I froze my killer instinct, shaking from the effort. The fear in Gioulio's eyes faded as they rolled, went white, and the last resistance in his muscles faded like a balloon losing its helium.

He was out cold. I grabbed him by the neck and dragged him up those stairs, quickly as I could. It wasn't easy. Every muscle in my body strained to haul his ass up. He'd been a muscular man in his younger years, but he'd clearly let it go, packing on fat while his strength faded like a bloated fucking guard dog in retirement.

Soon as I burst through the door, D and Lev were on me, helping me haul him to the main floor. Daniel aimed his gun at the ceiling and fired a few shots, screaming at the cowering servants. "Go! Get your asses out of here! And don't you think once about calling your boys outside or the goddamned cops."

The servants took off in all directions, screaming up the stairs and into the kitchen. Who could blame them after they'd spent the last five minutes wondering if it was their last?

Five minutes. Fuck!

Time was running out. My brothers and I hauled ass through the house, heading for the spa and gigantic pool in the back. We saw dark shapes lingering near the hill. My gun was drawn, ready to shoot our way out, even though we'd be fucked if we took any more delays. We were too fucking close.

Then one of the shadows signaled. Smoke seethed out my nostrils.

Vlad and our boys were waiting, right next to the SUV parked conveniently in the back for our escape. They helped us all over the gate. I got in the back with Gioulio, sat on his worthless carcass like a sack of potatoes, and we were off.

Just in time too.

Three police choppers descended on the mansion with their searchlights going the instant we were about a mile away. Soon, the ashes of Gioulio's empire were bathed in cherry red, glacier blue, and blinding white lights, dead and haunted to the authorities as the ruins in ancient Rome.

IX: One More Reckoning (Sabrina)

I woke up weak and sweaty. The pain was all gone. Amazingly, inexplicably vanished. I thought I was going to die, and I had to check myself several times to make sure I hadn't.

No ghost would ever feel she'd just survived a direct hit from a freight train.

I floated on a steamy high, thick and hot and invincible, the way you feel after getting over a bad illness. My memory took a few more seconds to follow.

My heart remembered everything that happened, and soon gave me some new pain to chew on.

Jesus. I'd really tried to kill him, hadn't I?

I'd saved him from swallowing the crap in the bottle and poisoned myself. I hadn't meant to, but as I slumped into the comfortable silk sheets, I wondered if I deserved it.

Everything feels like a distant dream when you're coming off a serious fever. But right now, the only thing I had to reach and hold onto was this weird and wonderful thing I'd built with Anton. I smiled when I thought about it, marveled at how it must've been unbreakable.

Somehow, I survived. *We* survived.

I couldn't understand it. Nothing made any sense, but my brain didn't lie. He hadn't squandered a second when he realized what was happening with the poison. Anton rushed me to the bathroom, kept me from dying until the doctor came.

It was more than lust, more than using me as a tool. I saw his love, his kindness. I felt his truth every time I took a new breath.

We'd both made mistakes. Our hearts were cruel, and they needed to be to survive the savagery constantly hammering away all around us.

Anton almost killed me by tearing out my heart with his betrayal, plus a little help from my twisted uncle. I'd tried to murder him for it, and I'd nearly died when I realized my mistake and my regret.

Sure, the poison was responsible for almost sending me into an early grave. But really, it was grief, brutal regret that I'd nearly destroyed the man I loved over a battered heart and a lie.

I still wanted to throw myself at him, tell him how sorry I was.

That didn't compare to the need I had for his lips, his embrace. I'd let him suck the last poison from my heart with every fiery kiss. Gioulio's toxin had faded and gone. Soon, I knew the rest of the venom he'd injected into my brain my entire adult life would go with it.

Anton. I needed to see him. I struggled to sit up, throw my feet over the bed to the cool floor.

I smiled when I was able to stand. Back when I was collapsing in his arms, puking out the poison while he held me, I never thought I'd stand and breathe again.

A window was cracked, letting in the cool autumn air. It was either dusk or just before dawn, judging by the little blue splash on the horizon. I didn't have a clue without something to tell the time.

I staggered to the bathroom and washed my face. The cool, refreshing water helped bring me back to life, made me halfway human again.

I was about to come out when the bedroom door burst open. Something heavy hit the floor, and someone was coughing outside.

"Shit!" Anton's voice.

A second later, he grabbed the bathroom doorknob and jerked it. I still had it locked. "Babe? Are you okay in there?"

I gave it a little push and flung it open, then fell into his arms. "I just woke up," I said, suddenly more energized by having his arms around me.

"Damn. I was hoping to have you in bed for the big surprise so it didn't give you too much of a shock. Nobody ever said this shit was gonna go perfect…"

I didn't understand what he was talking about. He held me, walked me out of the bathroom. I stopped when I saw his brothers standing against the wall. Lev and Daniel looked at us both, serious expressions on their faces. They wore matching black tactical suits like Anton.

Then I saw the bastard at their feet. Uncle Gioulio lay on the floor, squirming like an honest-to-God eel. His hands and legs were both bound by black cords. He turned his head, saw me, and started to struggle, grunting through his efforts.

The tape over his vile mouth prevented him from saying anything. For a second, my heart tried to have a flash of sympathy, but all the things he'd said and done came crashing home. The Russians weren't perfect, but they hadn't feigned love. They hadn't poisoned me. Anton and his brothers didn't twist my emotions the way he did – and he was fucking family!

My hand tightened in Anton's and he squeezed my fingers hard. We stomped over. I watched my man lean over the battered creature on the floor. In one fluid swipe, he ripped the tape off his mouth.

Uncle Gioulio coughed, looked at me, and swore. "Fuck. Don't let them do this to me, Brina. You can call it all off, save your uncle."

I shook my head. Amazing. I'd never seen him act so pathetic.

Anger bristled in Anton's eyes. He drew a handgun from the holster near his belt and pressed it to my uncle's temple.

"You heard her. No. Now, shut the fuck up! You don't talk unless she tells you to, understand?" Every syllable he spoke was a feral growl. "And quit your begging, asshole. Be a man for once in your miserable life."

Uncle Gioulio turned his head on the floor and closed his eyes. A harsh sob jarred his body. I came closer, pushed gently against Anton, pressing my lips to my uncle's ear.

"You told me about mama and how his father ran her down." I waited until my uncle saw me squeezing Anton's arm, looking lovingly into his eyes. I beamed back just as much hate at the bastard on the floor. "You didn't tell me about Mercedes, the French woman they were really after. Why?"

Gioulio sobbed again. He rolled, until he was flat on his back, miserably staring up at the ceiling.

"I loved that fucking woman. I'll go to my grave loving her like nothing else. Just do what you're gonna do," he said, a little strength returning to his voice.

"You lied to me." The words were so dry in my throat I choke back a cough.

I wasn't sure what I expected. Maybe an apology, an unselfish sob, something to tell me he was sorry for all this and wasn't just out to save his own ass.

Uncle Gioulio's eyes shifted to mine. They were narrowed, hateful. He looked at me like a pet who'd just disappointed him. Anton saw it, and he snarled, tightening his hold on the gun. He was ready to pull the trigger well over a minute ago.

"Not yet," I said, pinching at his arm. "Uncle, I need to know...did you ever care about me at all? Was I ever anything more than a loose end you couldn't tie up after you killed my parents?"

"I had you tied up," he hissed, bitterness in his voice. "Everything was fine. Perfect, until you decided to start interviewing this asshole in prison. You never would've found out shit. You would've been dumb, blind, and happy. I could've sent you overseas, left you the family fortune, more money than you'll ever see now. I've made ten times more each year alone than I ever did working with Gio."

I bit my lip when he said my father's name, and the asshole just kept digging.

"He wasn't strong enough. Neither was that fucking whore he married. She turned him soft. She twisted his arm into building more legit shit, riding my ass about leaving the real lucrative stuff behind. We had a problem with the Russians, and I saw my chance to kill two birds at once. It was Mercedes' idea. That woman never made mistakes. Fuck, if things hadn't gone to shit with her, I wouldn't be sprawled out on the floor like this right now!"

"But you are," I reminded him, running my sharp nails over his chest. "Thank you, uncle. That was all I needed to know."

Anton looked at me, his blue eyes burning like gas fires. "We ready to flush this turd, or what?"

"Do it," Uncle Gioulio insisted. "Let him put me out of my fucking misery."

The terror was gone. He was ready to die, resigned to his fate at the business end of Anton's gun.

Why did that make me feel so disappointed?

Anton looked at me. I nodded. His hand was up lightning fast, and he was about to pull the trigger when I reached up and slapped his shoulder.

"Wait. There's one more thing…" I crawled around on my hands and knees, until I was on the opposite side of him.

I put my hand on Gioulio's head and ran it backwards slowly. I'd inherited the same amazing Ligiotti hair, soft and dark and thick. The adrenaline numbing him made his jaw work like he was chewing on his own anxiety, sinking his teeth into the memories no doubt flashing before his eyes.

Several long, soft strokes calmed him down. He looked at me one last time with wider, softer eyes. There was the man I remembered. Kindly old uncle Gioulio.

Now, I was sure.

Somewhere deep down inside, he really cared for me. That made everything he'd done even more unforgivable.

I was ready.

"Niece, I'm sorry, sorry, so fucking sorry," he said, his voice breaking.

A thin, pleading smile pulled at his lips. I studied his pale face for a moment, leaning over him, finishing the last loop through his hair with my fingertips.

My face was right over his when I pursed my laps and spat. "I'm not."

I reached for the gun in Anton's hand while my spit was still in my uncle's eyes. I wrapped both hands tight around the weapon, pressed it to his forehead, and pulled the trigger.

The shot was deafening.

I jumped as its echo died. The gun slid out of my hands to the floor, and I backed away on my knees before my uncle's dark blood could touch me. Anton was on me lightning fast, pulling me up into his arms.

"You did good, babe."

"Just kiss me," I whimpered, stumbling away from the dead body.

He did. Anton grabbed me, jerked me close, smashed his lips to mine. His kiss carried me away, let me soar high above the hell below. I'd killed him, and hoped to God he was the only person I'd ever have to pull the trigger on.

Good thing I made it count, my one play at controlling life and death.

Anton's kiss swirled through the icy numbness inside me. With just his mouth, he warmed me, soothed me, told me everything was going to be okay.

We could rebuild after this. I just didn't know how.

"What now?" I whispered, stepping away with him so his brothers could start cleaning up the body.

"Glad you asked. The doc said you're good to travel. You just need a little extra rest, but you can make the trip."

"Travel?" I shook my head. "When? Where?"

"We're leaving, babe. Tonight. Half the Chicago police were swarming our asses looking for me, and that's before we caused a ruckus at your uncle's place. Now? Shit, I'll be surprised if the Governor hasn't sent out the National Guard."

"Oh my God."

My heart beat like a hammer. He really was one of the country's most wanted – something I'd easily forgotten in the chaos. I had to focus on my breathing, anything to prevent myself from falling back into another coma.

"Don't worry. We've already got our rat line worked out. My brothers are staying here. They'll be able to buy time and stay outta trouble with a few good lawyers. As for you and me, we gotta put some serious distance between us and the windy city."

"Where?" I whispered again, wondering all about the mechanics of loving a fugitive.

Hell, make that *living* like one too. We both killed the bastard at our feet, and we'd both go to jail if the law ever caught up with us.

Where? Where the hell was there anywhere on earth we'd be able to live above the surface, without looking over our shoulder every stupid second?

Anton just looked at me and smiled. "Come on, babe. You're a smart girl. You already know."

Early the next morning, we left for Lake Michigan. I watched Anton bid his brothers goodbye. The three men exchanged big manly hugs while I looked on.

When they were finished, the sophisticated Daniel came strutting over to me. "You're a lucky girl. Never thought I'd see the day when Anton's ready to run off and settle down. Listen, I'm sorry things had to start out so fucked up between us."

You and me both. I chewed on what he'd said for awhile, trying to decide whether he was being sincere or just diplomatic.

Grudgingly, I took his hand, and gave it one hard shake. Anton's brothers had good reason for mistrusting me after everything Uncle Gioulio had done. Of course, they'd been complete assholes and only made things worse.

But when had anything between our families been easy? If someone had told me I'd be standing in this house after a prison break and a near death experience, lovestruck by a man who'd scared my panties off the first time I met him, I would've made them bite their tongues.

"Chicago's in your hands now," I reminded him. "It'll be good to put some distance between us for awhile. Someday, when we come back...we'll see how I feel."

An arrogant smirk pulled at his lips. "You'll love us one day. Me and Lev both. I'm sure of it. One big, happy family. Whatever the hell I thought about you before, consider it gone. Clean slate. Take care of him for us, baby. You're good for him, and that's all that fucking matters at the end of the day."

He hugged me. A dozen emotions tangled in my belly. *Clean slate* resonated, and so did his tacit acceptance. When he let me go, the chauffeur was waiting impatiently.

Another servant carried down our luggage while Anton and Lev exchanged a few more words. I overheard them while I descended, taking the steps to the car, wondering if this dacha overseas he'd picked out had high stone steps too.

"By the time you get back, bro, we're all gonna have another eight figures to split between us. We're gonna make some crazy fucking bank without the Italians in the way." Lev looked past his older brother like he was waiting for gold coins to start raining from the sky.

"Whatever. You know I don't care about that shit. We're all in one piece. Blood before money. I want my family to prosper, but I'm outta the business for a good, long while. It's in your hands now. You make our old man proud filling up the bank, and I'll do it building this family."

Anton turned, looked at me. He seriously loved me.

Those lights in his royal blue eyes were as bright as the stars that first night we'd had sex. It was insane how fast I'd let his whirlwind pick me up and carry me away, but love and hate were always rocket fuel in huge quantities.

Part of me hoped we'd never fully settle down. This man made me *feel* like nobody else, even when I hated his guts and wanted him dead. He'd pulled me from my depths, saved my life, saved me ten times over. He delivered the lone bastard who reminded me I didn't deserve to crawl into a hole and die for what I'd done.

Killing Gioulio with him by my side drove a stake through the darkest parts of my heart.

I was finally free to experience everything. Free to live. Free to love.

"Shit, dude, at least put a ring on her finger before you try to breed her. You know cousin Strelkov did that much when he married his Italian princess out in Jersey." Lev grinned.

Anton gave him a dirty look. "Come on. This shit's not half as sloppy as that sideshow with the extended family. You saying I'm a bigger fool than David fucking Strelkov?"

"No, just a hornier one. You know I'm just busting your balls. Seriously, it'll be cool to have a nephew or niece talking Russian. Papa would've been proud." Lev gave him one last slap.

"Whatever. I'm gonna do it all right. Everything has its time and place. There'll be plenty of time to finally learn the ancestral tongue myself." He paused. "Take care of yourself, brother. You're the brawn now. Don't let D's brains cause any more goddamned trouble."

They both laughed, but I could tell it was bittersweet. Anton would be a wanted man with active investigators on him for a long time. It might be more than a decade before we ever set foot on US soil again, let alone returned to the only city I'd ever known.

I looked across the flat plains towards Chicago. The city was impossible to see from here. I wanted one last look, and I was still straining on my tip-toes when Anton crept up behind me. He grabbed me, pulled me toward him, wrapping both his big arms around my waist.

"What're you looking at, babe? It's time to go. Got a boat expecting us at ten o'clock sharp."

I turned, pressing my cheek to his chest. God, I'd never get tired of this rock hard contrast against my soft skin.

"Nothing. Everything I need's already right here."

One embrace changed my mind. I meant what I said. I'd miss the windy city, but it hadn't exactly been good to me. Chicago chewed my family up and spit me out a different girl than I'd been a couple months ago, and now I was ready to discover what kinda badass bitch the new Sabrina was.

It was a long couple days. The ship that took us across the great lake was more like an old freighter, and the waters were definitely frigid with November around the corner. Anton held me on his lap the entire time, whispering how amazing it was gonna be when we hit land again.

It seemed like we sailed forever, rocking in the cold, chaotic waves, all through the deep dark night. When the churning motion stopped, I woke up from the long nap I'd been taking with him.

Shoreline. Upper Michigan.

From there, it was a short drive to the border, and then one more boat ride across to foreign soil. We finally got to the airport in Sault Sainte Marie a day later, where the private jet was waiting for us on the Canadian side.

I'd never been on one before. Papa and my uncle could certainly afford it, but I'd never boarded one until now. It was strange to think the luxurious cabin with the big bed and the comfy chairs was a one-way rocket for taking us halfway around the world.

Half an hour later, we took off, on our way east for one last refueling stop before we crossed the wide Atlantic.

I stared out the window, gazing at the endless Ontario forests below. Anton slid into the seat next to me. "How you feeling, babe? Better than the boat ride in?"

"Yeah," I said, surprised my excitement cut through the melancholy tugging at my heart. "It's like the other night with Gioulio never happened at all...they said it should take a week to get over the poison. It's gone, all of it."

He smiled. "Course it is. You gave me one fuck of a scare, but I knew you'd get over that shit in the bottle. It was the motherfucker we finished off who was really dragging you down."

"I know," I said, reaching for the small glass of mineral water at my side and taking a long sip. "I keep wondering what's next. I've never been so far from home before."

"Shit, neither have I. Well, not that I remember. My old man always meant to fly us back to the motherland when we were kids, but it got to be a dangerous place after Soviet power crumbled. The seedy fucking underworld we both grew up in was a hundred times safer than that shock and awe shit Russia went through in the nineties." He grabbed me then, pulling me onto his lap. Instant heat. "You worry too much, babe. It's cute, but you shouldn't be wasting your precious energy. Long as we're together, it's gonna be amazing, wherever we end up. You know?"

He couldn't hide the raging hard-on against my thigh. Didn't think he wanted to. I looked down knowingly, a little smile curling my cheeks.

Okay, I was definitely feeling better than I thought, even with all this jet lag. Muscles clenched inside me, already drunk on his sultry touch. He reached for my thighs and squeezed, making me jerk on his lap, perfect for feeling the stiff rock beneath his trousers.

"Oh!" I whimpered. He silenced me with a long, deep kiss before I could say anything else.

"Quiet, babe, unless you want the crew to hear," he whispered, making me blush. "Honestly, I don't give a shit. It's about damned time we picked up where we left off. I know how much you like to fuck underneath the stars."

"Anton!" I was about to protest, but he reached up and pinched my nipple beneath my blouse.

Damn it. Just how thick were the walls on this plane anyway? The thing was airborne, so it couldn't be like a well built house. If I panted and moaned and came a little closer to screaming wrapped around him, I knew we ran the risk of the four man crew near the cockpit hearing everything.

He really didn't care. He flipped me over, meshing my legs around his waist. His friction hit my clit through our clothes, and I couldn't do anything but melt while he popped the buttons on my blouse.

"Keep making that beautiful music, Sabrina. You fight me, I'll rip your panties off and stuff them in your sweet mouth. We're fucking right now regardless, and I don't give a shit if you're gagged or howling like crazy when I'm emptying myself in your cunt."

He rubbed harder, faster. Jesus. I loved him, wanted him, and he was still a total bastard.

Naturally, I fucking loved it.

He did me a favor by clapping his hand over my mouth while he worked off my pants. A little turbulence jostled us when he slid down my panties, swinging them around my ankles like a pro. I watched them crumple in one hand.

"Fuck. You soaked every last inch of these bitches. You think you can keep it together without going to pieces on me, or am I gonna have to show you how good this pussy tastes?"

Growling, he pushed the gusset across his teeth, tasting my cream. My thighs started to shake. His free hand went between my legs and two rough fingers pushed inside me. He began fucking me before his cock ever came out, softening me up for him, adding to the napalm that drenched the lace in his fist.

"God damn it," he grunted, throwing them over his shoulder. "I can't kiss you and taste the real thing at the same time. Hold it together and don't cry on me girl. I'm gonna make you come so fucking hard you're never ashamed of anything again. The only whining I wanna hear is that little chirp you make right before your clit goes nuts on my tongue."

There I was. Lost at fifteen, maybe twenty thousand feet. He held my legs open, a powerful and unbreakable grip, ramming his face between my legs. Rough stubble braised my thighs. I arched my back when his tongue found the wet spot.

Jesus. Fuck.

I took every part of the heaven's name in vain, and then did it a few times more when his fingers clenched my ass cheeks, spreading me apart, wide and open just for him.

He dove in, fucking me with his tongue, licking and sucking until I pumped my hips back. Furious laps circled my clit. He did that thing where he sucked it between his teeth and growled, vibrating my entire pussy with his thunder, smothering me in total pleasure. The beast between my thighs wouldn't be satisfied until I gave it all up.

Fortunately for him, it wouldn't take long. My vision blurred and my head rolled to the side. I saw early evening stars shining out the window just as his tongue engulfed me.

It was like the whole plane exploded from a meteor strike, leaving us tumbling through the night sky. I let go, tearing at his hair for something to hold onto, screaming and coming so hard I forgot all about the crew.

They must've heard everything. It was filthy, shameful, and – like everything else with this man – absolutely mind blowing. His mouth sucked and licked and fucked my pussy in endless waves. Each movement lashed me higher, until I must've left the atmosphere for a few glorious seconds and slammed back into my body.

When I came out of it, he had me in his arms, jerking me against his shirtless body. "Fucking shit. You scream like that again, babe, and the pilots are gonna wreck this plane from jacking off, the jealous fucks."

I laughed. He took me by the hand and walked me over to the bed, completely buck naked. When we reached the edge, he tapped his knees on mine, pushed me down, tearing at his belt and dropping everything below the waist.

"Spread your legs. I *need* to be inside you, Sabrina. Right fucking now."

I obeyed. The firebird on his chest looked hungrier than before, ready to swoop down and fly through me while his thrusts rattled my body. I didn't need to touch its fiery wings to burn.

Anything but drawing him deep was unthinkable. I heard voices behind the thin door separating our cabin from the rest of the plane. Two stewardesses laughed, and then there was a manly, guttural chuckle with them.

Crap. The whole crew was enjoying our performance.

I locked up. Anton saw me struggling to wrap my head around fucking where these people could hear us. His face darkened, and the foreplay was over. He pushed his dick inside me in one rough thrust.

My pussy instantly clenched around him, obliterating any hesitation. That stud in his cock glided over places I couldn't even describe, massaging me from the inside out, making my pulse match the delicious throb in my pussy.

Perfection. I'd forgotten how incredibly well we fit together. His thrusts reminded me how good our rhythm could be when he started to get into it, rocking the little bed with his thrusts.

He was a mountain, a tidal wave, and hot lava all in one. My clit sizzled each time he swept low, cursing and whispering in my ear, nipping at my throat.

We fucked. Hard. We fucked and rocked and sweated out the last few drops of bitterness and betrayal we'd left behind in the States. Anton sped up, seized my hair in his fist, and pulled until my lips crashed against his.

I was coming when he pushed his tongue into my mouth, suffocating in him, and loving it.

Everything below my waist turned to tingly mush, pure hot pleasure racing to my brain. I tried to scream and gasp for breath, but he held me down, fucking me and swallowing every scream in his kisses.

"Oh, fuck. God!" I screamed when he finally let me up, never skipping a beat with his hips.

I wasn't sure how the plane wasn't crashing to the ground with his furious jerks. He pulled out, turned me around with a quick slap on the ass, and mounted me from behind, taking the reigns he'd formed out of my hair again.

"Not God, babe. It's me. You fucking scream my name when I make you squirt all over the sheets. I'm not holding your mouth shut this time. Let it go. Let it all fucking go."

He didn't suffocate me with another kiss, no, but he held me down even rougher. Every thrust battered me to the bed, a challenge posed in his hips. My body was ready to meet him. Primal instinct kicked in and I bucked back, grinding my ass as hard as I could on his pubic bone.

Big mistake. The friction only fed the manic fire he'd sparked in my pussy. Before I knew it, I was clenching my burning jaw and burying my face in the mattress, all I could do to stop myself from shrieking bloody murder before my body fried itself again.

Oh, no.

"Oh, fuck!" Anton pulled me up on his cock, whipped my head to the side by the hair, and sank his teeth into the soft nook where my shoulder and neck met.

He was growling when he started to come. I could practically feel his heartbeat each time his dick jerked, heaving his molten essence into me, so much seed my pussy numbed and overflowed. I tore at the sheets, screamed without thinking, lived and died in his amazing grasp.

We came for an eternity, rocking and snarling, draining every molecule of air from our lungs. His teeth didn't even start to hurt until I was coming off the high.

At last, he let go, lingering inside me for a good minute before he pulled out. The plane's engine droned on, sweet white noise grounding us on planet earth.

"Mister Ivankov? Is everything all right?" A fist knocked on the door ahead of the woman's voice.

"Bring us a couple glasses!" Anton shouted back. "Straight vodka. We're fine."

"God." I rolled over, and he pulled me to his chest, dragging me through several large wet spots on the bed. "I could really use a drink."

"We gotta get some water into you too, babe," he said, pointing to the wetness spattering the bed. "See what you fucking did? You've got about a minute to get into the sheets before she comes in and sees you buck naked."

He stood up, walked to the door nude, and left me to struggle into the bed. My mouth was still hanging open in disbelief when he returned with two crystal glasses of good vodka and an ice shaker.

"You're an animal," I said, hating the smile that killed all the mock venom in my voice.

He shrugged, handing me my drink. "You're an Ivankov woman now. I like my girls to give me everything and hold nothing back. Fucking nothing, Sabrina. You know it. I love this shit because it's the best damned trade in the world – everything love should be. We know the drill. I'll keep giving you the world, and you keep squirting all over this dick when I fuck your brains out."

"Really?" I quirked an eyebrow, feeling smooth vodka splash my belly like fire. "Is that all it takes to be an Ivankov's woman?"

"Yeah," he growled, pulling up the sheet and slipping into bed next to me. "That and keeping up with me."

He was hard, and ready to take me again. Unbelievable.

We fucked the entire trip across the Atlantic, all the way to European airspace. I'd never been happier. Little did I know there was so much more to come. This was a baptism of lust above the seas. By the time we landed in Moscow, I was purified. I'd had my final reckoning, and now it was time to enjoy my reward for the rest of our days.

It didn't take us long to prep. By the time the plane landed, we were cleaned up, dressed, and ready to face whatever new craziness was waiting for us in this distant land.

X: Home Sweet Home (Anton)

Russia was a whole different world. It took some serious wrangling to get this place in the country outside Moscow. My old man's rich cousins looked at me like I was a god, freshly arrived from the new world after leading our name to greatness.

Good thing respect is a powerful thing. The servants spoke with such thick accents it took my ears a couple weeks to get used to it. Shit, those real Russians know how to cook and party too. We spent our first week in the motherland blasted on our asses from vodka and overstuffed with caviar.

Sabrina took to the strange new world better than me. She was reborn, glowing around our manor like a second sun. Long rides on horseback and countless hours fucking through the night didn't exhaust her. She was up the next day with the breakfast tray from our butler, ready for more discoveries.

I thought she was beautiful before. Hell, I always thought that since the first time I saw her between the glass, taunting me, a ticket to butcher the asshole who'd done my kin so many wrongs. Never would've guessed she'd be my ticket to paradise too.

The girl spent most days pecking away at her new laptop. She was writing a whole fucking book, a tell all saga blowing open the rise and fall of crime boss Gioulio Ligiotti. The FBI could eat their bastard hearts out while the public snapped it up, unable to touch her while relations were frosty between Mother Russia and the States.

As it was, the Feds were fucked. Gioulio got dumped underneath a ton of concrete at an old construction site, closer to hell where he belonged. After a couple weeks of questions and agents roaming through every nook and cranny, the heat was off my brothers. We hadn't left a shred of evidence, and soon the boys were gonna get back to expanding business in the big city.

Me? It was a fucking relief to be away from all that.

I took up archery and plotted my next move. Maybe a legit import-export business between Moscow and the EU. If all went well, I'd have shit set up by the time relations started to thaw between East and West. We still had all the money in the world.

Swiss banks. Gotta love 'em. For everything else, there was bribery, which was even easier over here than back home.

It only took me a few weeks to lock down our little world. Like a good Muscovite Prince, I could ride right into town with my girl at my side, a whole army ready to serve us at every disco, bar, and art gallery as soon as I flashed my name.

The business moves would come later. There was just one more move I had to make, something to seal the crazy fucking deal Sabrina and me forged from the moment I pulled her outta the prison and into my brothers' truck.

She was writing when I came home that day.

"Save your shit and close that thing. We need to leave now."

She spun around as soon as my hand landed on her shoulder and squeezed. The look on my face told her she was in deep shit. It was hard keeping my voice grave as ice – I wanted to fucking laugh when I stared into her frightened eyes.

"Anton? Are we in trouble."

"You'll find out soon, babe. Come on."

I grabbed her by the hand, threw her coat on, and we marched out into the winter stillness. The old Russian man I'd hired to play driver rolled up in our limo after five seconds. She relaxed a bit when she saw the car. My girl was smart enough to know we wouldn't be going out in style if we really had to flee.

Still, I kept my cards close, tight to my chest as my own ink. Inside, perched on the leather seats, I handed her a glass of wine. I wanted her warmed up and relaxed for what was coming.

Shit, I needed a tall glass myself. For the first time in forever, I was nervous, and I stood a better chance of tripping all over my damned words sober.

"We're here, sir," the Russian driver called over the little speaker, about five minutes later.

Sabrina was eyeing me with curiosity and suspicion. I suppressed a smile. She had every fucking right. Ever since we'd landed, I kept trying to one up myself, make every surprise I had for her more special than the last.

"Anton? What is this place?" She must've asked the same question three times after we got out and I guided her onto the path to the old church.

The place was in ruins when I'd found it one day riding by myself. I knew there were ruins on my property, but I didn't think it was a whole honest-to-God church. The Bolshevik fucks had done a number on it almost a century ago.

It took a jumbo sized team to get the job done. Two months of round the clock work to put a new roof on and renovate the place. It cost a couple million, about twice as much as the heavy ring weighing down my pocket. But it was worth every fucking penny. I saw it on her face when the huge doors swung open and we stepped inside.

She knew. Same thing I knew the first time I saw it laying in pieces.

This was the place where we were gonna get married.

It looked like a living museum, all fancy with fresh wooden pews and glassy eyed saints staring down from the walls. The villagers fell to my feet and showered me in thanks for making it whole. It was a fine place to pray or worship, yeah, but that wasn't what I was after.

This was all about us. Her steps slowed as I led her to the altar. She *oohed* and *ahhed* a few times going down the aisle. I almost joined her. Those big glass windows really did something awesome to the light, turning dull winter rays into beautiful gold.

The walls shined like silver, gold, and ruby. Fuck, she was glowing herself when we got to where I wanted, like we were extensions of the glory all around us.

"Babe, stop right here. This is where you get your second surprise."

"Holy shit! Anton, I —" she clapped a small hand over her mouth. "Sorry. Cursing like that's the last thing I should be doing here."

I grinned. "It's fine. The only thing that'd really desecrate this place is refusing what I've got here." I reached into my pocket.

She started shaking her head, cherry red heat flaming on her cheeks, knowing what was coming. Fuck it. There was no more need to play sly.

I reached for the box in my pocket and popped it open, pushed it into her sweet hands cupped near her bosom. "Marry me. We've been through heaven and hell together, and here we are. You're already mine, babe, whatever the fuck happens from here. Now, let's make it official. Say 'yes' so I can slide that rock on your finger."

Her eyes almost popped out when she saw the ring. Fine jewelry was nothing new to her, growing up in wealth and splendor like me. I still managed to hit the mark. A few special connections and a million bucks bought more here than anywhere else.

"Anton!" She swooped into my arms, smashed the box between us, planting her lips on mine. "Of course I will."

Thank God. The phrase held extra power here. Not just because we were kissing in the middle of this beautiful renovated temple, but because I'd been scared as shit about something breaking down at the last minute, some creep of doubt, some kinda bad luck.

It was meant to be, and it took me a full minute of her hot little lips on mine to realize it always had been.

A few seconds later, I held her, plucked out the ring, and pushed it onto her finger. Perfect fit. Only kind there'd ever be.

We'd gotten our fairy tale ending after a twisted beginning. Sometimes, dreams do come true, and you can build them piece by piece, digging clay from the craziest fucking places.

"Bastard," she hissed in my ear, hot and salacious. "You scared me. You were planning this all along."

She laughed, and I shot her a serious look. "Shit, babe. We've christened this place with enough dirty talk for one day. Save some for the big day."

Another laugh. She gave my bicep a playful whack. I grabbed her, threw her over my shoulder, and led her to the back door carved in the nicely concealed wood behind the altar.

It was just a little passage I'd had built special for the church. Past that door, the right fork led to the priest's office, but we took the left.

"I'm not done with the surprises, babe." I set her down next to the new door, working at the lock with a key from my pocket.

Soon as it opened and she got a good look, she laughed and flapped her hair even harder than when I'd given her that ring. Fuck me. And here I thought those million dollar diamonds would be the greatest surprise.

"I can't believe you!"

Grinning, I cupped her ass and nudged her inside. She didn't need much help – she was drawn right into the small silver bedroom decked out with a red leather fold-down bed.

"Don't worry. This priest said it's kosher as long as there's a hallway and a seal between this place and the church. Besides, where else did you think I was gonna fuck you? Out in the snow? You know my dick's not gonna wait 'til we get back to the house. Not after hearing you're gonna be my wife."

My wife – fuck! I couldn't believe it. *Better fuck her long and hard to make it sink in.*

Just thinking it made me harder than the diamond and gold on her finger. It was all she was wearing a minute later when I laid her down and sank inside her.

We fucked. We kissed. We came together.

I was still growling her name like a holy mantra when my balls were milked dry, lost in this sweet slice of heaven we'd created. And I'd stay lost in its wonder 'til the day I died.

Thanks!

Want more Nicole Snow? Sign up for my newsletter to hear about new releases, subscriber only goodies, and other fun stuff!

JOIN THE NICOLE SNOW NEWSLETTER! - http://eepurl.com/HwFW1

Thank you so much for buying this book. I hope my romances will brighten your mornings and darken your evenings with total pleasure. Sensuality makes everything more vivid, doesn't it?

If you liked this book, please consider leaving a review and checking out my other erotic romance tales.

Got a comment on my work? Email me at nicolesnowerotica@gmail.com. I love hearing from my fans!

Kisses,
Nicole Snow

More Erotic Romance by Nicole Snow

KEPT WOMEN: TWO FERTILE SUBMISSIVE STORIES

SUBMISSIVE'S FOLLY (SEDUCED AND RAVAGED)

SUBMISSIVE'S EDUCATION

SUBMISSIVE'S HARD DISCOVERY

HER STRICT NEIGHBOR

SOLDIER'S STRICT ORDERS

COWBOY'S STRICT COMMANDS

RUSTLING UP A BRIDE: RANCHER'S PREGNANT CURVES

FIGHT FOR HER HEART

BIG BAD DARE: TATTOOS AND SUBMISSION

MERCILESS LOVE: A DARK ROMANCE

LOVE SCARS: BAD BOY'S BRIDE

Outlaw Love/Prairie Devils MC Books

OUTLAW KIND OF LOVE

NOMAD KIND OF LOVE

SAVAGE KIND OF LOVE

WICKED KIND OF LOVE

BITTER KIND OF LOVE

SEXY SAMPLES: OUTLAW'S KISS

I: Cursed Bones (Missy)

"It won't be long now," the nurse said, checking dad's IV bag. "Breathing getting shallower...pulse is slowing...don't worry, girls. He won't feel a thing. That's what the morphine's for."

I had to squeeze his hand to make sure he wasn't dead yet. Jesus, he was so cold. I swore there was a ten degree difference between dad's fingers in one hand, and my little sister's in the other. I blinked back tears, trying to be brave for Jackie, who watched helplessly, trembling and shaking at my side.

We'd already said our goodbyes. We'd been doing that for the last hour, right before he slipped into unconsciousness for what I guessed was the last time.

I turned to my sister. "It'll be okay. He's going to a better place. No more suffering. The cancer, all the pain...it dies with him. Dad's finally getting better."

"Missy..." Jackie squeaked, ripping her hand away from me and covering her face.

The nurse gave me a sympathetic look. It took so much effort to push down the lump in my throat without cracking up. I choked on my grief, holding it in, cold and sharp as death looming large.

I threw an arm around my sister, pulling her close. Lying like this was a bitch.

I wasn't really sure what I believed anymore, but I had to say something. Jackie was the one who needed all my support now. Dad's long, painful dying days were about to be over.

Not that it made anything easy. But I was grown up, and I could handle it. Losing him at twenty-one was hard, but if I was fourteen, like the small trembling girl next to me?

"Melissa." Thin, weak fingers tightened on my wrist with surprising strength.

I jumped, drawing my arm off Jackie, looking at the sick man in the bed. His eyes were wide open and his lips were moving. The sickly sheen on his forehead glowed, one last light before it burned out forever.

"Daddy? What is it?" I leaned in close, wondering if I'd imagined him saying my name.

"Forgive me," he hissed. "I...I fucked up bad. But I did it for a good reason. I just wish I could've done it different, baby..."

His eyelids fluttered. I squeezed his fingers as tight as I could, moving closer to his gray lips. What the hell was he saying? Was this about Mom again?

She'd been gone for ten years in a car accident, waiting for him on the other side. "Daddy? Hey!"

I grabbed his bony shoulder and gently shook him. He was still there, fighting the black wave pulling him lower, insistent and overpowering.

"It's the only way...I couldn't do it with hard work. Honest work. That never paid shit." He blinked, running his tongue over his lips. "Just look in the basement, baby. There's a palate...roofing tiles. Everything I ever wanted to leave my girls is there. It was worth it...I promised her I'd do anything for you and Jackie...and I did. I did it, Carol. Our girls are set. I'm ready to burn if I need to..."

Hearing him say mom's name, and then talk about burning? I blinked back tears and shook my head.

What the hell was this? Some kinda death fever making him talk nonsense?

Dad started to slump into the mattress, a harsh rattle in his throat, the tiny splash of color left in his face becoming pale ash. I backed away as the machines howled. The nurse looked at me and nodded. She rushed to his free side, intently watching his heartbeat jerk on the monitor.

The machine released an earsplitting wail as the line went flat.

Jackie completely lost it. I grabbed her tight, holding onto her, turning away until the mechanical screaming stopped. I wanted to cover my ears, but I wanted hers closed more.

I held my little sister and rocked her to my chest. We didn't move until the nurse finally touched my shoulder, nudging us into the waiting room outside.

We sat and waited for all the official business of death to finish up. My brain couldn't stop going back to his last words, the best distraction I had to keep my sanity.

What was he talking about? His last words sounded so strange, so sure. So repentant, and that truly frightened me.

I didn't dare get my hopes up, as much as I wanted to believe we wouldn't lose everything and end up living in the car next week. The medical bills snatched up the last few pennies left over from his pension and disability – the same fate waiting for our house as soon as his funeral was done.

Delirious, I thought. *His dying wish was for us, hoping and praying we'd be okay. He went out selflessly, just like a good father should.*

That was it. Had to be.

He was dying, after all…pumped full of drugs, driven crazy in his last moments. But I couldn't let go of what he said about the basement.

We'd have to scour the house anyway before the state kicked us out. If there was anything more to his words besides crazy talk, we'd find out soon enough, right?

I looked at Jackie, biting my lip. I tried not to hope off a dead man's words. But damn it, I did.

If he'd tucked away some spare cash or some silver to pawn, I wouldn't turn it down. Anything would help us live another day without facing the gaping void left by his brutal end.

My sister was tipped back in her chair, one tissue pressed tight to her eyes. I reached for her hand and squeezed, careful not to set her off all over again.

"We're going to figure this out," I promised. "Don't worry about anything except mourning him, Jackie. You're not going anywhere. I'm going to do my damnedest to find us a place and pay the bills while you stay in school."

She straightened up, clearing her throat, shooting me a nasty look. "Stop talking to me like I'm a stupid kid!"

I blinked. Jackie leaned in, showing me her bloodshot eyes. "I'm not as old as you, sis, but I'm not retarded. We're out of money. I get that. I know you won't find a job in this shitty town with half a degree and no experience...we'll end up homeless, and then the state'll get involved. They'll take me away from you, stick me with some freaky foster parents. But I won't forget you, Missy. I'll be okay. I'll survive."

Rage shot through me. Rage against the world, myself, maybe even dad's ghost for putting us in this fucked up position.

I clenched my jaw. "That's *not* going to happen, Jackie. Don't even go there. I won't let –"

"Whatever. It's not like it matters. I just hope there's a way for us to keep in touch when the hammer falls." She was quiet for a couple minutes before she finally looked up, her eyes redder than before. "I heard what he said while I was crying. Daddy didn't have crap after he got sick and left the force – nothing but those measly checks. He didn't earn a dime while he was sick. He died the same way he lived, Missy – sorry, and completely full of shit."

Anger howled through me. I wanted to grab her, shake her, tell her to get a fucking grip and stop obsessing on disaster. But I knew she didn't mean it.

Lashing out wouldn't do any good. Rage was all part of grief, wasn't it? I kept waiting for mine to bubble to the surface, toxic as the crap they'd pumped into our father to prolong his life by a few weeks towards the end.

I settled back in my chair and closed my eyes. I'd find some way to keep my promise to Jackie, whether there was a lucky break waiting for us in the basement or just more junk, more wreckage from our lives.

Daddy wasn't ready to be a single father when Mom got killed, but he'd managed. He did the best he could before he had to deal with the shit hand dealt to him by this merciless life. I closed my eyes, vowing I'd do the same.

No demons waiting for us on the road ahead would stop me. Making sure neither of us died with dad was my new religion, and I swore I'd never, ever lose my faith.

A week passed. A lonely, bitter week in late winter with a meager funeral. Daddy's estranged brother sent us some money to have him cremated and buried with a bare bones headstone.

I wouldn't ask Uncle Ken for a nickel more, even if he'd been man enough to show his face at the funeral. Thankfully, it wasn't something to worry about. He kept his distance several states away, the same 'ostrich asshole' daddy always said he was since they'd fallen out over my grandparent's miniscule inheritance.

All it did was confirm the whole family was fucked. I had no one now except Jackie, and it was her and I against the world, the last of the Thomas girls against the curse turning our lives to pure hell over the last decade.

A short trip to the attorney's office told me what I already knew about dad's assets. What little he had was going into state hands. Medicare was determined to claw back a tiny fraction of what they'd spent on his care. And because I was now Jackie's legal guardian, his pension and disability was as good as buried with him.

The older lawyer asked me if I'd made arrangements with extended family, almost as an afterthought. Of course I had, I lied. I made sure to straighten up and smile real big when I said it.

I was a responsible adult. I could make money sprout from weeds. What did the truth matter in a world that wasn't wired to give us an ounce of help?

Whatever shit was waiting for us up ahead needed to be fed, nourished with lies if I wanted to keep it from burying us. I was ready for that, ready to throw on as many fake smiles and twisted truths as I needed to keep Jackie safe and happy.

Whatever wiggle room we'd had for innocent mistakes slammed shut the instant daddy's heart stopped in the sharp white room.

I was so busy dealing with sadness and red tape that I'd nearly forgotten about his last words. Finishing up his affairs and making sure Jackie still got some sleep and decent food in her belly took all week, stealing away the meager energy I had left.

It was late one night after she'd gone to bed when I finally remembered. It hit me while I was watching a bad spy movie on late night TV, halfway paying attention to the story as my stomach twisted in knots, steeling itself for the frantic job hunt I had to start tomorrow.

I got up from my chair and padded over to the basement door. Dust teased my nose, dead little flecks suspended in the dim light. The basement stank like mildew, tinged with rubbing alcohol and all the spare medicine we'd stored down here while dad suffered at home.

I held my breath descending the stairs, knowing it would only get worse when I finally had to inhale. Our small basement was dark and creepy as any. I looked around, trying not to fixate on his old work bench. Seeing the old husks of half-finished RC planes he used to build in better times would definitely bring tears.

Roofing tiles, he'd said. Okay, but where?

It took more than a minute just scanning back and forth before I noticed the big blue tarp. It was wedged in the narrow slit between the furnace and the hot water tank.

My heart ticked faster. So, he wasn't totally delusional on his death bed. There really were roofing tiles there – and what else?

It was even stranger because the thing hadn't been here when I was down in the basement last week – and daddy had been in hospice for three weeks. He couldn't have crawled back and hidden the unknown package here. Jackie definitely couldn't have done it and kept her mouth shut.

That left one disturbing possibility – someone had broken into our house and left it here.

Ice ran through my veins. I shook off wild thoughts about intruders, kneeling down next to the blue plastic and running my hands over it.

Yup, it felt like a roofing palate. Not that I'd handled many to know, but whatever was beneath it was jagged, sandy, and square.

Screw it. Let's see what's really in here, I thought.

Clenching my teeth, I dragged the stack out. It was lighter than I expected, and it didn't take long to find the ropey ties holding it together. One pull and it came off easy. A thick slab of shingles slid out and thudded on the beaten concrete, kicking up more dust lodged in the utilities.

I covered my mouth and coughed. Disappointment settled in my stomach, heavy as the construction crap in front of me. I prepared myself for a big fat nothing hidden in the cracks.

"Damn it," I whispered, shaking my head. My hands dove for the shingles and started to tug, desperate to get this shit over with and say goodbye to the last hope humming in my stomach.

The shingles didn't come up easy. Planting my feet on both sides and tugging didn't pull the stack apart like I expected. Grunting, I pulled harder, taking my rage and frustration out on this joke at my feet.

There was a ripping sound much different than I expected. I tumbled backward and hit the dryer, looking at the square block in my hands. When I turned it over, I saw the back was a mess of glue and cardboard.

Hope beat in my chest again, however faint. This was no ordinary stack of shingles. My arms were shaking as I dropped the flap and walked back to the pile, looking down at the torn cardboard center hidden by the layer I'd peeled off. Someone went through some serious trouble camouflaging the box underneath.

I walked to dad's old bench for a box cutter, too stunned with the weird discovery to dwell on his mementos. The blade went in and tore through in a neat slice. I quickly carved out an opening, totally unprepared for the thick leafy pile that came falling out.

My jaw dropped along with the box cutter. I hit the ground, resting my knees on the piles of cash, and tore into the rest of the box.

Hundreds – no, thousands – came out in huge piles. I tore through the package and turned it upside down, showering myself in more cash than I'd seen in my life, hundreds bound together in crisp rolls with red rubber bands.

Had to cover my mouth to stifle the insane laughter tearing at my lungs. I couldn't let Jackie hear me and come running downstairs. If I was all alone, I would've laughed like a psycho, mad with the unexpected light streaking to life in our darkness.

Jesus, I barely knew how to handle the mystery fortune myself, let alone involve my little sis. I collapsed on the floor, feeling hot tears running down my cheeks. The stupid grin pulling at my face lingered.

Somehow, someway, he'd done it. Daddy had really done it.

He'd left us everything we'd need to survive. Hell, all we'd need to *thrive*. Feeling the cool million crunching underneath my jeans like leaves proved it.

"Shit!" I swore, realizing I was rolling around in the money like a demented celebrity.

Panicking, I kicked my legs, careful to check every nook around me for anything I'd kicked away in shock. When I saw it was all there, I grabbed an old laundry basket and started piling the stacks in it. I pulled one out and took off the rubber band. Rifling my fingers through several fistfuls of cash told me everything was separated in neat bundles of twenty-five hundred dollars.

I piled them in, feverishly counting. I had to stop around the half million mark. There was at least double that on the floor. Eventually, I'd settle down and inventory it to the dime, but for now I was looking at somewhere between one to two million, easy.

It was magnitudes greater than anything this family had seen in its best years, before everything went to shit. I smoothed my fingers over my face, loving the unmistakable money scent clinging to my hands.

No shock – sweet freedom smelled exactly like cold hard cash.

An hour later, I'd stuffed it into an old black suitcase, something discreet I could keep with me. My stomach gurgled. One burden lifted, and another one landed on my shoulders.

I wasn't stupid. I'd heard plenty about what daddy did for the Redding PD's investigations to know spending too much mystery money at once brought serious consequences. Wherever this money came from, it sure as hell wasn't clean.

I'd have to keep one eye glued to the cash for…months? Years?

Shit. Grim responsibility burned in my brain, and it made my bones hurt like they were locked in quicksand. Dirty money wasn't easy to spend.

I'd have to risk a few bigger chunks up front on groceries, a tune-up for our ancient Ford LTD, and then a down payment on a new place for Jackie and I.

It wouldn't buy us a luxury condo – not if we wanted to save ourselves a Federal investigation. But this cash was plenty to make a greedy landlord's eyes light up and take a few months' worth of rent without any uncomfortable questions. It was more than enough to give us food plus a roof over our heads while I figured out the rest.

Survival was still the name of the game, even if it had gotten unexpectedly easier.

Once our needs were secure, then I could figure out the rest. Maybe I'd find a way to finagle my way back into school so I could finish the accounting program I'd been forced to drop when dad's cancer went terminal.

It felt like hours passed while I finished filling up the suitcase and triple checked the basement for runaway money. When I was finally satisfied I'd secured everything, I grabbed the suitcases and marched upstairs, turning out the light behind me. I switched off the TV and headed straight for bed.

I sighed, knowing I was in for a long, restless night, even with the miracle cash safe beneath my bed. Or maybe because of it.

I couldn't tell if my heart or my head was more drained. They'd both been absolutely ripped out and shot to the moon these past two weeks.

I closed my eyes and tried to sleep. Tomorrow, I'd be hunting for a brand new place instead of a job while Jackie caught up on schoolwork. That happy fact alone should've made it easier to sleep.

But nothing about this was simple or joyful. It wasn't a lottery win.

Dwelling on the gaping canyon left in our lives by both our dead parents was a constant brutal temptation, especially when it was dark, cold, and quiet. So was avoiding the question that kept boiling in my head – how had he gotten it?

What the *fuck* had daddy done to make this much money from nothing? Life insurance payouts and stock dividends didn't get dropped off in mysterious packages downstairs.

He'd asked for forgiveness before his body gave out. My lips trembled and I pinched my eyes shut, praying he hadn't done something terrible – not directly, anyway. He was too sick for too long to kill anyone. He'd been off the force for a few years too.

I lost minutes – maybe hours – thinking about how he'd earned the dirty little secret underneath my bed. Whatever he'd done, it was bad. But at the end of the day, how much did I care?

And no matter how much blood the cash was soaked in, we needed it. I wasn't about to latch onto fantasy ethics and flush his dying legacy down the toilet. Blood money or not, we *needed* it. No fucking way was I going to burn the one thing that would keep us fed, clothed, sheltered, and sane.

Jackie never had to know where our miracle came from. Neither did I. Maybe years from now I'd have time for soul searching, time to worry about what kind of sick sins I'd branded onto my conscience by profiting off this freak inheritance.

Fretting about murder and corruption right now wouldn't keep the state from taking Jackie away when we were homeless. I had to keep my mouth shut and my mind more closed than ever. I had to treat it like a lottery win I could never tell anyone about.

Besides, it was all just temporary. I'd use the fortune to pay the rent and put food in our fridge until I finished school and got myself a job. Then I'd slowly feed the rest into something useful for Jackie's college – something that wouldn't get us busted.

It must've been after three o'clock when I finally fell asleep. If only I had a crystal ball, or stayed awake just an hour or two longer.

I would've seen the hurricane coming, the pitch black storm that always comes in when a girl takes the hand the devil's offered.

An earsplitting scream woke me first, but it was really the door slamming a second later that convinced me I wasn't dreaming.

Jackie!

I threw my blanket off and sat up, reaching for my phone on the nightstand. My hand slid across the smooth wood, and adrenaline dumped in my blood when I realized there was nothing there.

Too dark. I didn't realize the stranger was standing right over me until I tried to bolt up, slamming into his vice-like grip instead. Before I could even scream, his hand was over my mouth. Scratchy stubble prickled my cheek as his lips parted against my ear.

"Don't. You fucking scream, I'll have to put a bullet in your spine." Cold metal pushed up beneath my shirt, a gun barrel, proof he wasn't making an empty threat.

Not that I'd have doubted it. His tight, sinister embrace stayed locked around my waist as he turned me around and nudged his legs against mine, forcing me to move toward the hall.

"Just go where I tell you, and this'll all be over nice and quick. Nobody has to get hurt."

I listened. When we got to the basement door, he flung it open and lightened his grip, knowing it was a one way trip downstairs with no hope for escape.

Jackie was already down there against the wall, and so were four more large, brutal men like the one who'd held me. I blinked when I got to the foot of the stairs and took in the bizarre scene. They all wore matching leather vests with GRIZZLIES MC, CALIFORNIA emblazoned up their sides and on their backs.

I'd seen bikers traveling the roads for years, but never anything like these guys. Their jackets looked a lot like the ones veterans wore when they went out riding, but the symbols were all different. Bloody, strange, and very dangerous looking.

The men themselves matched the snarling bears on their leather. Four of them were younger, tattooed, spanning the spectrum from lean and wiry to pure muscle. The guy who'd walked me down the stairs moved where I could see him. He might've been the youngest, but I wasn't really sure.

Scary didn't begin to describe him. He looked at me with his arms folded, piercing green eyes going right through my soul, set in a stern cold face. He exuded a strength and severity that only came naturally – a born badass. A predator completely fixed on me.

An older man with long gray hair seemed to be in charge. He looked at the man holding my sister, another hard faced man with barbed wire ropes tattooed across his face. Jackie's eyes were bulging, shimmering like wide, frantic pools, pulling me in.

I'm sorry, I hissed in my head, breaking eye contact. One more second and I might've lost it. The only thing worse than being down here at their mercy was showing them I was already weak, broken, helpless.

They had my little sister, my whole world, everything I'd sworn to protect. No, this wasn't the time to freak out and cry. I had to keep it together if we were going to get out of this alive.

"Well? Any sign of the haul upstairs, or do we need to make these bitches sing?" Gray hair reached into his pocket, retrieving a cigarette and a lighter, as casually as if he was at work on a smoke break.

Shit, for all I knew, he probably was.

"Nothing up there, Blackjack." The man who'd taken me downstairs stepped forward, leaving the basement echoing with his smoky voice, older and more commanding than I'd expected. It hadn't just been the rough whisper flowing into my ear.

"Fuck," the psycho holding Jackie growled. "I like it the fun way, but I'm not a fan when these bitches scream. Makes my ears ring for days. Can't we gag these cunts first?"

Nobody answered him. The older man narrowed his eyes, looking at his goon, taking a long pull on the cigarette. My head was spinning, making it feel like the ground had softened up, ready to suck me under and bury me alive.

Oh, God. I knew this had to be about the mystery money the moment those rough hands went around me, but I hadn't really thought we were about to die until he said that.

Gray hair turned to face me, scowling. "You heard the man, love. We can do this the easy way or the hard way. I, for one, don't like spilling blood when there's no good reason, but some of the brothers feel differently. Now, we know your loot's not where it was supposed to be – found this shit all torn up myself."

Blowing his smoke, he pointed at the mess on the ground. I could've choked myself for being too stupid to clean up the mess earlier.

"You've got it somewhere. It couldn't have gotten far," he said, striding forward. "Look we both know me and my boys are gonna find it. Only question left is – are you gonna make this scavenger hunt easy-peasy-punkin-squeezy? Or are you gonna make all our fucking ears ring while we choke it out of you?"

I didn't answer. My eyes floated above his shoulder, fixing on the man across from me, stoic green eyes.

"Well?" The older asshole was getting impatient.

Strange. If Green Eyes wasn't so busy hanging out with these creeps and taking hostages, he would've been handsome. No, downright sexy was a better word.

My weeping, broken brain was still fixed on the stupid idea when Gray Hair grunted, pulled the light out of his mouth, and reached for my throat...

Look for Outlaw's Kiss at your favorite retailer!

Made in the USA
Lexington, KY
26 July 2015